RUSS MORGAN, PI

Lloyd A. Meeker

A NineStar Press Publication

Published by NineStar Press
P.O. Box 91792,
Albuquerque, New Mexico, 87199 USA.
www.ninestarpress.com

Russ Morgan, PI

Printed in the USA
First Edition
March, 2020

Print ISBN: 978-1-951880-78-1

Also available in eBook, ISBN: 978-1-951880-77-4

Warning: This book contains sexual content, which may only be suitable for mature readers.

Private Investigator Russ Morgan solves cases, using more than his wits.

Enigma

Who's blackmailing the high-profile televangelist whose son was miraculously cured of his homosexuality many years ago? Threatening letters using old Enigma songs from the 90's have got Reverend Howard Richardson spooked. Psychic Denver PI Russ Morgan uncovers obscene secrets shrouded in seeming righteousness, but must make peace with a sword of justice that cuts the innocent as well as the guilty.

Blood & Dirt

When Russ Morgan investigates a vandalized marijuana grow in Mesa County, he lands in the middle of a family feud that escalates into murder. Who is willing to go that far to get what they want? Russ's personal life is escalating, too—he has to figure out if he's brave enough to begin a relationship with Colin Stewart, who is half his age.

This book is dedicated to everyone whose intuitive sensitivities add extra challenges to daily life. May your gifts become good companions and allies on your journey.

ENIGMA

The little man in the expensive suit sneered as if I should have known what brand he wore and wilted before its awesome power. Armani? Versace? Burberry? I had no idea, and it didn't matter to me that I wasn't current on suits likely to cost more than my monthly mortgage.

His sneer had come from a designer collection, too. Men more generous than I am might have imagined he'd meant his lip movement as a smile that had come out deformed, but every time his lip curled, his aura came up spiky and dark. No, it was a sneer.

He was not happy to be in my office. In fact, he'd walked in carrying some kind of grudge. Since I'd never met him before, I figured his issue wasn't mine to fix until he shared. I let him stew.

He leaned forward and snapped his business card on the middle of my desk like it was an ace of trump. "My client wants you to find his son's blackmailer."

I picked up the business card and studied it, although I already knew what it said. *Andrew Kommen, Managing Partner, Stelnach, Kommen and Breyer.* On the phone, his assistant had spoken the name with outright reverence, expecting I'd be awed or at the very least grateful for this visitation.

I pulled one of my own cards from the desk drawer. It said *Rhys (Russ) Morgan, Investigations* and listed my license number, address, and phone number below my name in a perfectly professional manner. Granted, it wasn't embossed on the same quality stock as Mr. Kommen's, but I offered it to him anyway, the second half of the business card minuet. When he smiled, thin lipped, and didn't take it, I smiled back and placed it gently on the desk in front of him.

He gazed at it for a second, just long enough to let me know touching it was beneath him. I had to hand it to him—his sense of nuance and timing was impeccable. I tried to imagine him doing stand-up comedy. It didn't work.

According to reputation, Andrew Kommen's firm had enough money to hire every detective in the city for a whole year and still never think of cutting back on the Jamaican Blue Mountain coffee beans in the general staff room. But here was the managing partner, sitting opposite me in my modest too-close-to-Colfax-Avenue office, slumming.

"I'm a little surprised you've come to me," I said. "We don't usually travel in the same circles."

"Believe me, you were not my first choice."

He didn't like me, and I didn't like him. That made us even. "Who's your client?"

"Until you sign this nondisclosure agreement, there will be no names." He lifted an attaché case too sleek to be made anywhere but Italy onto the desk and popped it open. Out came two documents, which he pushed across to me.

I read far enough to learn they would ruin me if I breathed a word about this case to anyone but an authorized representative of the firm or its client. Recovery of fees, punitive damages, etc., etc. I stopped before getting to the paragraph stipulating grievous bodily harm if I divulged any information, but I'm sure it was in there somewhere.

I looked up. "You guys play hardball."

"I'm so glad that registered with you. It would be unfortunate for you if that were to slip your mind. Ever." He smiled again, this time showing teeth. "On the other hand, we will pay you well for your services. Very, very well."

"There are limits to what I can keep confidential with the police, for example. I won't violate those."

"Of course." Kommen shrugged, a tiny gesture dismissing a tiny concern. "You will receive no harassment from the police in this matter, I can assure you."

That smelled bad. I shifted my focus to check his aura. Calm and probably quite clear for him. At the very least, he believed what he was saying to be true. I watched him for more clues but didn't see any.

Could he and his firm work their connections with the police to deliver on that promise? If so, did I really want to do business with a lawyer who could pull strings like that? I wasn't eager. I gave him another chance to change his mind. "Surely your firm could do better than hiring me for what is obviously a very sensitive case involving very sensitive people."

"Yes."

I had rarely heard that word so carefully filled with insult yet so calmly delivered. It was the perfect smackdown. I couldn't help smiling in admiration. "Nice. But?"

"You're a known homosexual, with knowledge of homosexual activists." This time the disapproval was front and center. "We believe vengeful homosexuals are behind this attack on my client and his family. This matter requires extensive knowledge of your...*sub*culture."

Got it. Sub, as in lower than. I struggled not to laugh. "I see." I imagined several generic scenarios, all involving the gay son of some prominent figure. I already knew whose side I was on. I reached for the nondisclosure agreement.

"Well, I think I'd like to help your client's son."

"He's not the one who's important," Kommen snapped. "Your job is to help my client. The rest of the family's affairs are none of your business."

I studied the man across from me with a sudden twinge of pity. He looked even smaller now—pinched and dried out. Mean and empty.

"I think we both know you may not be able to control the scope of the investigation like that, so please don't pretend." I signed both copies, and he signed for his firm and his mysterious client.

Then he pulled out the letter of engagement, check attached. "Your base salary will be $7,000 a week plus expenses for which you will provide receipts. My client wants this matter finished expeditiously. If you solve the case within four weeks of engagement, you will receive a $25,000 bonus. Payment in the method of your choice."

My pride thought he put just a little too much emphasis on the *if*. "Before I sign anything else, you need to brief me on the nature of the assignment. Otherwise, we're finished already."

He stared at me for a minute. I stared back, prepared to wait him out. He was in my office, after all, and he'd already made it clear he didn't enjoy slumming with known homosexuals who might even know a vengeful activist or two. Me, I was perfectly comfortable. I often dealt with jerks.

"*Your* client will be Stelnach, Kommen and Breyer, Mr. Morgan. *Our* client," he said as if giving me far more than I deserved, "is Reverend Howard Richardson. It is likely you will never meet him or speak with him. All your communication concerning this matter will be directly with me. Under no circumstance are you to initiate contact with Reverend Richardson or any of his family. Is that clear?"

I nodded. I appreciated that Richardson would want to keep as far as possible from an investigation of blackmail against his gay son. At least, I assumed his son was gay. Even before Proposition 2, Richardson had been a powerful figure in every anti-gay political pushback in Colorado as well as nationally.

Oh, the irony. A high-profile family values advocate with the very abomination he sought to eradicate lurking in his own household.

"And he wants to keep his family aberration a secret?"

"Oh, no." Kommen looked way too pleased at my wrong guess, as if it confirmed my inadequacy. "He made no secret of his son's illness."

He leaned forward, apparently to drive home the point. "In 1993, when James first admitted to his father that he was afflicted with homosexual desires, the Reverend enrolled James in a therapeutic program. He hid nothing from anyone. Indeed, he called to his congregation to pray for his son's victory over darkness."

My stomach lurched. Reparative therapy. The devil's work if ever there was a devil. I kept my face neutral. "And how old was James then?"

"Seventeen. Committing him to the rescue program was perfectly legal."

"I have no doubt." I stuffed my nausea, deciding I wanted more than ever to help James to recover from his father's abuse, although I didn't know if I had the skills for that. I could read auras, but I'd never tried to heal them. "So what then?"

"He was transformed. His father declared it a miracle. James joined his father in ministry, although not in a political way. He now supervises a number of successful educational and outreach programs for the church as well as the publishing operation."

The story was way too tidy. "Let me guess. James married, and they've got two children."

"Three." Kommen's smirk made his whole face quiver. "They're very happy."

"But it's not all harmony and light in paradise, is it?" I wasn't asking a question.

"About two months ago, threatening letters from someone calling himself Enigma began showing up. In very disturbing ways."

I wanted to make sure I understood. "You're saying that the way the letters arrived was disturbing, in addition to their threatening content?"

Kommen shook his head. "First, the letter of engagement," he said pointing to the paper on my desk. I signed. He signed. He put his copy in his attaché case and snapped the latches.

"The Enigma letters are in our keeping. Come to our offices tomorrow at nine, and you can examine them. You may make copies, but the originals remain in our custody."

Kommen stood, and I followed suit. I offered my hand, which he shook for less than a second. I retrieved my spurned business card from the desktop and watched him leave. The documents from my new best friend went in the safe, and I stared out the window at Pearl Street, taking my time to decide where to have lunch. I like taking my time with important decisions. At fifty, I figure I've earned the right.

*

The next morning at ten minutes to nine, I entered the hushed LoDo palace of glass, metal, thick gray carpet, and perfect understatement that was Stelnach, Kommen and Breyer.

The sleek receptionist behind the minimalist desk asked me to make myself comfortable, which I did, and looked around. Original artwork lined the foyer walls, western and mountain themes. Regional Estes Park gallery stuff, but top-end.

At 9:01, an adorable young man with scrubbed-pink cheeks, sandy hair, and elfin green eyes appeared and introduced himself as Colin Stewart, one of Mr. Kommen's assistants. On his invitation, I followed him down the hall.

I couldn't help admiring the way he walked. *Sweet butt of youth*, I thought, apologizing half-heartedly to Tennessee Williams. I was pretty sure Mr. Williams would have enjoyed the view, too. Colin ushered me through a glass door set in a floor-to-ceiling glass wall and into a small conference room furnished with laminated-wood-grain furniture. He sat me down and handed me the folio of letters.

"I'm going to have questions," I said opening the folio, wishing I wasn't curious whether Colin was gay. He was a quarter century younger than I was. "Are you the one to answer them?"

He sat down across from me, polite and sweetly enthusiastic. "That's what I'm here for. Mr. Kommen briefed me for it."

I looked at his aura, full of genuine goodwill and inexperience. He'd do his best.

Still, as sincere as he might be, Colin was another layer of insulation holding me at distance from those who had direct knowledge of these events. That annoyed me and stirred shadows of self-doubt. I relied on my psychic contact with people who had firsthand knowledge or experience. Without that, I was traveling blind.

There were four letters in all. Not really letters— poetry. None of them contained a specific threat or clear demand. Maybe they were coded so only the Richardsons would understand them.

I knew the physical messages had been handled by a lot of different people, but I held them for a moment hoping I could connect with their origin. It took a while, but I got something. Rage. The kind of fury that can lead to serious harm. The danger was real. That was a good start.

"Mr. Morgan, are you okay?" Colin Stewart's voice pulled me back. "Do you want a glass of water or something?" I looked up. He hovered, half out of his chair.

"Hm? No, I'm fine. I was just thinking. Sometimes I go far away when I think."

"Sure. Of course." Colin's puckish grin showed slightly uneven teeth. He sat back down, looking eager again, all worry erased. "All the time you need."

"Your boss mentioned that somehow these letters are intended to blackmail James Richardson. How did he come to that conclusion?"

"Well," Colin said, blushing, "they're poems. Mr. Kommen thinks they're from an old lover of Rev. Richardson's son."

"On the assumption that if they're poems, this must be about James Richardson's gay experiences. Because poetry is just so gay." I shook my head, disgusted by Kommen's knee-jerk analysis. That wasn't analysis, I corrected myself. It was mere prejudice.

Colin had referred to James as Rev. Richardson's son, and so had Kommen. Was that who James Richardson was to these people, even though now in 2009 he was a thirty-three-year-old husband, father of three, and a successful businessman? Maybe he was little more than a potential chink in Rev. Richardson's armor to them.

I spread the letters on the table and scowled at Colin. "Why would an old lover wait sixteen years to send him poems?"

Colin looked uncertain. "It's a long time to wait, isn't it?"

"I know I wouldn't wait that long. Unless something happened only recently to open an old wound." I looked at the first one again. Laser printer, black ink, standard size Times New Roman. Nothing unusual except it was 24-weight paper. Enigma liked nice paper.

April Fool's Day, 2009—but you can't fool God!

This is The Cross of Changes

There followed several lines of free verse, part New Age vision, part Delphic warning, talking about universal justice. Signed Enigma.

It didn't sound like something from an old lover to me. It felt more like an allusion to wrongdoing. Illegal money? Sexual harassment or maybe an affair? It certainly wouldn't be the first time in the history of church leaders.

"Do we have any input from the Richardsons about the letters?"

"Not that I know of. Mr. Kommen just said they were really bad poems."

"That's it?" I looked up at him, amazed. "You've had these things for weeks and no one thought to find out more about them?" Colin squirmed but kept silent.

"C'mon. Let's find a terminal."

Colin logged me into the library computer and sat in an adjacent chair, holding the letters. I found Google, pecked in "This is the Cross of Changes" and hit return. A page of links to lyrics for a song called "The Cross of Changes." By a group called Enigma. A few more clicks. The album was *The Cross of Changes*, released in 1993, the very year young James Richardson had been sent away to be cured of his deviant lust.

I pointed to the screen. "You think that might be relevant, Colin?"

The poor kid flushed scarlet as he read. He looked down at the letters in his lap. He had nice eyelashes. He was almost certainly straight, and even if he wasn't, he was way too young for me. But he had pretty eyelashes just the same.

"I think we should have a little chat with your boss, don't you?"

His eyes popped wide. His mouth opened, but it took him a couple of seconds to speak. "Please wait here while I see if he's available, Mr. Morgan." He disappeared into a stairwell. A few minutes later he came back, looking frazzled. I guessed Andrew Kommen disliked being interrupted.

"He says he can give you five minutes. Please come this way."

We took the stairs up two flights, and Colin swiped us onto the floor with his badge.

*

Andrew Kommen's office was vast. He sat on a little throne behind about fifty square feet of carved mahogany desk, its dark gleaming expanse unblemished by anything resembling work. Other than the big desk, the room was sparsely appointed—bookshelves, conference table, expensive cool artwork. Classic unimaginative power-attorney decor for a temple of litigation. Nothing personal, not even a family photo. The big space felt barren to me.

He didn't invite me to sit, so I stood. As I began talking, he leaned back in his chair, steepling his fingers against the tip of his chin. If he thought that made him look clever, he was wrong. It made him look silly.

I wrapped up. "The album was released in 1993, the year James was introduced to the joys of heterosexual orientation. I'm amazed your earlier investigators didn't learn that."

"In fact, we did know it."

"What?" I shifted focus. The muddy spikes in his aura said he was lying through his teeth.

"I said," he repeated, voice dripping with condescension, "we did know that connection."

I folded my arms across my chest. "Mr. Kommen, you're lying. You didn't know."

His eyes narrowed. He pulled in a sharp breath and sat up straight. "How dare you!" He was clearly not used to being challenged by contract labor.

"How dare I? It's easy, believe me. I have a sixth-sense kind of thing that goes off when someone lies to me. It's very valuable and very reliable. You just made it ring, big time."

I dropped the letters on his desk. "Find someone who doesn't mind your bullshit, because I don't have the patience for it. I'll send your check back by courier this afternoon."

"Wait." He leaned forward, pushed the papers back toward me. "What I meant was that we were confident there was a connection to James Richardson's past." He paused. "It's true, we didn't actually know about the connection to the music album."

"Still not interested. You don't bother taking the most obvious step of researching the text of the letters, then you obstruct and mislead the efforts of the people you hire to help. I can imagine you've gone through investigators like shit through a goose. No wonder you finally ended up in my office."

I turned toward the door and caught sight of Colin, standing behind me, slack-jawed, eyes wide as a spooked horse.

"What will it take to keep you on the case? I'll double your fee." The voice from behind the big desk actually sounded frightened.

I stopped and turned back. "I don't want double your fee. I want your cooperation. No more games. That's what it'll take. Starting with in-person interviews with the Richardsons. All four of them."

"Very well." Kommen sounded contrite. His aura sparkled with fear.

I pointed to the letters. "By themselves, these don't constitute blackmail. There's no demand. There's not even a target. How do you know James is being blackmailed?"

"Reverend Richardson is convinced it's aimed at him. I've just assumed he has good reason to do so."

"And what does James think?"

Kommen only hesitated for a second. "He agrees."

"I look forward to confirming that. If you jerk me around again, Mr. Kommen, I will quit, and you will pay me two weeks additional fee as the cost for your bullshit games. Please amend my engagement letter to say if I quit, you owe me two weeks."

"Very well," he repeated.

"Set up the Richardson interviews as soon as possible, please. I want to meet with each of them separately. Let me know when and where."

I picked up the letters. "Colin, can you make copies of these for me?" I followed him out of Kommen's office without looking back.

After he'd made the copies, Colin and I walked to the elevator together in silence. Once the doors closed, he grinned at me. "You're gutsy. I'm impressed."

I shook my head, and a wave of sadness washed through me. Or maybe it was just fatigue. "No, not really gutsy. Just beat up enough to know there are things that leave bigger holes in your life than money, if you lose them."

I could tell he didn't really get it. But then when I was his age, neither had I.

"Still," he said, looking at me sideways with a bashful smile. "I liked it. Kinda hot."

Had he batted his eyelashes on purpose? *Oh, damn. Don't, Morgan. Bad idea.*

*

On the thirty-minute walk back to my office, I thought more about what I'd told Colin. I knew something about those larger holes firsthand, the ones left by integrity and love, when they've been lost.

I'd been sober just over fifteen years now—the same length of time, I realized with a start, since James Richardson's conversion. We'd both started a new life in 1993.

Whatever he felt about his, I was grateful for mine. I'd worked hard to find a new sense of myself as a human being, one that I could live in with a little contentment.

When I was drinking, I'd told myself that I drank to insulate myself from the constant bombardment of other people's auras, and that was probably true, at least in part. A few stiff drinks served as insulation that would last all night. My sensitivity wasn't a big deal until I came out and began my new life. Somehow suppressing my sexuality had also kept my sensitivity damped down. When the door to everything I'd kept locked in the basement finally blew off its hinges, I found not only did I have to build an authentic life, but cope with new receptivity that made me feel very vulnerable.

I had no idea how to keep enough distinction between me as an individual and those wild sensations that could literally bring me to my knees without warning, usually when I was near someone in rage or grief. I ended up on my knees a lot. Alcohol numbed me out at first, which was helpful when I felt overwhelmed. Eventually, alcohol taught me not to care at all, and that's when it stopped being helpful.

I finally made it to AA and learned that an alcoholic could rationalize his drinking six ways from Sunday. Whatever the given reason, it was never as important as the behavior it sought to excuse, and the resulting wreckage was just as terrible.

In my case, I'd driven away a smart, gentle, loving partner by hiding in a bottle and hadn't seen much of love since I crawled out. Maybe I never would. But I wanted another chance at it now. I may have been fifty, flawed, and a little psychic, but I was as real as I'd ever been in my life. Some nights I wanted another chance at love so bad the longing was a metallic tang along my tongue.

As tasty as Colin looked, he was an hors d'oeuvre for a man my age, not a full meal. Above the belt, I knew very well he wasn't what I was hungry for, but if he made it clear he wanted to play, I wasn't convinced I'd be strong enough to say no. Was a snack better than no meal at all? Maybe, but more complicated, too.

I wondered if James Richardson's hunger for love had been satisfied, but that was well outside the scope of my assignment unless he'd started fooling around with men again and someone was blackmailing him about it. But if this really was blackmail, it felt to me like the letters were aimed at Howard, not James.

I pushed all those question marks aside as I unlocked the door to my office and my home. A few years ago, I bought half an old two-story red brick duplex on the corner of 16th Avenue and Pearl Street. I'd set up my office in the front room downstairs, in what had been the living room, complete with a small but functioning fireplace, expanded the kitchen, and half bath in the back, then made my living quarters upstairs.

I'd furnished the place with comfortable, well-made used items. Maybe it was a reflection of my age and condition, but I found most new furniture to be soulless and uninteresting. I preferred something unusual, sturdy, and a little beat-up any day.

I loved my little place. It represented so much of what I'd managed to build in sobriety. It wasn't huge, but it was plenty big for one. In fact, it was plenty big for two, but that was a different problem altogether.

I made fresh coffee, went upstairs, and parked in my favorite armchair next to the front windows overlooking the street.

A little more internet research showed all the messages used lyrics from the same album. I shut down the laptop and put it away, then spread the letters in chronological order.

April Fool's Day, 2009—But you can't fool God!

This is The Cross of Changes

That one I'd already looked at, so I turned to the next.

April 15, 2009—Tax Day! Soon it's time to pay...

The Silent Warrior

This one was more ominous, a promise of a judgment day for those who abuse the name of God. "The Silent Warrior" was the title of the song, but Enigma also had to be saying it's time to pay some silent warrior, presumably him- or herself.

May 1, 2009—Beltane, sex and fire! Who have you been screwing?

Out From the Deep—come terrible secrets...

Clearing ancient debts and learning over lifetimes were the themes of this one. New Age blackmail? Interesting concept.

May 31, 2009 — And then it's all over.

I Love You—I'll Kill You

The title alone gave me chills. Mixing love and hate, the song was a poetic declaration of enduring love and a promise of imminent death.

Was it a literal threat? The police probably wouldn't think so even if Kommen had wanted them involved. If the threat was less than literal, there still had to be a skeleton or two in the Richardson closets that danced to these tunes. My incentive of 25k told me just how seriously they took the letters.

Mr. Enigma—or I suppose Ms. was a possibility—had a strong attachment to *The Cross of Changes*. I could easily understand how this stream of oblique references to wrongdoing and the inevitable working of justice could make the Richardsons nervous. Some intuition whispered at me about that, but I couldn't make sense of what it wanted me to see.

I closed my eyes to listen better. Nothing came for a while, but I'd learned how to wait.

When I'd settled into the stillness, I glanced down at the letters in my lap and read through all the lyrics again. A line about playing games with ones who loved you called to me from the last song. Okay, good. That felt right—a clue that family issues might be at the heart of this case. Not very specific, but a working start. Maybe there was more.

I closed my eyes again, and Colin showed up, fresh and eager. Or not Colin, but his face reminding me of what I wanted, what I'd thrown away by playing games with one who had loved me.

"I'm so fucking sorry, Robbie," I whispered into the hole in my heart, knowing there would be no answer, since he'd packed up his stuff and moved out over fifteen years ago.

Again, I saw him standing sadly at the front door holding his last box, his tears all cried out weeks earlier.

"You love him more than me, babe," he said, pointing to the bottle in my hand. "I wish I still loved you like I used to, but I just don't. Can't. I can't compete, and I can't stay to watch you kill yourself." And then he was gone.

Even though I was five years sober when he and Eric got married, I couldn't go to the ceremony. I couldn't bear to see the man I threw away marry someone else, knowing I could have had him if only I had…

If only. That was pure bullshit. If nothing. I hadn't, and I was living with the consequences. If I kept swigging from my favorite barrel of self-pity, a tumbler of booze might not be far off, and that was one hell I did *not* want to revisit. They say in AA you learn not to regret the past nor close the door on it. Apparently, I wasn't finished working on that.

I stared at the papers again for a long time. They felt incomplete.

Was this really blackmail, or something else? Knowledge of wrongdoing was clearly implied, most explicitly in the third letter: *"Who have you been screwing?"* But was that literal or figurative? Then again, maybe the blackmailer was just preparing the ground for a demand more specific than *"soon it's time to pay."* Regardless, he/she was definitely sending loaded messages to the Richardsons. Enough to make Howard Richardson call his high-powered and, no doubt, very expensive lawyer.

I needed to listen to the music, see if I could get some other lead from it. I phoned Pete at my favorite indie music store, Wax Trax. He had a used CD, and I asked him to hold it for me until I could pick it up. Pete was eager to give me the whole history of the album over the phone, but I asked him to hold off until I could get it in person.

As soon as I hung up, Kommen called. He'd regained his aggressive tone, but to his credit, he kept most of the sneer out of his voice. I had appointments tomorrow with the Richardson men at his office, Howard at nine, and James at one-thirty. Colin would arrange any other appointments I needed, and I should call him directly.

Finally, some traction. This was good. I headed out to Wax Trax for the album and Pete's enthusiastic history lesson.

*

The next morning, Colin met me in the foyer right on time. He was so deliciously puppy-eager, I began to worry about what I might do if he was hitting on me. Neither of us needed that complication.

I opened my vision to take a quick look at his aura. It's hard to describe what I do for that, even though I have better control over it now. I kind of expand the energy around my head and shoulders, making space, and then relax my eyes until my vision shifts—pretty much like when an optometrist clicks away one of those obscuring lenses and suddenly you can see things you couldn't before.

Colin wasn't flirting, although I thought I saw the warm glow of attraction. His aura was more professional than mine, congruent with his full-bore Eagle Scout mode. The kid just loved helping others. I understood. In my own jaded way so did I. I hoped he wouldn't get too badly hurt for his natural generosity, even though I knew it was inevitable.

Odd. I was both relieved and offended he wasn't flirting with me. I'm impossible to please sometimes.

This time we marched directly to the elevator and went up to the big shots' floor. Once inside Kommen's office, Colin led me past the massive desk and through a door behind it into a spacious sitting room. He backed away, and there was a soft click as he closed the door behind me.

Kommen and the Reverend Howard Richardson sat next to each other in a pair of overstuffed leather chairs against the far wall. They'd been talking for a while; I could feel it. The air between them hung thick with their conversation.

I looked around. Very comfy in a bland way. Private. The place shouted with whispers it was so full of secrets. A wall of glass looked south and west over the Platte, and off through the tawny Denver haze to the mountains. On the opposite wall, a kitchen and fully stocked wet bar waited for customers.

Neither one stood as I crossed the room, but I stretched out my hand to Richardson and waited.

After a beat of silence, Kommen introduced us. "Reverend Richardson, this is Rhys Morgan, our investigator." The reverend stayed put as he shook my hand. His grip was firm and crisp with a fast release. Very professional, and not as oily as I'd expected. But underneath the smooth polish, panic sparked off his hand, stinging mine. Sometimes, it still physically hurt to be an empath.

Richardson reached up to caress his hair into place. He needn't have worried. It remained fixed in silver perfection. His whole face was so smooth I figured it had benefited from a little cosmetic surgery.

I gave him a polite smile. "Please, call me Russ. Nobody uses Rhys."

Richardson turned businesslike. "Well, Russ, thank you for your help with this unfortunate business." He turned on a just-between-us grin. "I hope Andrew hasn't been too hard on you. He's my fiercest protector in the entire congregation, and I know he can be, ah, intimidating."

So Kommen was a congregant. That explained a lot about his behavior, including his fear at losing another PI while his spiritual leader panicked.

I sat on the near end of a cream leather-covered love seat where I could see both of them at the same time. "I'm sure he's doing the best he can to protect you and your ministry, Reverend. And I'm not intimidated in the least." I saw that register in both.

"Good for you. Good for you." Richardson sat back in his chair and raised his hands, palms turned slightly out and up, a gesture of openness, welcome, and benediction all in one. "You have some questions for me."

"Yes." I pulled out my pocket recorder and set it on the coffee table in front of me.

"No recordings. Absolutely not." Kommen's voice dropped the temperature in the room about fifteen degrees.

I raised an eyebrow at Richardson, who shrugged an apology. I put the recorder back in my pocket and took out a pen and notepad. "Okay, no recording. This will take more time, then. I'm pretty slow at taking notes."

I got myself set and shifted my vision so I could watch Richardson's aura. "I'm told that these threatening messages are blackmail against your son. Is that your take?"

"It's the only explanation that makes any sense to me." His aura spiked. A serious lie. I nodded studiously and made a note.

"What's your most likely scenario?"

"I believe someone wants to harm me and my ministry by discrediting my son."

He fixed me with an intense gaze worthy of a biblical prophet surviving in the desert on locusts and honey. "As you know, since he was delivered from the chains of homosexual desire," he intoned, dragging out the bad word as "HOE-moe-SEX-shul", "he's become my right arm in Abundant Life and Gospel Ministry Church."

My body contracted at his pronunciation as if I were fifteen again, braced against my own father's righteous fury pouring from the pulpit. It's sad, in a way, how the body can remember the pain of darkness long after the soul has found the light switch.

"How might they attack your son and your ministry, Reverend?"

"You don't need to answer that, Howard," Kommen cut in. He glared at me. "That's your job, to find out how."

"With all due respect, Mr. Kommen," I said, putting more emphasis on *due* than was polite. His aura darkened. He got it. "That's not true. You hired me to find out who's sending the letters. It seems to me that understanding how the letters might be effective in doing damage to your client could yield some idea of who might be behind them."

"Now, Andrew," Richardson's mellifluous pulpit voice wafted sweet as the balm of Gilead across Kommen's darkening face. "I'm sure the man means well. We must let him do his job no matter how uncomfortable that makes us."

Kommen's hands turned into claws on the arms of his chair, but he said nothing.

Richardson turned to face me, his saintly smile radiant. "If someone were to cast believable doubt on my son's commitment to the true path of Christ, it truly would be like cutting off my right arm." He shook his head with ineffable sorrow at the prospect. "All we've built together would fall into terrible jeopardy."

"Specifically, you mean cast doubt on his sexual orientation?"

"Yes, in spite of his miraculous healing years ago, and his exemplary life as a family man ever since."

I nodded and made another note. "And he's never, um, slipped up in that?"

"Absolutely not. Never. His healing is full and complete, praise the Lord." A significant lie. And behind it something even darker, I couldn't tell what. That warranted much more exploration when I could find a way to do it.

"When did your son go into treatment?"

"Let's see, that would have been 1993. November."

"And he left treatment when?"

"Just before Easter of the following year." Richardson's voice swelled, lofty as a pipe organ. "He was resurrected from Satan's darkness on that blessed anniversary by the blood of Our Savior, and the stone over his tortured heart was rolled away by angels." He cleared his throat, as if stopping himself from a longer sermon.

I forced myself to write carefully as a way of countering my nausea:

Easter, 1994. Check date.

Howard Richardson's bloated certainty was suffocating, and some claustrophobic part of me wanted to end this interview so I could run away and breathe again. But I'd committed to the case. I'd never bolted before just because I didn't like the person I was supposed to be helping, and I wouldn't now. Keeping a promise was bedrock to me, part of my living amends; a sober man being in the world the way it is. I couldn't betray that.

I changed focus to watch his aura. "I'm told the letters were delivered in disturbing ways. How did the first one arrive?"

"It was in the interoffice mail." True.

"Envelope?"

"Yes. Addressed to me." True.

"Who can I talk to about your interoffice mail system?"

"Our office manager, Marianna Stokes. I'll arrange it."

"Thank you." I wrote down her name.

I decided to push the good reverend a bit more. "If the letter was addressed to you, why would you think the threat was directed at James? Could it have been about something else?"

"The threat is to me, using James as the weapon." Richardson's aura spiked. Anger as well as fear. Something there he didn't want to talk about. Maybe this wasn't really about his son at all.

"Did you recognize the source of the words?"

"No. I simply recognized them as a threat."

"All the messages are lyrics from an album by a group called Enigma, called *The Cross of Changes*." Kommen must have already briefed him on that because Richardson didn't even blink.

"It gets even more relevant," I continued. "The album was released in December of 1993, while your son was undergoing reparative therapy. Do you think James knew about this music? Any lover he'd had before his therapy would certainly learn about it right away. The album was very popular, especially among gay men."

"James would never listen to such soulless rubbish!" Richardson's voice cracked, along with his composure. "He enjoys Christian music exclusively. In fact, shortly after he joined us in ministry, he took charge of our outreach, music, and publishing programs. He singlehandedly spearheaded our very successful efforts to extend our offerings into Latin America, including drawing on Latin American music to reach those wonderful people's hearts."

I felt obliged to offer a slightly different perspective. "I can understand that you might think the album rubbish, but a lot of people loved it. And bought it."

I gazed at Richardson. "Are you sure you didn't receive another note, one that contained the lyrics to that particular song, *Return to Innocence*?"

"Absolutely." He was telling the truth.

"Well, then, I'll bet you a dollar that it's on the way. Maybe Enigma has saved that song for last. How did letter number two arrive?"

"It was mailed to my home. That address is closely held information, but this Enigma knows it." His aura writhed into coils as he spoke. Enigma knew where he lived, and that terrified him.

"How closely? Could you make a list of who knows your home address, or is it more generally known than that?"

"More general. Still, those who know would never divulge it."

"You do realize, then, that someone you trust probably sent that letter."

Richardson didn't respond, but his aura twisted and sparked with fear. I let the silence stretch a little. "Letter number three?

Richardson cleared his throat. "I have a modest bathroom in my office at ministry headquarters. It was taped to the shower door."

I looked at Kommen, then at Richardson. "Another indication Enigma has close access to your life, Reverend, or at very least an accomplice among your staff."

"It seems that way, even though most of them have been with me for years." He shook his head at the sad likelihood of such betrayal.

"May I interview your secretary?" In my peripheral vision, I saw Kommen glowering at me, a guard dog I was glad had been leashed. "I promise to be discreet," I added. "And kind."

Richardson glanced at Kommen, who nodded. "I suppose you must," he sighed. "Gladys has been my secretary for twenty-five years. I trust her completely."

I nodded. "I understand. And the fourth letter?"

"It came to this office," Kommen cut in.

"Addressed to whom?"

"Reverend Richardson, but to my attention."

"By courier or mail?"

Kommen's aura flashed. He was getting angry. "Courier."

"Which one?"

"Colin can look that up."

"I'll need to talk to their dispatcher. Will you authorize that?"

Kommen gave me a tiny nod, looking deeply inconvenienced.

"Were there any viable fingerprints on the messages?"

"No. We had a very good lab do the tests. There weren't any. Enigma wore gloves."

Kommen was trying to take control of the interview. I figured he wanted to end it, so I decided to help him out. I could tell I'd gotten everything I was going to get from Richardson. At the moment, anyway.

"Okay. Well, thank you, Reverend. I'll wait to hear from Mr. Kommen when I can interview your office manager and your secretary."

I put away my notebook. "I may need to ask you some clarifying questions after I interview your wife, son, and daughter-in-law. But for the moment, I'm all set."

Apparently Kommen wasn't done flexing his muscle as gatekeeper. "Another interview may not be possible," he huffed.

I stared at him. "If it's necessary, it will be brief. And I sincerely hope, Mr. Kommen, that your desire to insulate your client from my investigation doesn't become counterproductive. My request would not be frivolous, and denying it could be problematic."

I stood up, and stuck out my hand again. When Richardson got up, so did Kommen. "Thanks for your time, Reverend," I said. "We'll get this cleared up, I promise." I didn't feel quite that certain, but I wasn't going to hedge in front of Kommen.

Even though the day was heating up, it was a relief to get out onto the street. I bought an early and unhealthy lunch from a street vendor, then walked down to Confluence Park. Traffic on the Speer Boulevard Viaduct shimmered in the heat, and a dozen thunderheads were already building against the mountains—a typical June morning in Denver, if any weather could be called typical here.

At the park I found a little shade on the bank opposite REI, where I could watch the kayakers bob and twist through the man-made rapids, eat my lunch, and ponder my interview with Richardson senior.

Now I understood why Kommen had been unconcerned about the police. They weren't involved because there was no crime for them to investigate. Not until Richardson got a demand for money, at least.

The bad news was that most of the customary lines of inquiry surrounding a crime were also missing. No police report, no witnesses, no known motive. Not even an apparent one. I did have leads, though. I was far from stymied.

On the surface, the level of Richardson's panic at receiving the letters seemed strangely disproportionate to what they contained. He had to see something in them that he wasn't talking about. I'd find out what that was.

Then there was the question of his son's sexual orientation. Had father really expected reparative therapy to fix his son? Regardless of Howard's expectations, James hadn't been the poster boy for its success as proclaimed. Howard knew his son hadn't been cured. He also knew he was vulnerable because of its failure.

Something else was out of joint between father and son, too. Something he didn't want to talk about. The afternoon's interview with James promised to be more fruitful than I'd first thought.

*

I got back to Kommen's office in time to cool off a bit in their air-conditioned foyer while waiting for Colin to appear. He did, radiating his rosy-cheeked sincerity, precisely at one thirty.

He'd already collected the contact info for the courier, Rocky Mountain Mercury, and their tracking number for the fourth letter. He was quick—a smart, decent gay kid trying to do his job right in what was undoubtedly a very precarious environment, and more power to him.

Colin didn't lead me back to the big suite off Kommen's office, but to a smaller, still well-appointed conference room down the hall. He parked me in one of the upholstered armchairs and scurried off, I assumed, to fetch James. I wondered if Kommen was always this obvious in his messages about status difference between father and son. Given how he'd behaved toward me, I figured it likely.

In a moment, Colin opened the door and Kommen appeared with Richardson Jr. beside him. James sat down opposite me, but Kommen stayed at the door.

"I have a meeting," he announced, glaring at me like it was my fault. "No recording this. I've instructed James to refuse to answer any question he feels uncomfortable with. Afterward, he'll be reporting to me on your conduct. In detail." He wheeled and was gone.

As he closed the door, I caught Colin's eye. He knew his boss was an asshole, too. I watched him through the glass wall as he scooted down the hall. I could see that some days, he'd have to work hard at being cheerful.

I wanted the atmosphere to settle a bit before I got started, so I took my time pulling out my pen and notebook and getting set up. When I looked up, Richardson was sitting back, waiting with his arms on the chair and his knees wide apart. He had big thighs, and not from fat. Very fit.

He was an attractive guy, in a button-down collar, perfect teeth, only slightly weathered collegiate kind of way. Solid intelligence in the eyes, but I saw more pain than kindness there. Good jaw, but also hard, somehow. Dark hair like his father's in the old press photos I'd looked up. James had a bigger, more athletic frame, though. He obviously worked out, but not obsessively. His features reminded me more of his mother, although I'd seen only one photo of her. Pretty nice overall, but not gut-grabbing sexy.

I gave him a conciliatory smile. "I can't promise to ask you only comfortable questions, but my goal here is certainly not to harass you."

He shrugged dismissively. "I know. Kommen is a martinet, and it gets old in a hurry. I'm a big boy and can take care of myself."

"I have no doubt of that," I said, grinning.

I shifted my focus to watch his energy. "I've learned a lot about the Enigma album containing the lyrics used in these letters," I said, pen at the ready. "Do you think there's any significance to the fact that it was released while you were in therapy?"

"No, I don't," Richardson said. Big lie—his aura blazed with it, plus anger. I made a note as slowly as if I were just learning to print block letters. I was half tempted to stick my tongue part way out with the effort.

"Do you have any idea at all as to who might be behind these letters, even just a wild guess?"

"None at all." Again, a big lie, highly charged. Instead of anger, this time I saw searing pain. He had an idea, for sure. And now so did I.

"Your father believes that these letters are an attack on him, using you and your background as the point of attack. Do you think that idea is at all valid?"

"It could be. Leaders of some other churches would love to see my father disgraced. The math says donation dollars that go to one church don't go to another, and our draw for members and donations is growing fast."

"Is it possible that this is an attack on your father directly? Church funds, moral misconduct?"

"No." Big lie. "Our books are rigorously audited and summarized annually for our members." True.

I waited for him to address the moral misconduct part of my question. He didn't. If his first answer was a lie, but the second was true, then moral misconduct sat big and broad in the equation somewhere. I'd gotten my answer from his silence.

"Your dad also says that you've been instrumental in expanding your ministry into Latin America. Do you think the threat comes from there?"

James shook his head. "I really don't think so. Our membership there doesn't care much about the competition between churches in the US. On top of that, our presence in Latin America extends back only a few years, probably no more than about 2002. Long after my experiences as a teenager."

"Do you think they would know about those experiences?"

"Certainly. It's a story worth repeating as often as possible." He gave me a smile radiant with the Gospel's glory, but his aura swirled up dark and angry. "My personal salvation is a testament to my father's faith and the invincible power of our Lord Jesus Christ."

"I'm glad for you." I wanted to sound sincere, but I don't think I made it. "Has any spark of that old temptation ever presented itself since those days?"

"No, thank the Lord." His lie spiked out, even bigger than the others. James sighed a deep breath and gazed out the window, as if savoring his God-given liberation for the first time. Poor guy. What kind of hell was he living in, pretending the hand of God had fixed him, living a straight man's life?

"Were the methods of your therapy harsh? I've heard they often are."

Richardson's aura boiled up with pain, grief, and rage, but his face remained an angelic mask. "I don't have to answer that, but I will. Yes, they were harsh. But they were warranted. My very soul was at stake." He paused, his eyes opaque with the flat stare of a bouncer. "And that's a closed chapter you and I will not be visiting."

I nodded. "Got it," I said making my note. "Is there any other light you can shine on this business right now?"

"Not at the moment." To my amazement, he was telling the truth. He knew a lot about this, but he couldn't shed light on it now. James Richardson was in this up to his neck. But how? Why?

I leaned forward, caught his eye and held it for a few heartbeats. I wanted him to know I knew he knew something else. I pulled out one of my cards and offered it to him. As he took it, I said, "In case anything else comes to you, I'd really appreciate a call. I promise not to badger you or anyone in your family. I'm just trying to solve this."

"I will do that, Mr. Morgan," he said, sounding thoughtful. "Something else may come to mind, and if it does, I'll be sure to let you know." He pulled out one of his cards and wrote on the back before he gave it to me.

I must have looked as surprised as I actually was, because he gave me a little smile, aura welling up in sadness. "My cell. In case you think of other questions for me," he said.

"Thanks," I said, tucking the card in my shirt pocket, pretending I didn't understand the gesture was a significant invitation, maybe even a request. We shook hands. I tried not to wince. James Richardson was a man in serious pain, and some of it burned in my knuckles. We headed down the hall.

Colin appeared before we'd taken half a dozen steps, steering Richardson away on some vector that didn't include me.

I headed on to the elevator.

As I walked down the Sixteenth Street Mall, I called Rocky Mountain Mercury and set up an appointment with the dispatcher in an hour. It was Friday afternoon, and they were already slowing down. I gave them the document number so they could be ready. I promised to be in and out in just a few minutes.

*

The dispatcher at Rocky Mountain didn't hand me a case-solver, but I did get a couple of interesting pieces.

Delivery of the fourth letter had been charged to the account of Stelnach, Kommen and Breyer. It had been picked up at the front desk, only to be delivered back to the same location an hour later. The same receptionist had signed off on the pickup as for the delivery.

That seemed strange, but when I asked the dispatcher about it, he just shrugged. The courier's pay was a low hourly base with a per-item delivery count determining the remainder. Even if the courier noticed that the letter was to be delivered to the same place where it was picked up, and he probably did when he scanned it into his handheld, he'd do it anyway. The rationale behind the letter's origin wasn't his problem, and the delivery meant another dollar in his pocket.

On my walk home, I pondered the varied nature of the deliveries—inter-office mail, regular post, taped to a shower door, and courier using Kommen's own account number. Two things became clear.

First, Enigma had at-will access to the innermost workings of Richardson's life. I'd got that already, but using Kommen's corporate account number for this delivery and having it physically picked up at the law office showed significantly broader access than I'd imagined. There weren't many with access to both Richardson's shower door and his attorney's office downtown.

Second, Enigma was bedeviling Richardson with item one. The deliveries had been orchestrated to that end. There was no other reason to use such a variety. Enigma was toying with the good reverend like a cat torments the mouse it will eventually kill.

No wonder Richardson's aura had fried with panic. He could feel hot cat breath in his whiskers, but he couldn't squirm out from under its paw. Howard Richardson was being punished.

*

I was just toweling off after a shower when my phone rang. It was Colin.

I looked at the bedside clock. It was six o'clock. "Do you always work this late on Fridays?" I asked.

"More often than I'd like, Mr. Morgan," he said. "I don't mind today, though. I've arranged Monday interviews for you, first at the church, then with Ann Richardson and James's wife, Leigh. I've got the details here if you want to write them down."

"Hang on," I said. "I just stepped out of the shower and don't have anything to write with." That was probably more information than was professionally appropriate, but it was fact.

"Oooh," he said softly. He hesitated, and I could imagine him looking over his shoulder to make sure no one else was within earshot. "I'd have worried if you had a pen in the shower, Mr. Morgan."

I chuckled. "That's good. Please call me Russ." If we were going to talk about my showers, we deserved to use first names.

"Okay." He paused again. "Russ. That sounds nice."

Now he was flirting. It felt good. "It's a good enough name, I guess."

Colin's voice dropped to a whisper. "No, I meant the shower thing." I felt my body respond. *Fuck. No, wait— wrong word.*

I laughed to hide my embarrassment at wanting him. "You'd better stick to the appointment details, or you're going to get us both in a lot of trouble, young man." *And it might be worth it.*

I wrote as he spoke. The church headquarters was down south, almost to Castle Rock. I could meet the office manager, Marianna Stokes, at eight o'clock, then Richardson's secretary, Gladys Everton, at nine. He gave me numbers in case anything came up. I'd have to leave at six thirty to make sure I got there in time.

Neither Ann nor Leigh wanted to come downtown to Kommen's office, so I was to meet with them at their respective homes in Highlands Ranch. According to Colin, they didn't live far apart. I'd check everything online anyway, now that I had the addresses.

As I finished writing, Colin chatted about the weather forecast for the weekend. I could see him being an outdoors kind of guy, biking or hiking maybe. It was a nice visual.

I wanted to ask him what plans he had for his weekend, but managed to resist the temptation. Instead I just thanked him, maybe with a little more warmth than was wise, told him to have a good one, and hung up, feeling unjustifiably proud of my virtue.

*

Simply driving into the multi-acre parking for Abundant Life and Gospel Ministry Church was a reminder that religion was also a business. I figured there were spaces for at least three thousand cars, and the soaring white structure looked like it could hold twice that many people.

Attached to one side of the church were the offices, with a separate entrance. I checked in with the concierge a little before eight.

At ten minutes after, a trim, young, short-haired Hispanic woman dressed in a gray business suit and modest black heels strode into the foyer and headed directly toward me. I stood. Marianna Stokes was polite as she introduced herself but offered no social niceties. Her wedding band was her only jewelry. She was all business.

She led me to the mailroom, describing the in-house mail system as we walked. By the time we arrived, she'd told me pretty much everything I needed to know. It was a generic open system and nearly anyone in the building could have put the first letter into it or even dropped it off directly in the mailroom without raising any question marks in anyone who noticed.

Even before eight thirty, three people were busy in the mailroom. One of them was running copies at a huge machine on one side of the room, the other two were sorting baskets of mail for delivery. Marianna saw nothing unusual in any of that. It was always a busy place. In fact, use of the copier for big jobs had to be scheduled.

I asked her if we could go to her office and talk for a moment. I promised I would take no more than ten minutes.

We took stairs to the second floor, where I was amazed to encounter a maze of easily two thousand square feet of offices, cubes, and conference rooms. The place was bustling.

She led me to her office, motioned me into a chair, and sat behind her desk. "I have a meeting in a few minutes, Mr. Morgan," she said, giving me fair warning.

I nodded, wondering why office managers always had shelves of three-inch black plastic ring binders with hand-printed labels lined up behind their desks. Maybe it was a badge of office.

"I have only a couple of questions," I said. "This won't take long."

I pulled out my notebook. "Do you know of anyone on staff whose spouse, girlfriend, or boyfriend might object to him or her working for the church?"

She shook her head firmly. "Absolutely not. Commitment to the ministry is number one priority for us. If someone was feeling pressure from family or loved ones about working here, they would speak up and ask for support. I'm certain of that."

I nodded. "One of the letters I'm investigating was taped to the shower door in the reverend's private bathroom. Is it possible that someone other than an employee could have stuck it there? The janitors? Some other contractor?"

"No." She shook her head again. "No one but an employee gets into the building without being cleared first at the front desk, twenty-four seven." She looked slightly apologetic. "Not everyone is as enthusiastic about the work we do as we are, Mr. Morgan. There are even those who would do mischief to us."

"As evidenced by the letters."

She gave a curt nod of agreement and glanced down at a handwritten page of notes on her desk. She was well prepared for me.

"The reverend asked about the janitorial service the day he found that letter," she said. "Shining Kingdom Janitorial does all our on-site work. They weren't scheduled the night before the letter appeared. They do the rest of the building as well as the offices, but they wouldn't have gotten into the office that night at all, even if they'd been on the premises. And they weren't."

And that was that. I stood, and so did she. "Thank you, Mrs. Stokes. I appreciate your time. If you'd have someone point me toward Gladys Everton's office, I'd be grateful."

Marianna pushed a button on her phone and summoned a plump, bright-eyed young woman with a glittery valentine heart containing a crucifix hanging at her throat. "Tracy will show you to Gladys's office, Mr. Morgan," she said. "She'll stay with you until Gladys is free."

I got it. I wasn't allowed to be on my own. Even once past the front desk, no stranger was allowed to wander unchaperoned. Without a doubt, the shower door letter was an inside job.

Marianna and I shook hands, and then I was speed-walking my way down a hall with Tracy before I could tuck my notebook and pen back in my pocket.

Gladys Everton was a quiet soft woman probably pushing sixty who wore her age well. Her bright blue eyes sparkled, and her voice was firm. Whether it was a difference in generation or background, she was gentler than Marianna Stokes, warmer and more gracious.

I asked her the same question about the possibility of a disgruntled employee or perhaps a family member.

Again, the answer was no. "Our little group begins each day in a prayer circle and sharing," she said with a den mother's kindness. "No one in my office has said anything about that—and they would."

She showed me Howard Richardson's office, and the bathroom he'd described to me as modest. "Modest" was clearly a relative term. The shower in question was a glass-walled walk-in, and the whole bathroom was at least twice the size of my bedroom.

The office itself was comfortably, unimaginatively appointed, with the exception of a big portrait of an olive-skinned, dark-haired Christ painted against rough golds and browns, hanging on the wall behind the desk. This was the virile son of a carpenter with strong arms and flashing teeth, not just some holy wimp. Interesting.

I didn't see any plants or a single living thing in the room. Not even cut flowers. I decided not to ask Gladys about that. There was an allegorical painting of a wheat field at harvest, though, with laborers bent over the sheaves. Maybe bringing in the sheaves was enough for the good reverend.

The walls had a few enlarged photographs of Howard beaming at the camera or beaming at people. Lots of beaming. He had an industrial strength smile, and he clearly used it a lot.

Gladys didn't know how anyone could have taped a message to the shower door, either. That baffled her. She would have certainly noticed, she said. Yes, she was at work the day in question, and the day before. She hadn't missed a workday in over a year.

I could feel the fear and confusion in her as she spoke of the letter. That was quite a contrast to when she spoke of Howard Richardson. She'd worked in his ministry for decades, she said proudly. Every time she mentioned his name her aura glowed with warm devotion, perhaps even love. A true follower.

I asked if she'd show me James Richardson's office. He wasn't in yet, but she unlocked it and stood in the doorway while I looked around. No private bathroom. It was smaller than his dad's but plenty big enough.

The desk had actual work on it, in tidy stacks and folders. James was organized, by the look of it. The walls were covered in photographs of Mexico or some other Latin American country: colorful groups assembled for the camera, singing and dancing, landscapes, seascapes. A group of children enacting La Posada, with Mary on a donkey and Joseph at the halter—*los peregrinos*, searching for shelter.

There were only two family photos behind the desk on the credenza, one of Leigh smiling, looking formal and brittle, and a larger one of their three kids. He'd have his back to them when he was seated at the desk, but anyone facing him would see them. Were they there just for show?

I wandered around the room a second time, studying the photos. They felt significant, somehow, with lots of energy attached to them. Sunny south of the border. It was the happiest looking room I'd been in so far. Still nothing living. Odd.

Then I was being escorted down to the entrance and walking toward my car. It looked lonely in the middle of all those vacant spaces. Most of them had been filled yesterday morning for Sunday service, I had no doubt.

*

Even though it was early for lunch, I'd had no breakfast and I was hungry. I got an Americano and a sandwich at a Starbucks and ate it on my way to interview Ann and Leigh Richardson, who waited for me in their enormous Highlands Ranch homes nestled among very white, very conservative, very Christian, and very comfortable folk just like themselves.

A little frisson of excitement made me shiver as if I were a spy parachuted into enemy territory, driving down the long curving streets with trees no more than thirty years old everywhere. Although maybe I didn't exactly qualify as an enemy spy. I'd actually voted Republican once. Long ago. Years before Proposition 2.

I didn't learn much about the letters from Howard's wife, Ann, or from James's wife, Leigh. But I learned a lot about the kind of family they had.

Ann reminded me so much of Laura Bush it hurt to think about it. She was gracious, perfectly coiffed and dressed—sweet and serene, in a pill-induced way. Detached and more than a little tragic, committed to appearances that didn't ring true to what little I could see of her inner life.

Anti-anxiety benzodiazepines affect the aura as well as whatever else they do. They create a signature fuzziness to a person's energy that Ann's displayed constantly. She said all the right things, and while I could see frequent incongruities between her answers and her energy, it was as if I connected from a great distance. Whether that meant a distant past or a chemical haze, I couldn't really tell.

I got an overall impression of regret and loyalty from her, as well as a wistful, genuine kindness that skewered my heart whenever it showed. Over the course of the interview, it became pretty clear that she appeared at functions when needed, addressed women's groups when asked, and basically stayed put in her bland and immaculate suburban mansion watching life roll by around her.

She had a few close friends in the church circle, of course. She didn't spend a lot of social time with Leigh—different generations, you know—but she doted on her grandchildren and loved taking them whenever their mom was busy.

She apologized that she couldn't shed any light on this terrible matter.

Leigh, on the other hand, was a barracuda. Intense, hair-trigger defensive, and ready tear the throat out of whoever was trying to blackmail her family. And her fury was genuine. She said she'd give her life to protect Howard's ministry and her family, and her aura confirmed it unequivocally.

She was keeping her share of secrets, though. When it came to questions about her home life with James and the children, she insisted everything was perfect as could be expected in this troubled world, but her aura flared all over the place. Not outright lies, but partial truths and withheld information. I probed gently and was told to back off in no uncertain terms. Her icy protectiveness was very real, and more than a little chilling.

She'd started volunteering at Abundant Life and Gospel Ministry Church as a teenager and stayed on to become an office employee. She'd met James in March of 1995 when Howard introduced them at a relief drive for victims of the previous month's big earthquake in western Colombia. They'd married three months later, a June wedding. In just over a week, they would celebrate their fourteenth anniversary with a quiet night at home. The children were six, eight, and eleven.

Most of her time was taken up with being a mom, but she would fill in wherever she could, however Howard needed her help. Her father-in-law was a true man of God and deserved all the assistance those around him could provide.

I was glad to get in my car and thaw out.

On the drive back into Denver, I wondered what it was like for James to live with Leigh. What kind of relationship did they have? Her aura had lit up when she spoke of her love for her children and for the church, but was much less vigorous when she spoke of James.

She was obviously intensely loyal and devoted to their kids. But there was something else in her, a religious fanaticism I'd first seen in my own father that neither James nor Ann displayed. That unquestioning ferocity had terrified me as a child, and Leigh's had frightened me now. Even Howard hadn't shown that kind of fervor. Maybe his had calmed over the years into a smoother certainty, like stones in a river.

My cell rang. It was Kommen, more agitated than I'd ever heard him. Another letter had arrived at his office, this time with a demand for money—two cases, each with $144,000 in cash. I was to meet him there immediately. I told him I was at the Tech Center, and it would be forty minutes before I could get to his office. He hung up and I sped up.

A hundred and forty-four thousand: the number of the blessed in Revelation, standing with the Lamb on Mount Zion. Doubled. Enigma had a sense of humor. No, scratch that. Enigma had a marvelous sense of irony.

*

When I got to the reception area, Colin was waiting for me. He practically dragged me into the elevator, down the hall, and into Kommen's office. What I guessed to be the new letter was the lone object on the gleaming expanse of his big desk, but Andrew Kommen himself was standing at the window, hands clasped behind his back. He didn't turn around when Colin ushered me in and then backed out, closing the door behind him.

"You said there would be another letter with the lyrics of that other song. You were right." It felt odd, getting that acknowledgment from him.

I walked to the desk and picked up the letter.

June 15, 2009—In honor of the approaching Solstice, REPENT!

"Return to Innocence"

Here it was; the famous song. Redemption, wild joy, and innocence. And then at the bottom, paydirt. Literally.

> *PS—To avoid complete destruction of the Abundant Life and Gospel Ministry Church have two cases, each containing $144,000 USD in non-traceable bills at Stelnach, Kommen and Breyer, ready for delivery, at 1:00 pm on Thursday, June 18th.*

The traces of this letter's origin were still fresh and easy to feel. A vortex of old pain, acute grief, and rage churned through me. I immediately recognized that particular blend of misery. I'd sat across from it for an hour last Friday. James Richardson had sent this letter, I was certain of it. I wasn't ready to share that little discovery with Kommen just yet.

"Well, now it's officially blackmail," I said. "Or extortion, if you prefer."

"I don't prefer," Kommen snapped without turning around. "I want a report. What progress have you made?"

"Actually, I'm pretty close to being able to provide you with Enigma's identity," I said. That got his attention. He turned around, his face comical with surprise.

"I have a few more things to confirm," I continued, "but I should be finished with the investigation by Wednesday. That would be the seventeenth."

I put the letter back on his desk. "My unsolicited recommendation is to have the money ready for Thursday as Enigma requested. I believe he can make good on his threat."

"Your unsolicited recommendation is a crock of shit," he spat. I watched him wrestle with his curiosity and lose. "He?"

"Yes, he." I shrugged. "Ignore my advice if you wish. But if I'm right about Enigma, you'll wish you'd listened."

I paused, almost feeling a little sorry for him. "That said, if I'm right, you won't like my answer no matter what."

Kommen leaned forward on his desk. "I insist you tell me who you suspect." I hoped he wasn't going to pound his fist on it, because I knew that in spite of my best efforts to the contrary, I'd laugh out loud at him.

"I will. On Wednesday. Keep a half-hour slot in your morning open for me, any time after 10:00. Reverend Richardson should be present, too. I'll call Colin sometime tomorrow to get the appointment time."

I drove home. I'd never solved a case where I'd known so little about what had happened in it.

Once I'd settled in my favorite armchair with a cup of coffee, I put *The Cross of Changes* CD in my computer and copied "Return to Innocence" onto my desktop. Then I dialed James's cell.

"I recognized your number, Mr. Morgan," he began. "I was wondering if you might call today."

"And here I am." I tried to sound light and conversational, but really, how do you ask a blackmailer if he knew he'd just sent another letter? I figured the direct approach was best. "Did you know that another letter arrived at Kommen's office?"

"I've heard." James's voice was cautious, but to my surprise, completely unafraid. Happy, in fact.

"I'd like to talk to you about it, but somewhere..." I hunted for a diplomatic word for 'well away from everyone else,' "neutral. Is it easy for you to meet, say, at Washington Park around lunch time tomorrow?"

There was a tiny hesitation. "Just checking. Sure. I can do that."

"Great. Let's meet at the parking lot on the west side of the lake. Bring a sandwich, and we can find some shade, eat while we talk."

"Sounds like a plan. What time?"

"Can you do early? Eleven-thirty?"

"Sure. See you then."

I sat for a moment, letting the conversation recede. On a hunch, I sent one of my favorite poems of all time to the printer downstairs.

Then I didn't want to think about the Richardsons or their problems anymore. I needed to focus on something else. I remembered getting an email from The Center, calling for LGBT volunteers to help with their new SAGE program outreach mailing. I'd see if they could use another volunteer for a few hours.

*

I was waiting in Wash Park's main lot when James climbed down out of his honking-big SUV and waved a cheerful greeting. He must have known that I suspected, but he seemed strangely carefree, as if he was confident I couldn't prove anything. Or maybe he truly didn't care.

As he strode toward me, something about him struck me as different. His dark hair was now blond. I decided not to mention it.

We shook hands. His aura sparked happy excitement, and I got still more confused. Maybe I'd got the whole thing wrong. "Thanks for coming," I said.

"Perfect day for a picnic," he answered. "What did you bring?"

"I like the custom deli sandwiches at King Soopers," I said. "Roast beef, cucumber, and provolone on light rye, with sprouts and lots of horseradish is my current favorite."

He hoisted a Subway bag, grinning. "Meatball marinara with double extra cheese. A contraband treat. Don't tell Leigh."

"My lips are sealed," I said, instantly struck by the irony. He must have got it, too, because he barked out a short laugh but didn't say anything.

We strolled around the north end of the tiny lake, mostly in silence. All the benches seemed to be out in the open, and I was going to need shade.

"Do you mind sitting on the grass?" I asked. "I don't do very well sitting in direct sun."

He loosened his tie. "Shade is definitely preferable for me, too," he said.

We found a cluster of trees right at the edge of the water and set up shop, unwrapping our sandwiches. I was still a little unnerved by James's calm atmosphere. He was as relaxed as if we were old friends who'd done this a hundred times, having a routine lunch at a favorite spot.

When we finished eating, we stuffed our trash into the Subway bag. As if James could sense that I was unsure of how to start, he stretched languorously and said, "About that letter."

"Yes." In that instant, I saw how to begin. I reached into my bag and opened up my laptop. "I want to play something for you. The sound isn't very good on my machine, but it's good enough for you to get the drift."

I clicked on "Return to Innocence" and the media player blossomed into action. "Ayy-yi-YI, Oh, ayy-yi-yii..." The haunting call of the song rose around us like ancient spirits finally set free to dance.

James closed his eyes, and his aura swirled and pulsed in the same dance. Before the words began, he was crying. When the song ended, we sat in silence for a while as the conifers all around us breathed their scent down on us in pungent whispers.

James wiped his eyes. "I'm glad you figured it out. Now you can tell Kommen and Howard, collect your fee, and move on."

"And you? Won't they press charges?"

His smile turned hard. "No, it's time for me to move on, too. And they won't press charges. I've had fifteen years to plan this. They can't touch me."

"Why? And I mean that question in the broadest sense. I'd like to understand."

He leaned back on one elbow. "Is it good, living openly gay?" he asked. "I have no choice, nor do I want one, but I'm scared."

I recognized that state, and compassion flooded me like a river breaching its banks. "It's very good." I closed my laptop and put it away. "There are surprises, though. Many of them unpleasant. Straight white men in this country are generally blind to how privileged their lives are. You will become part of a marginalized minority overnight, and that can be very scary."

"But spiritually. There's an inner life there, right? Something to navigate by, other than the physical?"

It was my turn to feel the burn of incipient tears. "Oh, yeah. It's there, I promise. Maybe involving a religion or maybe not, but there's a spiritual life for you as big as you have courage to make it."

"It's not easy, though, is it?" It wasn't a question.

"Not for me, not so far. All the standard paradigms in our culture are tooled for straight people. You'll have to build your own. It's worth it, though."

James sat up and brushed dirt from his sleeve. "Good. I needed to hear that. Thank you." He stared out over the lake, his aura thoughtful and determined. I got a flash of him locking the door to his Highlands Ranch house and walking to a waiting cab, on his way to his new life. He wasn't carrying luggage. I wondered about the children.

I waited for what I hoped was an appropriate length of time, given the magnitude of what he was facing.

"Can you tell me more about why, and some of how?" I asked quietly. "And about the kids? Not that any of that is really my business."

Slowly, James turned to face me as if coming back from very far away. "Sure. You'll get most of the story Thursday when I come to Kommen's office for the money and my grand exit." He grinned. "You'll have a front row seat for the fireworks. It'll be worth every penny, I promise you."

He looked back out over the lake. "The main reason," he said in a calm voice, "is because Howard Richardson is a brutal, cunning animal with the conscience of a crocodile. His moral compass is self-aggrandizement and power. He trades on the suffering and hope of others like a trader on the floor of the stock exchange. His hubris..." James's voice tightened, and he swallowed hard, "is about to be chastised."

I stayed quiet. James's profile was as grim, competent, and resolved as a soldier's.

"As it affects me directly, Howard Richardson's use of people started with my mother. She was the daughter of another prominent evangelist, Jimmy Evans. Howard worked for him as a junior pastor. She got pregnant, not by Howard, but someone else. I've never learned who. The scandal would have destroyed her father, and an abortion was, of course, out of the question.

"Maybe she confided in him, but somehow Howard learned about her situation. He approached her father with a deal. He would marry my mom, pretend the child was his, and in return he would inherit her dad's ministry. That's how Howard got his head start."

James paused. It's a powerful thing when someone tells a story that's been kept at the bottom of the heart's well for a long time. Each word seems to weigh fifty pounds, and it has to be hauled all the way up to the surface and into the daylight. It's hard work. I gave him space, knowing that as much of the rest of the story as he wanted to tell me was already on its way.

"He used that knowledge to bully my mom into submission. He bullied me with it, too. When I was ten, he told me I wasn't his son, and that I'd been conceived in sin. Said I should be grateful he'd rescued us both. He blackmailed us into the behavior he wanted from us."

He threw a little stone into the lake. After it splashed, and the ripples softened away, he smiled as if he approved of the calm water "The blackmailer is finally on the receiving end of the stick. Seems more than fair to me."

He fell silent, but I could tell his heart was busy processing. "He even made me dye my hair dark so it would look like his. By the time he went for the phony silver wisdom look, it was too late to change."

He turned to me with a broad grin and pointed to his head. "This is my real hair color, and I'm liking it a lot."

I smiled and nodded acknowledgment. "I noticed. Looks good on you."

"I'm going to pause the story in a minute, but there's one more piece that you should hear today.

"My mother didn't want me committed to reparative therapy. The plague was everywhere in 1993, and she was terrified for me, but she wanted to let me live my life.

"Howard was adamant, though. To his followers, my conversion would be another marquee triumph in his ministry. My ˋmom refused to sign the commitment papers. Howard signed them, which he had no legal right to do since he wasn't my biological father and hadn't adopted me. He couldn't adopt me, because my birth certificate already said I was his son.

"But because of all the earlier lies, he got away with it. That's when she started using tranquilizers. She's been adrift ever since. I truly believe she'll be happy I'm doing this."

He stared out at the lake for a moment, and his aura softened into tenderness. "I love her, and I'll miss her. She doesn't know it yet, but I've arranged a way for us to stay in touch, maybe even get together once in a while. With or without Howard's knowledge, I don't care."

He turned to face me, his energy hard again. "While I was a prisoner in that torture camp—which is what it was—I realized my only chance of surviving intact was to pretend I'd been healed. As fast as I could, I learned what they expected as results from my 'sessions' and fed it back to them. Theology was the key. The torture got less severe, and little rewards started showing up. More food. The occasional warm shower, with soap, even. Less slave duty. But it still wrecked me. After I got out, I couldn't have an orgasm, even on my own, for at least two years without feeling sick to my stomach, followed by a kind of paralyzing dread that I have no words for."

He turned toward me again and pulled off his tie, putting it in his jacket pocket. "An old saying goes that if you give a man enough rope, he'll hang himself. I've given Howard fifteen years of rope. He's now trapped in a web that he's spun all by himself, and when all is said and done, he'll be damn grateful I cost him so little." He almost giggled. "Ooh. I said damn! That felt good."

He punched me on the shoulder like we were veteran teammates. "The rest of the story is for Thursday. Go give Kommen your solution. Let him know I'm Enigma, and I'm not kidding about the money."

He stood, and I followed suit. "I wish I could see his face when you tell him, but I'm prepared to forego that little pleasure."

He reached into his jacket and pulled out a piece of paper. "I deliberately left my fingerprints all over the original of this one, but here's a copy of the letter. Kommen will understand I couldn't have made it without knowing what the original said. He'll get it. He's a weasel, but he's a smart weasel."

We walked back to his car in silence and shook hands. "I wish you all the best on your journey into a new life, James."

I pulled the poem out of my bag and gave it to him. "This is something that helped me more than I can say. It's a poem by Mary Oliver, called *The Journey*. I kept it taped to my dresser mirror for a couple of very dark years."

"Thanks, Russ. It feels good to tell all this to someone besides Raul."

"Raul?"

James laughed. "I met him three years ago, doing the Lord's work in Mexico. Thursday." He climbed up into the cab of his SUV and the beast snarled to life. The window slid down. "I'll be so glad to leave this monster truck behind, along with the monster house, and the monster wife. The kids I will miss, but I can't do anything about that."

The window slid up and he backed out. I waved, watched him drive away, then headed for my own car.

Telling Kommen tomorrow morning was going to be an interesting adventure. In the meantime, I'd type up my report and attach the letter James had given me.

I needed a change of pace. There was a Rockies game this evening, and I decided to splurge on a high-end ticket. *Maybe Colin would like to come with me, too. Three hours in the soft Colorado evening with Colin, side by side, knees brushing now and then. No. Still a bad idea.*

*

Andrew Kommen pushed away from his desk and marched to the window, clutching my report in a fist. Apparently, the view from the window wasn't any more comforting than the one he'd just left, so he returned to his desk. He hadn't taken the news that James Richardson was Enigma gracefully. His face was as ashen as his office walls. His hands shook. "You bastard. You don't know how much damage you've done to good people."

"Don't shoot the messenger, Mr. Kommen." I picked my words with care. "I'm not responsible for the behavior of others. It may be your practice to lay blame like that, but you can't make me the bad guy."

I stood up. "I'm glad you refused to have Rev. Richardson here for this. He can learn the news from you, rather than me. I'm guessing he's a messenger-shooter, too. Good luck with that."

I stopped at the door. "You'll get my invoice for $39,000 this afternoon. That's two weeks at seven thousand, and the bonus of twenty-five for solving the matter within four weeks of engagement. I'd like it in a cashier's check, please. All as agreed in our contract."

This time I got all the way to the elevator before Colin caught up to me. I was genuinely glad to see him. His face told me he was glad, too.

*

At five minutes to one the next day, Colin fetched me from the reception area and delivered me into Kommen's inner sanctum. Everyone else was already there, and the atmosphere felt like sharks circling in chummed water. Two closed briefcases sat on the coffee table in front of Howard. I assumed it was the payoff. Colin bolted, and I sat down without anyone acknowledging my arrival.

I wasn't offended. I was just a spectator in this drama now. In fact, I figured that both Howard and Kommen had objected when James insisted I be present. He'd promised me all the answers and the fireworks, though. Right now, it felt like they were going to be prizewinners.

James got up and poured himself a drink at the bar. "Anyone else for a drink?" Ugly silence was his answer. "Right, then," he said, sitting back down. "Let's do the money exchange first, then you can ask me questions."

He pulled up a battered gray and black duffel from beside his chair, then a green one from inside the first. "Andrew, would you please transfer the money to these bags?"

"No," Howard Richardson jumped up as if his chair had ejected him, his face an unhealthy red. "Answers first."

James shrugged and sat back. "Ask away, then."

Howard paced. "Why in heaven's name are you doing this?" he fumed.

James was as relaxed as he'd been at the park two days ago. "Because you took my life away from me, and now I'm taking it back. With interest."

"But why now, when my ministry is doing so much good work—work that you've done so much to accomplish?" Richardson's voice had a whine in it, and I almost felt embarrassed for him.

"You are so fucking blind, Howard." James shook his head. Apparently, he'd been practicing his swear words, because this time he didn't even blink. "Why now? Because I'm finally ready, and because there's a lovely symmetry to this timing."

He took a swig of his drink. "I was released from the prison you sent me to on March 31st of 1994. Easter was April 3rd that year. On that morning, you paraded me like a prisoner of war in front of the congregation and the cameras, claiming I'd been raised from the depths of temptation, restored by everyone's prayers."

James Richardson had probably never had such complete attention from the Reverend and Kommen. They were spellbound. Maybe it was the first time they realized how serious he was.

"Easter was April 4th this year. Enigma's first letter arrived on April Fool's Day. So close to Easter, so apt. This time, I sat quietly on stage while you postured and pounded and prayed, knowing that it would be the last time I'd have to do it." He took another sip of whatever he'd poured himself and smacked his lips.

"In the fifteen years between those two Easters, I spent every moment I could planning my escape and your punishment. At first, I wanted you dead." Everyone's eyebrows went up, including mine.

"But I realized that would be far too easy on you. I want you to live a long time with the knowledge of how you crippled your little empire, and how you have no one to blame but yourself."

"But I've done nothing—"

"Nothing? Shut up, Howard, and listen. You ready?" James started counting on his fingers.

"One. You turned my mother's pregnancy into a bargaining chip to seize control of old man Evans's church. And money.

"Two. You signed my commitment papers to reparative therapy illegally, since you are not my father but only my stepfather.

"Three. You were already fucking Leigh when you introduced her to me, and you didn't stop when we got married. And yes, there have been others. I have only a partial list, but it's plenty long." It was as if all the oxygen had left the room. Both men stared at James in silence. Neither one of them moved for several seconds.

"Four. Most importantly, once you realized I wasn't going to sire children to support your conversion myth, you got busy. You've had three children by the wife that you arranged for me. You had the gall to pretend they were mine. Leigh readily agreed, of course, because she'd do anything for you. Anything. Your willingness to use people," James choked up, shook his head as if to open the pipes again, "is staggering."

James let his hands drop. The room was utterly silent. I looked at Kommen. His aura was shocked flat, in full defensive mode. I guessed he hadn't known this stuff, and now it looked like he was busy figuring out how to distance himself from the good reverend.

"I'll deny it." Howard stood up straight in what he must have thought was a gesture of defiance. "Leigh will support me."

"You idiot!" James shouted. "How can you be so fucking stupid? Do you really think you can pray away reality? Pray away the gay? Pray away the DNA?" James slammed his glass on the table and stood up. "Reality, especially *inconvenient* reality, is part of God, Howard. It's time you figured that out."

He knocked back the rest of his drink, strode to the bar, and got himself a glass of water. "Do you think I've just been doodling on a notepad for fifteen years? No, you don't think at all. I have no Richardson genes. Thank heaven. But I do have DNA samples from myself and the children recorded at two different labs, both of which are recognized by the courts. Enough of the blood tests were authorized by Leigh for other reasons, so you can't claim I've committed some kind of fraud. And I have certified copies of all of them.

"Those are documents beyond your control. They will prove your paternity beyond a doubt." James raised his glass in a cynical salute. "Copies of the relevant ones are poised to be mailed to some of your fiercest brothers in Christian ministry. I suspect you know what they might do with those. The very same thing you would do with them if the shoe were on the other foot."

Howard Richardson's face had gone grey. "Please—"

"Oh, you want mercy? You are so pathetic." James laughed, joyless and hard. "You cruel, selfish little man. Long ago you abandoned the last scrap of human decency you may have once had. But now when you're caught with your pants down, you want mercy?"

James dashed to stand in front of Howard, and I braced for physical violence. None came. "When did you show me mercy?"

His voice became a wail. "You let those men fucking torture me! A boy died while I was there, and not by suicide. Death by therapy." He took a deep breath and blew it out. "Do you even know what they did to me? Do you?"

He wiped a string of spittle from his chin. "No, you don't. You didn't want to know."

He turned away with a sob. "Listen to the songs on that album again, Howard. You might get a whiff of how bad your shriveled, decaying heart stinks. What's the term our HR department uses in our employment agreements? Moral turpitude? That's you, Howard. You should be fired."

Richardson's face crumpled, but James wasn't finished. "It's your turn now. It's time you climbed up on the cross of changes. For the rest of your pathetic life."

I surprised myself by breaking the long silence that followed. "Tell us about those lyrics, James?" Three heads swiveled in my direction.

Howard opened his mouth, but James cut him off with an abrupt hand wave. "Sure."

He raised one hand, thumb and forefinger an inch apart. "That following summer, 1994, I was this close to suicide. I couldn't function with a woman, didn't even want a woman, and I didn't dare touch a man. I was drowning, without hope. I was eighteen, trapped in his phony righteousness." He tilted his head toward Howard.

"Then I heard that song, 'Return to Innocence.' It saved my life. I knew it was a sign from the real god, the one that wanted me to be me. I played that song over and over. I wore out tapes, then I wore out CDs. It was my secret treasure. It became my battle cry."

He took a drink of water. "I had to be patient. But I knew that if I kept the faith, the next step would come. Meanwhile, Howard, you just kept digging your own grave without any help from me or anyone else.

"I found men here and there, decent guys, all very short term, since I wouldn't tell them who I really was. Then I met Raul. I knew he was the one. We've been lovers for three years, and we're very happy together. We'll live in Mexico."

His eyebrows arched, as if he'd just remembered something. "Oh, by the way. I've emptied all the church accounts I had signing powers for. That came to about a hundred grand, in case you're wondering."

James pointed to the duffels next to the briefcase. "So now it's time for this money. Andrew, you can do the honors."

Kommen got a nod from Howard, clicked open the briefcases and began putting the bundled bills into the bags. It didn't take long. "How do we know you won't keep asking for more money?" he snarled, stepping back.

"You don't. I don't expect to ask for more, but you never know. I'll be happiest, though, if I don't."

James turned to Kommen. "Speaking of money, have you paid Mr. Morgan yet? If not, that should happen now."

Andrew Kommen made his pissy face but said nothing. He pulled out an envelope and gave it to me. Feeling cynical, I opened it and checked. Right instrument, right amount.

"What about the children?" Howard was whining again. "They'll grow up without a father."

James barked out a short laugh. "What do I have to say to make this sink in? They *will* grow up with their father, their *real* father, and you'll take good care of them. Leigh will no doubt make me out to be the villain, but while I'm genuinely fond of the kids, they're not mine. They're yours and Leigh's, you take care of them. Be decent to them. And to my mom, too. I'll know if you're not. You don't want that to happen, believe me."

James stood up, took the bags and hoisted one in salute, as if he were getting on a plane. Maybe he was. He'd had plenty of time to make reservations. "Don't try to come after me, Howard. If you do, you'll lose everything."

James smiled. No, he was gloating. "See, you're the one in the closet now. One mistake from you is all it will take. One email from me to a particular attorney somewhere in this great country, and your sordid story—complete with proof—comes blazing out of the closet to be splashed over every Christian network station there is."

He winked at me and then he was gone. Nobody moved or spoke for what seemed a very long time. I was the first to leave.

*

I drove home slowly, so sad my chest hurt. For an empath, it's never easy witnessing a family, no matter how dysfunctional, tearing itself apart. The pain goes so deep, the wounds are so grievous. Pain is pain, and even with practice you can't always keep a wall between your own and what belongs to others.

Worst of all, it's usually the innocents who get ground up the worst in battles that never should have injured them in the first place. The sins of the fathers. If this scandal became public, the three Richardson kids would be exposed horribly. At best they would simply suffer abandonment by the man they believed to be their father.

Later, hopefully when they were strong enough to bear it, they'd probably discover the grotesque truth that their real father and grandfather was the same man, that both he and their mother had lied to them, just as James had. Children may fib, but it takes an adult lying to a child to do real damage.

On the other hand, I believe deeply that at least once, maybe twice in a man's life he has to choose between his own truth and all the stories the rest of the world tells him about what he owes others.

James Richardson had faced a terrible choice. He could be true to himself or be what others wanted him to be. He'd been brave enough to take the path of authenticity, and I couldn't fault him for that, no matter how many people got hurt. Maybe he should have made the choice earlier, but I'm in no position to judge, given my own story with the bottle.

That was what Mary Oliver's poem, the one I'd given him yesterday, was all about. Save the only life you can save.

I was tempted to rescue the kids myself somehow, although I knew as rough as this was going to be for them, their wounds weren't mine to heal. Someone else would have to do that. Someday.

From what I'd seen of the Richardson adults, it wasn't likely to be them, either. Howard wouldn't have a clue about where to start. Maybe Ann, one day, if she could find her way back to earth. But not Leigh. She was still too certain of her own righteousness to acknowledge her part in this mess. The kids' suffering would forever be James's fault, not hers.

I parked behind my house and got out. I imagined making a placard saying, "Be good to your child today!" and marching up Colfax Avenue with it. That made me cringe. I was getting maudlin, and that's not a healthy place for me, even just to visit.

I needed a meeting. There was one at three on weekdays over at the York Street Club. If I started out now, I wouldn't have to drive. I figured the walk and the open air would do me good.

Maybe after the meeting, if I felt brave enough to take a risk that could end up hurting both of us, I'd give Colin a ring and ask if he liked baseball.

BLOOD & DIRT

A Note from the Author

When I wrote *Enigma*, the first Russ Morgan mystery, I wrote it as a one-off submission for an anthology. *Enigma* didn't make the anthology, but to my delight another publisher picked it up.

Even after the publisher contracted it as a standalone, I didn't see it as the beginning of a series. It was only after readers responded enthusiastically to Russ as a PI that I realized he might have more stories to tell. It's true, sometimes the author is the last to know. So here is the second Russ Morgan mystery, set in current time as all others will be in future. In a miracle of fiction writing, nobody has aged in Russ's leap into current time. I trust you don't mind...

Chapter One

Saturday

"Russ Morgan Investigations is invisible," Evan Landry said as he settled elegantly in front of my desk. It was an accusation, but I assumed he meant well and intended it for my own good. "You don't even have a website. You really should embrace the twenty-first century."

By all accounts, Mr. Landry was a successful restaurateur, so I was sure he knew all about promotion through websites and social media. I'd also heard he was ruthless and domineering. I got the domineering part right away.

I nodded, unashamed. "It's true, I probably should, although personal referrals seem to work best for my business. Isn't that how you found me?"

"Yes." He seemed oblivious to the implication. "I want you to find out who trashed my sister's marijuana grow," he said, as nonchalant as if he'd asked for more coffee. His aura, however, was a mess, swirling bright red with fury. He was very good at hiding his feelings.

"You'll find out it was my nonbiological *sister*," he said, making disdainful air quotes around the word sister, "Marianne Ellis. But I want proof."

In Colorado, a case involving marijuana was inevitable, I supposed, but this was my first.

He brushed something seemingly offensive off his slacks. "I'd like you to start today on-site at the ranch, which is just south of Grand Junction. I'll pay whatever your rate, travel, and per diem are. I want the bitch nailed. Quickly."

I smiled, hoping I didn't look too amused by his unexamined sense of entitlement. "Assuming we come to an agreement, I'll be glad to drive up Monday."

He frowned. "I want you there today. It's Saturday. Even with weekend traffic, you can be there by four at the latest."

It might have occurred to him that I had obligations preventing me from jumping into my car at that moment, but apparently, he'd dismissed that possibility as unimportant.

He fixed me with a glare that was undoubtedly successful on his sous-chefs. "You said on the phone you were available to take a new assignment."

"And I am. I'll be glad to get there Monday. I have a commitment here in Denver tomorrow I need to honor."

"You came highly recommended," he said, changing tack. "I hope I haven't been misled. You don't strike me as being very responsive to a client's interests."

"Just the opposite," I said, only mildly offended. "I take my commitments very seriously, including one to you, should I make it. That means you don't have to worry about me jumping ship if someone comes by with a more attractive offer. I won't do that for you, but I won't do it to you, either."

He pursed his lips. "Okay." He sounded miffed. "Monday, then."

"So, can you give me a little background before I say yes?"

"Of course." Landry never missed a beat, all practicality. "My sister Sarah started growing marijuana when it became legal a few years ago. She found a couple of good strains and learned how to grow the stuff. She's very good at it.

"The laws around cultivation are complex, and bank loans aren't possible. I loaned her money to get started and helped her navigate becoming part owner of a dispensary that's now a retail outlet as well. Last year she began to make real money at it and invested her profit in the systems to take her operation to a much larger scale."

He waved his hand in a vague, dismissive gesture. "Large, very expensive lights, a drip irrigation system, some kind of chemical regulation equipment for the hydroponics. From rooting a cutting to its harvest, marijuana runs on a four-month cycle. She staggers those cycles to sustain a monthly yield from her new system. Last week, when she was nearly ready to harvest her current crop, someone broke into the barn, doused all the plants with gasoline, smashed half the lights with a baseball bat, and tore up the irrigation system."

I shifted my vision to check on Landry's aura. It was seething. "And you suspect your stepsister Marianne Ellis? Statistics show vandalism is usually the work of an angry male."

"I'm certain of it." Landry's smile was grim. "But I wouldn't put it past her to have hired a thug to do it for her. I'll brief you on our toxic family constellation if you're wondering about the different last names, but I'll wait until you agree to investigate before I show you all our family's filthy laundry. For the moment, I'll just say Marianne is a ruthless bitch with embarrassingly bloated social pretensions. Having a sibling growing marijuana in a conservative ranching community does not advance them.”

“What do the police have to say about it?”

Landry’s face darkened. “I haven’t filed a complaint and won’t. There’s no point. It’s complicated. For one thing, it’s essentially a family matter because it happened on family land.”

An ambulance pulled up at the corner of Pearl and Colfax a block away, its siren howl dying as it stopped. Landry glanced out the front bay window at the sound before turning his attention back to me.

“The Sheriff’s Department is not thrilled with the arrival of marijuana cultivation in the county. All over the state, one hears stories about ambivalence of law enforcement in protecting the interests of grow operators, so I’m not sure how much help they would be, even if I did report it. But the real reason is that the Ellis name still carries some prestige in regional society, and the Ellises want to keep this as quiet as possible.”

He looked up from examining his fingernails, and a genuinely soft, sad expression crossed his face. “It’s pathetic, really, that belief in the clout of a family name persists long after any actual significance is gone.” His face hardened. “This is the twenty-first century. Ranching fell on hard times a long time ago, and the once great Ellis Ranch is on the verge of bankruptcy. More of that story later, too.”

“But isn’t this pointless, then?” I asked. “If you don’t want to go to the police, or the sheriff, I guess, if you’re in unincorporated territory, what are you going to do when you find out for sure who did this? And if Marianne did it, what difference would that make? It strikes me that you’re merely set on getting even. Why would you need proof that it was Marianne? If you're certain, why not just take your retribution now?"

"I may be an aggressive businessman," he said with a sharp, cold light in his eye, "and make no mistake that is exactly what I am, but I like to have facts before I take—" He paused and gave me one of the most chilling smiles I'd ever seen, a predator licking his chops in anticipation of an easy kill. "—appropriate measures."

"I imagine it takes a lot of guts and determination to succeed as a restaurateur," I said, appalled at the venom in his aura but trying to be tactful. "From what I've heard, it's a perilous profession."

Landry chuckled, cold and humorless. "The world will carve you up and eat you raw if you aren't ready to fight back, Russ." He lifted one elegant, long-fingered hand. "And a chef is only as good as his knife skills. I have no intention of letting that happen to me. Ever."

Landry uncrossed his legs, leaned forward, and put his forearms on the desk. The motion pushed up his sleeves, exposing a fancy square Tag Heuer watch on his wrist. "So. Do we have an agreement?"

I'd never been able to figure out why, but without trying I had become a specialist in dysfunctional families. Landry was obviously no saint, but then who is? Besides, a private investigator who worked only for saints would starve.

I couldn't deny family intrigue was fascinating to me. Over the years, I'd encountered a long parade of bizarre relationships, toxic secrets, competition for affection or mere attention, and vendettas. However, I'd also seen reconciliations and witnessed the most beautiful demonstrations of compassion and forgiveness and understanding. I smiled at my own discovery. Maybe I had just figured out why I'd become a specialist in family complexities.

I stuck out my hand. "Yes, I'll take your assignment. I've never had anything to do with marijuana cultivation, so this should be especially educational."

"Good." Landry gave my hand a perfunctory shake that said my answer was no surprise to him—he'd expected my agreement before he walked in. At the same moment, he slid his other hand into a jacket pocket and handed me a check. Already made out to me. "A retainer," he said with cool nonchalance. "You don't need to create an invoice until you're done, then we can see what's left to cover."

Nodding, I tucked the check into my desk drawer and pulled out my simple one-page engagement letter.

"Now," Landry said as we finished up the formalities, "you get all the dirty laundry."

I got ready to take notes.

*

It was a convoluted story, with all the elements of a classic family melodrama, a perfect breeding ground for bad blood. Stanford Ellis, the current owner of the Ellis Ranch, was in his sixties. He'd married young and sired three children: Stanford Jr., Marianne, and William, who everybody called Billy even though he was now in his late twenties.

When Billy was four, Mrs. Ellis decided the rancher's life was no longer for her and disappeared, leaving her husband with three small children to raise and a ranch to run.

Stanford, being an old-school rancher, knew a rancher needed a wife, so he got himself another one—

Carolyn Landry, who already had two children of her own by a previous marriage.

Although Carolyn had frequently asked Stanford to formally adopt her two children, Evan and Sarah, he'd refused. Maybe it was some vestige of arrogance about the Ellis name and Ellis blood that prevented him from saying yes. Maybe it was something else, but while Stanford Sr. was perfectly decent to his second wife, the two children she had brought into the family remained Landrys.

According to Landry, Stanford Sr. might have been obstinate about that particular issue but was indecisive about everything else. After Carolyn's death, his refusal to take a firm stand with his brood left the children to cope with each other without boundaries except, strangely, at the dinner table. There, Stanford controlled everyone's behavior with a dictator's fist.

By middle school, an internecine rivalry had begun, with the Ellis children pitted not only against the Landrys, but against each other as well. Each child developed their own way of fighting, or at least coping.

Sarah had become something of a Birkenstock hippie, spending more time with animals and plants than people. She did passably well at school and began working for the local rancher's co-op after graduation.

When she could show that marijuana was a viable cash crop, she negotiated a very favorable lease with Stanford Sr. for space in an old barn the ranch no longer used, complete with water rights.

Evan had stayed under the radar of family conflict as much as possible until he came out in high school, then he defiantly took on all comers. He'd escaped as soon as he could, moving to Denver where being gay wasn't such a big deal, got a grunt job in a restaurant. and learned the business as he worked his way up to chef, managing partner, and, finally, owner.

Stanford Jr. had never really accomplished much of anything. He was smart but chronically unrealistic. He daydreamed, was undisciplined and grandiose, and drank far too much and too often. Marianne was the most social of the Ellis children and went off to study journalism after high school. She was now part of the TV news team at the Grand Junction station. She made sure she was part of all the social circles on the western slope that counted, few as those were.

Billy wasn't the sharpest knife in the drawer but was kind and reliable. He and Ellis Senior did all the physical work on the ranch. Billy had gone through high school as a member of Future Farmers of America and 4-H. He'd raised prize-winning animals to show at the county fair. He was born to be a rancher.

Stanford Sr. had made the competition and distrust among the siblings worse by making vague promises and threats about who would inherit parts of the ranch land when he died, and the story changed all the time.

Maybe he thought that was the only club he had to maintain control, but whatever the reason, the lion's share of blame for sibling animosity rested at the patriarch's door, as far as Evan Landry was concerned.

"Even though our family dynamic puts a nest of vipers to shame," Landry said, winding up his story, "Ellis insists that when we are on ranch property, we all eat dinner together." He gave me a joyless smile. "And you'll get to join us in that unique pleasure on Monday night."

That didn't sound particularly attractive to me.

Landry stood and shrugged his sport jacket into place. "Arrive at the ranch as soon as you can. I'll introduce you to Stanford Sr. before dinner. He's promised everyone's full cooperation, and he's the only person who can make that promise. So be aware you'll be operating under his aegis as well as mine."

He laughed bitterly. "My aegis is not half as far-reaching as Stanford's, so stay alert. The only reason I'm still tolerated on the property is because I've got money and because Sarah's marijuana operation is now a more reliable income stream than the ranching operation."

He shook his head. "The Ellises have the land, and the Landrys have the money. You'd think that would offer an easy solution, but family blood and pride seem thicker than poverty and envy. Or their cure."

"How do I get to you on Monday?"

"Oh, right." He reached into his pocket and pulled out another piece of paper. "I sketched this map. It's easy. The ranch is on the west side of the Gunnison. South from Grand Junction to Whitewater on 51, then west on 141 a few miles. You'll see the sign for Ellis Ranch, north side of the road. Get there no later than four o'clock. Call me if you get lost."

We shook hands again, me agreeing to his instructions. He let himself out, and I watched him cross the street toward a high-end Mercedes sedan. Its lights blinked, ready and obedient, as he approached. Evan Landry was used to being the boss.

Chapter Two

Sunday

I worked hard to keep my breath rhythmic and steady, if only so I wouldn't embarrass myself with ragged gasping. Men at different ages had different things to prove, I mused, focusing on my diaphragm to push used-up air out of my lungs.

At twenty, few men needed to prove they could get an erection; at seventy, it might be different, setting aside magic pills. On the other hand, at twenty it was hard to prove excellence in your chosen field, if you even had a chosen field at that age. At seventy, you'd probably have made peace—or at least a truce—with your career. From my vantage point at fifty-three, I seemed obliged to prove most everything. I was about to draw a deep conclusion to my train of thought, but some scree gave way under my boot and derailed it. I nearly fell on my face.

Here on a steep Flatirons trail outside Boulder, Colin Stewart didn't need to prove he was equal to the climb, whereas I felt obliged to keep up with him even though he was half my age. Pride can be a bigger bully than a drill sergeant.

Colin's sturdy calves bunched and released as he clambered up the escarpment ahead of me, his hiking boots bouncing from one toehold to another. The trail wasn't heart-stoppingly difficult, even for me, and following his firm shorts-clad backside at close range certainly made the tougher parts of the trail more rewarding. The Sunday morning sun, still fairly low behind us, warmed our backs and turned the fine hair on his tanned legs to spun gold. Lust for spun gold was another powerful inspiration to keep up.

As I pulled myself up around a boulder already May-morning warm, I admitted that hiking with a young man who, for some unfathomable reason, found me desirable was the standard stuff of midlife fantasies. Most gay men my age would be trembling with excitement, asked out on a date with an adorable young thing who made no secret he wanted more than just a date. But adorable and young as Colin was, he definitely wasn't just a thing. He deserved much more than I could give him.

The trail's incline eased, and I filled with more gratitude than I should have felt.

The way I saw it, the reality of a fifty-something-year-old man being pursued by someone as young, intelligent, and sweet as Colin Stewart posed a much more complex problem than any midlife fantasy. I had serious reservations. When I thought about a relationship with him, I immediately felt responsible for his happiness, and my sobriety had no room for such bald codependence. Worse, I was fighting a losing battle to suppress an old shame I didn't want to face.

Sweat tickled down my spine in a steady little stream. With a mixture of relief and arousal, I stared at a moisture-darkened V forming on the back of Colin's khaki shorts, starting just below his belt. Never mind he was carrying our lunch and all the water in his daypack. At least he was sweating, too. It seemed only fair.

He twisted to look down at me, his face damp, radiantly happy under the wide brim of his hat.

"Let's stop for water," he said. "Even on a trail like this, it's important to stay hydrated."

"What do you mean, even on a trail like this?" I panted, trying not to feel embarrassed.

Colin laughed, pulling a big blue bandana from his hip pocket and tilting his hat back to wipe his forehead. "I didn't mean it that way. Really. This is work for me, too." He hitched his pack into place. "I meant a short outing. We'll be back in Denver in a few hours."

"Still plenty of time to see the rest of my life flash before my eyes, I guess."

"You're doing great," he said, holding out his hand to me. I took it, and he pulled me up next to him. Close. He cocked a thumb at his backpack and turned away from me. "Dig us out some water."

As I pulled out a bottle, I admitted he was right. I was in much better than average shape for my age. But I wasn't twenty-five like Colin, and he certainly wasn't fifty-something. And therein lay the root problem for us, as I saw it.

Us. I handed Colin the water and watched him tilt his head back to drink, watched his throat move as he swallowed. I wanted to feel that motion under my tongue. There couldn't be any "us," not in the long run.

He must have felt me staring, because he gave me a knowing smile and slowly licked his lips. "Like what you see, Russ?"

"You know I do."

"Well, I like what I see, too." He handed me the water bottle and stared me in the eye. "A lot."

I couldn't bring myself to accept what he said was true, but I knew he wasn't lying. His aura showed no guile when he said it, not a flicker. I got vertigo when he talked like that. I took a long pull of water, not wanting to think about what the lust in my own aura might look like in that moment.

"Time for us to get back on the trail, don't you think?" It was weak of me to change the subject like that, but I wasn't feeling brave. Colin gazed at me for a moment, eyes cool, and shrugged.

Ashamed of my cowardice, I stuffed the water back in his pack and off we went again.

*

"I love the climb, but I love the view from the top even more." Colin made a slow three-sixty, turning first to the mountains and foothills to the north, then the flatland stretching out to the east under its Front Range brown cloud, and finally, endless mountains to the south and west.

"It's magnificent," I agreed, pulling in lungfuls of air so fresh the ozone stung my nostrils.

"That's what I wanted to do to you, too," he said, not breaking his gaze from the higher hills behind us. "First time I saw you, I wanted to climb you so bad."

"Climb the mountain just because it was there?"

"Not at all," he said, turning to scowl at me. "And it's not just physical. When you told me about how you read auras and what it felt like, that was it. I wanted to move in with you right then." He laughed. "And climb your mountain." He gave me his evil grin, the one that scared the crap out of me because it cut straight through my rational defenses to fire me up. "I'll bet the view from your peak is fabulous. Bet I'd see shooting stars."

I laughed in spite of myself but kept staring at the snow-covered peaks to the west. I could feel Colin's eyes on me as he waited for me to say something. I filled my lungs with air and let it out slowly, grateful I was no longer panting. He deserved my honesty, if nothing else, even if I wasn't proud of what I had to say.

I turned to face him. "We should talk."

Colin grinned and shook his head in mock amazement. "I was beginning to think you'd never say that." He pointed to a flat rock at the edge of the lookout and shrugged out of his backpack. "Let's eat while we do." It was a little intimidating to see how patient and together Colin was. How mature. I followed him to the ledge, feeling like I was the one who needed extra care.

"So," I said as he spread out the sandwiches. "I should start by saying that I'm really flattered by your interest in me."

"But," Colin said quietly.

"No but. Full stop. I can't describe how good it feels to be desired by someone as young, smart, and beautiful as you." I stared into his elfin green eyes, fascinated at their almond shape and hypnotic depth. I felt naked—and not in a good way. I looked away. "It's also terrifying. I need to tell you a little story."

I put down my sandwich, knowing I couldn't eat until I got this out. "Almost fifteen years ago, shortly after I got sober, I met a beautiful young man. I was pushing forty, he was in his twenties. We liked each other. A lot. We dated. We had great sex, we shared a lot of interests in spite of our age difference. I fell hard."

The memory hurt so much I had to close my eyes. "Fell so damn hard." My voice cracked, so I took a drink of water and wiped my mouth with the back of my hand. I felt Colin watching me, but I couldn't look at him.

"One day, a few weeks into our affair..." My throat stopped working. In a moment, I tried again. "He'd stayed over, we were having breakfast. I pushed a set of keys to my house across the table to him and asked him to move in with me. He put down his coffee cup, looked at me, and said, 'I've thought about that, and realized that in twenty years I don't want to wake up next to a sixty-year-old man.' Then he got up from the table, kissed the top of my head, gathered his things, and left. We never spoke again." As painful as it was, it felt good to have said it aloud.

"Jesus, Russ."

"I felt so incredibly ashamed. I might have been able to change my behavior or my work or any number of other things to keep us together, but I could do absolutely nothing about my age. My 'best used by' date had long passed, apparently, even though I was so sure it hadn't." I laughed because I didn't want to cry. "And now it's over a dozen years past that."

I shifted to face him square on. "It sounds melodramatic, but it nearly killed me. I came within a cat's whisker of picking up a drink again, and for me to drink is to die. I can't risk getting drunk again, I don't think I'm strong enough to survive it."

I stared at him, cherishing the way the sun lit the sheen of sweat on his ruddy cheeks. "I wish to hell it weren't so, but I'm just too old for you, Colin. A relationship with you would be wonderful, I'm certain. But I'm not resilient enough to survive another breakup like that, just because I'm too old."

"But I—"

"No, let me finish. You're twenty-five—"

"Twenty-six."

"Twenty-six. You've got your whole life in front of you. I've lived most of mine. As wonderful as our life together might be, a moment would come when you looked at me with disgust. You'd ask yourself what the hell you were thinking when you took up with me." I hoped my smile didn't show my pain at saying goodbye to something precious. "I'm sorry. But thank you just the same. Your interest makes me feel young, even if I'm not."

Colin didn't say anything, just stared out at the prairie as he chewed on his sandwich. I tucked into mine, grateful to have something nonverbal to do. Halfway through my sandwich, I saw him put his down.

"I know how old you are, Russ. I like how old you are. Maybe you think there's something wrong with me for wanting you, some psychological kink that makes me a freak." He took a deep breath, sighed it out, and shrugged. "It sure would be more convenient if I could find partnership material in younger men. Believe me, I've tried, and I never have."

He smiled at me, looking sad. "I have a story for you, too. About two men in Ireland. I want you to listen with an open mind. Really open." He patted the back of my hand like a patient teacher encouraging a struggling child.

"Their names are Patrick Scott and Eric Pearce. Eric was twenty when he met Patrick. Patrick was fifty-six. They were partners for thirty-seven years. Do you know the statistics for any couple staying together that long, regardless of age? They did pretty well. When they got married in October of 2013, Patrick was ninety-three, and Eric was fifty-seven. Patrick died the next year. Maybe they knew that was coming, or maybe they just decided to get married because they finally could. Whatever the reason, they did. They had a long and wonderful life together."

He looked at me, as if checking my face for a sign of agreement, or at least comprehension. "So, don't tell me it's impossible. Sure, it's rare, and maybe we don't go the distance like they did. All I'm saying is, don't rule me out just because of our age difference. I'm sorry someone else hit you over the head with that, but I can promise you I will never say what he said to you."

He gave me his devilish grin again. His teeth were a little crooked, and to me, they made him even more adorable. Mischievous. He patted my bare knee this time, and his warm hand was an angel's touch.

"There are plenty of other reasons out there for parting ways, that's for sure. If we break up, it will be for one of them." He threw his head back and laughed, wild and free. "Here we are talking about breaking up, and we haven't even started yet. How crazy is that?"

I nodded, forced to agree. "It's crazy, all right." His logic was impeccable, even if it didn't do much to change the knot in my guts. That was the trouble with logic. It can peel away the most rational arguments and still never touch the heart. Below the neck, logic is the flimsiest form of persuasion.

Unpersuaded, my heart was walking along a precipice without so much as a path to follow. One sudden gust of wind, one misplaced foot, and I could be dead. I hated that the beauty of the view from this deadly cliff was so exhilarating.

"I'll have to go slow," I said, feeling strangely liberated at giving in. "I can't... In spite of your story, I'm still scared. I'll need all your patience. Lots of it."

His smile was glorious as a sunrise and every bit as triumphant. Without another word, he took out his phone and took a selfie of us sitting side by side on that rocky ledge above a chasm. *Our first photo*, I thought, as if we were starting a scrapbook. *Don't say that*, I scolded myself. *That's way too fast.*

*

By the time we got back to Denver, it was late afternoon. We were happily tired, dusty, sweaty, and hungry.

"Thank you for today," Colin said as soon as we were inside my apartment. "For everything."

He stepped into my space and wrapped his arms around me, tentative and warm. *Our first hug*, I thought as my arms hauled him in. He lifted his face to me, asking silently for a kiss. *Our first kiss.* Sweet and fresh as a tree-ripe peach.

"Let me take a shower here, and I'll make you dinner out of whatever you have in your fridge." He wriggled in my arms. "Or maybe take a shower with me?"

I shook my head. "Too soon" was all I could croak out, even though I knew he could feel my erection through our clothes.

"Can I shower here, though? I have fresh clothes in my pack."

"Sure," I said, feeling cornered. "I'll get you a towel."

While Colin showered, I rummaged around in the kitchen for what we could eat, finding enough for a decent omelet and salad. I was arranging things on the counter when I heard the floorboards creak behind me. I turned and stopped breathing.

He stood wrapped in my towel and nothing else—wide-eyed, vulnerable, lips parted, his blond hair spiked damp and wild, his creamy lean body graceful and glowing. Without taking my eyes from his, I let my loaf of bread land somewhere on the counter behind me.

"My god, you're...so beautiful." It was all I could say. I could hear the awe in my voice, but I wasn't embarrassed by it. It was the truth.

He walked to where I stood paralyzed, put his arms around my neck. His towel fell, bunching around his feet.

I reminded myself I had the right to say no. I didn't. My hands found his waist, and the smooth small of his back. Then some dam inside me crumbled, and the crashing flood from behind it seized me. My mouth was on his neck, on his forehead, lips, eyelids. My hands caressed everything they could touch, frantic to discover. He began pulling my shirt out of my cargo shorts.

"I should shower first," I muttered.

"Don't you dare," he said, breathing hard. "I want you just the way you are. Let's go upstairs."

*

Significantly delayed, the omelets and salad turned out pretty well. We made them together, navigating my tiny kitchen with only minor collisions. We laughed at where I'd decided to put spices, staples, and utensils in my kitchen, bantered about how illogical my choices had been.

Dinner itself was quiet, comfortable. It was clear neither of us wanted to be anywhere else. Eventually, we agreed to do the dishes.

"I have to be at work early tomorrow," Colin said as he stretched plastic wrap over the leftover salad. "Is it okay if I stay here tonight? You're a lot closer to downtown than I am."

"Ah," I joked. "A relationship of convenience. Now it all comes clear."

He stuck his tongue out at me. "Sure. It's taken me months of dogged pursuit to run you to ground, just so I wouldn't have to go home tonight. That was my evil plan all along."

I laughed. I couldn't help it. "Well, I have to go to work tomorrow, too, for a new client over on the Western slope. I'll have to be out of here by nine and gone for four or five days. Strange business. I probably shouldn't say more." His face hardened, and I hurried to head off any misunderstanding. "I'm not holding out on you. I just... I feel protective of you. I didn't think you really wanted to be burdened with the details of my work, which are seldom pretty."

I watched his face and aura soften again. He smiled. "I know. It's sweet of you, really, but eventually you'll realize I'm not made of glass. Anyway, I'll be long gone by the time you leave. I have to be at work by seven. Big trial coming up, and all us paralegals will be going through discovery documents for at least a week."

A fear niggled at me. "Do you think I was a jerk for not talking about my assignment?"

Colin shrugged. "I hope we get to share parts of our work life, too. I want that, whenever you're ready to do it."

So the answer was yes, or at least probably. Was my reticence mere habit or real discretion? It wasn't really a virtue to keep secrets just because I'd had no one to talk to for so long. I'd have to relearn how and what to share.

When we'd finished tidying, I fired up the dishwasher. "Do you want to watch a movie? I have Netflix on my TV. Or the Rockies game is playing on Altitude tonight, I think."

"We'd have to sit on the bed to watch, right? Is that your only TV?"

I could feel my neck and face heat up. From guilt, mostly, because although I was looking forward to cuddling, I hadn't tried to arrange it. "Yup, that's the only one."

"Good," he said, running his tongue along his upper lip. "No place I'd rather be right now."

We locked up, pulled the blinds, turned out the lights, and climbed the stairs. Doing those things with him felt...comfortable, familiar. Was that prophetic? Wishful thinking? I had no idea.

After the third inning, Colin stood up and shucked his clothes, folding them on an armchair. "I can't stay awake any longer," he said, yawning. He looked over his shoulder at me, caught me staring at his sweet tan lines, and twerked his perfect little ass at me. "No more of that tonight. Hope you don't mind. Gotta save my energy for tomorrow."

In a swirl of lust and relief, I tried to decide if I minded. I didn't.

"So do I," I said, feeling stupidly happy. I got up and found a new toothbrush for him.

After I turned out the light, Colin curled himself into my side. I don't think I'd ever held anything so angelic. I kissed the soft-spiky top of his head, feeling my solitary life ready to scatter into chaos.

Maybe it was a mistake to have him in my bed. What if it was? I wanted him there anyway. I watched over him until his breathing shifted into the languid waves of sleep.

Chapter Three

Monday

In the morning, I cranked on the coffee at six, fed Colin, and kissed him goodbye at the door. I watched him bounce down the steps, his youthful energy sparking off him in every direction, happy and optimistic. He must have felt me watching, because he turned and waved, a goofy schoolboy grin on his face as he slung his backpack over a shoulder and headed downtown.

Feeling disoriented in my own home, I nursed my coffee and rattled around the upstairs of my pre-WWII duplex. I'd opened it into a sleeping area with bathroom in the back, and a pleasant sitting nook at the front looking out over 16th Avenue. I loved my little home, but Colin's absence sat in every corner like a thick cloud.

Apparently, it had been too long since I missed someone, because it felt like a big deal. One of my voices said I was getting involved too deep, too fast. But missing him felt good, too—a sweet ache with an exquisite cure. I'd insisted he leave his hiking clothes for me to wash, so I threw them into a load of laundry. After burying my face in them for a hungry huff. Or two. Miraculous and intoxicating.

Bewitching, green-eyed Colin. I'd met him on an assignment last summer, when he'd been my liaison in a case involving an especially dysfunctional family.

We'd flirted a bit, very mildly at the time, and after the case had been resolved, I invited him to a baseball game. Whether or not that had been a good idea, I'd never know. It was far too late to change the past.

But as he'd said last night, I'd been elusive. He really had run me to ground. He asked me to go on hikes last fall, and I'd declined. He invited me to go to the aquarium, and we spent a wonderful afternoon strolling through the tanks and exhibits.

He wasn't aggressive in his pursuit; he just wouldn't let up, relentless and gentle as a starfish opening an oyster. He badgered me into seeing the movie "Pride" with him, even though I told him I didn't go to movies much because the sound overwhelmed me, got too far inside me. But he persisted until I said yes, promising he would take care of me. And he did, holding my hand while I bawled like a baby as a hall full of Welsh mining families sang *Bread and Roses*.

Then he showed up on my doorstep last Christmas Eve wearing an elf costume, complete with green tights and curly-toed shoes, looking more edible than any sugar plum. He had a present for me—a book we'd discussed weeks earlier. I couldn't help myself and asked him if he minded going out to a restaurant as an elf. We ended up at Le Central and had a magical, candlelit Christmas Eve dinner. That had been the real beginning, I saw in hindsight.

Now, as I cleaned out my fridge and packed for a week on the western slope, I reflected on how defensive I'd been against Colin's advances, again ashamed for my cowardice. It wasn't that I was too fearful or passive, a voice pretending to be common sense insisted. I just wanted to be sure I wasn't taking a wrong step and setting us both up for heartache.

But surely that was a risk shared by both of us, another voice said. I told the committee in my head to shut up. Colin and I were both adults. Still, my gut insisted more of that responsibility was mine. I was the older, experienced one, after all. Wasn't that the way responsibility usually worked?

I set the security alarm and locked up the house, stopping next to my car for a moment to enjoy the heat of the morning sun, already sharp on my skin. I threw my backpack and duffel in the trunk and headed for 8th Avenue, my best route out of town.

The five-hour drive to Grand Junction gave me plenty of time to reflect further on developments with the young Mr. Stewart. I had to stop being so skittish. If Colin really wanted to date, I had to stop pretending he didn't know what he was doing. He was an adult, and I had to respect that. Colin was challenging me to change.

I came to that lofty realization driving through Glenwood Canyon with the ageless Leontyne Price singing Madama Butterfly, soaring and tragic, filling the car. The drama queen in me said I might be setting myself up to be Butterfly, but that was silly. I could take care of myself. And Colin wasn't Butterfly either. I just had to make sure I wasn't Pinkerton.

The directions to the ranch were simple and clear. Before long, I turned off the highway at a ten-foot sandstone cairn holding a wooden sign, painted white with green lettering, announcing this was the Ellis Ranch, founded 1906. The sign had needed repainting for a few years.

The red dirt road rose in a gentle climb and curved off to the left. A billow of dust swirled out behind my car even though I drove slowly. The dormers of the house eventually rose from behind a stand of massive rough-barked cottonwoods. They'd been shielding the house from road traffic for a long time.

By the time I'd parked in front of the house, also painted white with green trim, Evan Landry was waiting for me on the deep veranda that ran the full length of the structure. The clock in my dash said two thirty.

I got out and closed the car door, glad to stand up. Warm, sweet, pine-scented air flowed over me like a welcoming gift. The house was big, and while it wasn't exactly falling apart, it certainly hadn't been kept up to its original standards.

Landry and I shook hands. "You should park around back later, but there's no rush," he said crisply, very much the employer in charge. Which he was. "I'll show you to your room first, then give you a quick tour around the main buildings."

I nodded and locked the car, leaving my things in it. City habit come to the country, maybe, but I was here to investigate a crime, most likely committed by someone who lived here. Better to be safe than sorry.

He led me into a room two stories high, easily twenty-five feet deep and at least as wide. After driving in the bright daylight, it took a moment for my eyes to adjust to the dim interior. Except for the daylight from the windows opening to the shaded veranda behind me, the only source of light came from the ceiling twenty feet up.

"Welcome to the ancestral seat," Landry said. He swept his arm in a sarcastic, grandiose gesture. "Behold its glory."

I did. It still had some. Above the dark wood paneling of the main floor, the tired yellow walls were dotted with antlered game trophies interspersed with a few large Western-themed paintings.

Three large carpets covered parts of the plank floor, creating sitting areas set with heavy, simple furniture. The carpet under my feet, a dark red Persian, had worn through in several places. I could imagine it had survived generations of boots traipsing across it before fraying. To my left, a giant fireplace laid with unlit firewood dominated one wall. The long mantel held the usual stuff—a plate held vertically for display, candlesticks, a brass tray dark with tarnish propped against the wainscoting, and a cluster of photos in pewter-colored frames.

Just beyond the fireplace, a wood-paneled hallway led somewhere. In line with it on the opposite side of the room, a matching hall led away in the other direction. From above each opposing lintel, a large cougar head snarled down at us with fangs bared. Beyond the hallways and off to the right, a wide staircase led upward, attended by its own rising procession of frames and plaques.

It had taken generations of successful Ellises to build this house. I guessed it had been finished post-WWII. Not really that old, but it smelled ancient and defeated. I opened my sensitivity a bit. Not a happy place. Full of...bitterness was the first word that came to me.

Landry pointed to the hall beyond the fireplace. "Stanford's office is just in there. We'll check in with him later."

He marched across the room, leading me to an arch opposite the door we'd come in. "Through there on the left is the dining room and the kitchen. You'll see those soon enough. And at the end of the hall, the back door opens to the barns and outbuildings. That's where we're headed as soon as we get you settled."

He waved at the staircase. "All our bedrooms are upstairs," he said. "Yours, too." We headed up.

When we got to my room, I noticed my door had no lock, but it seemed impolite to point it out. As we exited, I again got a shadow of uncertainty about its security, and I couldn't ignore my intuition twice.

"I'm a little concerned about how safe my computer and records might be in here," I said. "What do you think?"

Landry looked offended at first, but as I watched him think about it, I could tell the risk was real. "No one would dare." He didn't look as confident as he sounded.

"Someone dared trash Sarah's business. You suspect someone who lives in this house, maybe even on this floor," I said. "It's not much of a stretch for me to imagine that whoever did it would be quite willing to come in here and take my notes or anything else that might cause a problem for them."

"Let me think about it," he said. "In the meantime, make sure you hold on to everything you want to keep safe."

At the top of the stairs, he paused. "To be honest, I hadn't thought about that," he said, as close to an apology as I'd seen him get, "but you're right. We need to find you a solution. I'll introduce you to Stanford now," he said brusquely. "I assume you'll want to interview him first."

"I think I'd prefer to interview your sister first and inspect the damage to the property while it's light. Then I think an interview with Ellis Sr. would be good. Does that timing work all right with him?"

"You still need to check in with Stanford first. It's the way things are done."

We crossed the great room and headed down the hall past the fireplace.

"This is his office," he said, knocking softly on the door. It was a surprisingly tentative knock from the in-charge Evan Landry I'd seen so far. From inside, a gruff, slightly raspy voice ordered us to enter.

Stanford Ellis Sr. sat at a giant roll-top desk, but he pushed away and swiveled to face us as we came in. He didn't get up. Behind him, next to the desk stood a trestle table with stacks of files and loose papers. It didn't look well organized.

Ellis was dressed in a worn work shirt, jeans, and boots. He looked the quintessential lean, tough, tall rancher, complete with square jaw and large, work-roughened hands. His eyes, however, were flat with despair. Frayed regret held him in a cloud. His aura hung dull and dense, odd for a man who had spent most of his life outdoors.

He looked first at Evan with what seemed to be irritation, and to my amazement, Evan cringed. His shoulders sagged, and his aura pulled in small. Was that a childhood response? Was he still afraid of Ellis in spite of his scorn and bravado? Something to think about.

When he was done silently putting Landry in his place, Ellis turned his attention to me, his leathery face impassive.

Evan cleared his throat. "This is Russ Morgan, Stanford. Russ, Stanford Ellis."

I stepped forward and shook Ellis's hand, not surprised at the firm dry grip of authority.

"So you think you can find out who tore up Sarah's greenhouse?"

He was daring me to say yes, so I did. "Yes, sir, I believe I can."

"Good. I've told everyone that I expect them to cooperate with you completely." It felt like he was dismissing me. "They may not want to do that, but if they know what's good for them, they will." He turned his attention back to the papers on his desk.

Evan caught my eye and cocked his head at the door. We were done for the moment. When Evan had closed the door, he straightened his back into his usual elegant bearing. I wondered if he'd noticed his body's responses to his stepfather's presence.

"I'll take you to Sarah now," he said. We walked to the back of the great room, past the dining room with its French doors wide open. We finally reached a back door that opened on to gravel paths heading in various directions to a number of outbuildings, two of them large barns. We headed for the barn on the right.

*

The interior of the barn was dim and smelled sharply of damp and marijuana. And gasoline. Sarah Landry, in rubber boots and overalls, was shoveling debris into a wheelbarrow.

"Sarah, I'd like you to meet Russ Morgan," Evan said. "I've hired him to find out who did this to you."

Sarah kept shoveling. "Finding out who did it isn't going to get me back in business any faster, Ev," she called out over her shoulder. "I've lost over a hundred thousand dollars' worth of equipment and product. I can't afford to wait around for someone to figure out what happened." In the dim light, I couldn't tell what she looked like. Her long brown hair was tied back in a ponytail, but her heavy overalls obscured her frame.

"But you might have destroyed some kind of evidence that could identify who did it." Evan's voice sounded petulant, as if his inner spoiled child hadn't got its way.

"Does it really matter?" Sarah snapped, turning to face us, glowering at her brother and dragging the back of her hand across her forehead to wipe away the sweat. "I think that matters a lot more to you than it does to me."

She was clearly Evan's sister. Her facial features weren't as fine-boned as her brother's, but stronger, with a more generous mouth, her energy more open and warm. She had the same intelligent light in her eyes, but it shone kinder through her, even in her irritation.

She turned her attention to me, and her energy was like a firm swat on my shoulder. Friendly, but with a tough, no-nonsense focus. She waved at the wall behind her. "Whoever it was used Billy's old baseball bat over there. It's all scarred up from the blows, even has white paint from the light fixtures on it. It had to be done by someone in the family. That means the police won't be called in, and no one will be prosecuted. We already know that, too." She looked back at Evan. "And that's really all we need to know."

That rang like a challenge in the barn's dusty air.

"I understand you've got a lot on your plate right now, Sarah," I said, "but when you're ready for a break, could I ask you a few questions?"

"Sure. But if you want more than five minutes, you may as well help me clean up. We can talk while we do."

"Great idea," I said. "Glad to supply some unskilled labor."

"You don't have to do that, Russ," Evan interjected. "She's got to stop sooner or later. She's been at it all day."

"Well, I've been sitting in a car for five hours, and I'm grateful for a chance to move around a bit. Besides, I figure I need to talk to Sarah before I talk to anyone else, so this is a good way to do both."

Evan shrugged, looking peeved. Interesting. Was he peeved at me for helping, or at Sarah for not stopping? I guessed whatever it was had not been the way he wanted things to go. He left us to it, our longer tour unfinished. Sarah found me some work gloves and a shovel, and I got busy.

"So tell me a little bit about what you had going here before all this happened," I said, putting a mangled white fixture in the wheelbarrow. "These lights couldn't have been cheap."

"They're not cheap to buy and they're not cheap to run," Sarah said, grunting as she moved the wheelbarrow to her new pile of junk. "I had thirty-six of them. You figure five plants per light, that's a hundred and eighty plants, with forty-five to harvest every month. A good yield is just over a pound, maybe a pound and a quarter of dried bud per light. At twenty-five hundred dollars a pound for quality product, that puts my peak revenue at twenty-eight thousand a month. I wasn't at full production yet when this happened, but I would've been there in a month."

"What were your expenses like?" I asked.

Sarah stood up and looked at me thoughtfully. "Why? Do you think someone did this because I was making too much money? I've been thinking someone didn't want my grow on the ranch."

"I have no idea. I'm just trying to get a sense of what your operation was like. I don't really know anything about marijuana cultivation."

Her shovel scraped harsh and loud across the concrete floor of the barn, pushing another smashed light fixture toward a pile. "You should go take a look at a few of the Denver grows. Some of them have it down to a perfect science," she said with a note of awe in her voice. "I would love to be that well-funded, skilled, and have that kind of operation going."

"I'll bet that would be interesting," I said.

"You might find it more than interesting. Maybe inspirational. I'll give you Rick Saxon's contact info tonight at dinner, and I'll let him know you might call. He's one of the most knowledgeable guys in the business, and he's been a generous mentor to me."

"Thank you. But about your lease? Your other expenses, too, I guess."

Sarah bent over her shovel again. "Stanford's the only one who took me seriously, at least at first. He saw the potential, and he gave me a decent deal on the lease, water included. I didn't have to pay any rent, only electricity, until I started making money." She straightened and massaged the small of her back.

"This is important," she said, looking me in the eye. "My grow's never cost the ranch a penny, to get back to your earlier question about why." She cocked her head at the wheelbarrow. "Help me get this load out to the Dumpster."

I picked up the handles, ready to push it outside. She steadied a tangle of conduit lying across the top, but shouted, "Wait!"

She reached under the metal and pulled out a white plastic tag with a barcode on it. "I hope to hell I haven't thrown any of these out already. We're going to have to chuck this into the trash a piece at a time."

"What is it?"

"A headache I haven't had the heart to address yet. It's a plant tracking number."

"You tag every plant?" Growing marijuana suddenly seemed a lot more complex.

"Don't get me started about the regulations. This is a MITS tag."

"Not as in mittens, I take it."

"Marijuana Inventory Tracking System. Medical and retail products are handled and tracked separately from beginning to end. Every plant is given a barcode, then that number is referenced to a new tag for every five-pound bag, then referenced to the new barcode on every individual item sold to a customer. I've got to account for every ruined plant. It'll take me hours to go through my spreadsheets."

We went through the load of trash piece by piece, but we didn't find any more tags. I suggested that was good news, but Sarah didn't look encouraged. When we brought the empty wheelbarrow back, I waited for her to start speaking again. She didn't, so I offered a nudge.

"So you've been in the black for a while, then?"

"I started turning a profit last year. Now I pay two thousand a month flat rate, plus fifteen percent of sales. Starting next month, the ranch would be taking in over six thousand a month." She wiped her brow with a sleeve. "Given the financial situation of the ranch, I think we can be fairly sure Stanford didn't do it. An extra six grand a month could keep this place going forever."

"Evan thinks Marianne is responsible for this. Do you?"

"No," Sarah said with a note of disgust in her voice. "Marianne can be a bitch, but she's a coward. She wouldn't have the guts to do this—too much risk to her precious reputation. Although I'm sure she was delighted when it happened. I think Stan did it. Vandalism is more his style than Marianne's. Not that it matters. It won't happen again, I promise you," she said grimly. "I was far too trusting about my security."

"Stan is Stanford Junior?"

"Yes, Stanford is senior, Stan is junior. Although Evan uses Stan's childhood name Stanny when he wants to piss him off. Which is often."

"What about Billy?"

Sarah shook her head. "Billy doesn't have a violent bone in his body. He loves ranching, and he loves his animals. Money from my grow has kept the ranch going. Billy would never do anything that might jeopardize the future of the ranch."

I was running out of suspects in a hurry. "Then you suspect Stan?"

"He's my first choice, for sure. He's a Grade A alcoholic asshole. Grandiose ideas, extravagant promises, zero results." She pulled a blue bandana from her hip pocket and blew her nose. "No, actually that's not true. Usually somebody loses money on his ideas. Not him, of course, because he never puts anything on the table but talk."

"Why do you think your brother suspects Marianne, then?"

Sarah laughed, harsh and dismissive, leaning on her shovel. "Because he wants Marianne to be the culprit so bad he can taste it." She shook her head. "They despise each other. Ev's never said so explicitly, but he's hinted Marianne tried to straighten him out, so to speak, back along the way, and he probably laughed at her and cut her to shreds. Whatever started it, it's escalated into full-blown warfare now." She pushed a strand of hair behind her ear and looked at me full-on. "Evan can be quite cruel, you know. I wouldn't make all that only Marianne's fault."

She wasn't afraid to name her brother's flaws. Maybe I'd get more reliable information from her than I'd expected. "Is the ranch really in that bad shape financially?"

"Before I started growing medical marijuana, the ranch was on the ropes—dangerously behind in its taxes and a sky-high unpaid feed bill at the co-op, among other things. A list of deferred maintenance long as your arm."

She squatted, stretching out her back, stood, and did side bends. "A hot bath and yoga tonight," she said with a grin.

"So the ranch was in rough shape," I nudged.

"Ranching anywhere is hard at the best of times. Real estate developers were beginning to gather around this place like vultures over a dying calf. Stanford would've had to sell out in another year, two at the most. Maybe that's what Marianne and Stan didn't like about my success. Maybe they were hoping for a windfall from the sale of the land."

"And you were about to set your business on cruise control and get rich? You would have netted a tidy amount every month, I'm guessing."

"What?" Her eyes widened, and her aura flashed angry spikes. "Cruise control? Hardly." Then she grinned. "You said that just to see if you could get a rise out of me, didn't you?" She nodded, confirming her own suspicions. "It almost worked, too."

I smiled my apology. "It would have been more direct, I guess, to ask you what your goals for the business are."

"Well, there's no room for complacency, that's for sure. Once I hit my stride, I can probably handle three hundred plants without having to hire anyone. That's sixty lights, and just under ten grand a month to the ranch."

She waved at the rest of the barn. "That's what all this extra space is for. But I didn't want to grow too fast. I get chills thinking about where I'd be if I'd invested in a full-scale grow before this happened."

"Twice the expense to get going again, I guess. Much harder to recover."

"I'm not sure I could have." She grunted and scraped her shovel across the cement floor, pushing debris in front of it. "Scale of operation aside, shifting from a medical grow to both medical and retail is a ton of work. Do you know all our transactions have to be done in cash? The DOJ has promised some provision to allow banks to handle marijuana-derived money, but so far nothing but promises. Hundreds of thousands of dollars, maybe millions, exchanged every day in this industry across the state. All in cash."

She was on a roll now, her passion incandescent in her aura, and I couldn't bear to interrupt her.

"...the oversight is intense," she was saying. When I refocused, I'd apparently missed a point or two. "But we harvest only the buds and destroy the plant. We're required by law to do that, and it's such a waste."

"What would you do with it otherwise?"

"If we could legalize use of the rest of the plant for manufacture, we could create an entire cottage hemp industry." Her eyes gleamed with a visionary's fervor. "Imagine hemp cloth, oil, rope, mulch, the possibilities are immense. This plant family is one of nature's greatest gifts to us. Imagine the local jobs. We could form a co-op and ship a truly sustainable range of essential goods all over!" She grinned. "I guess Evan told you I was a bit of a zealot about these things."

I nodded. "I'm interested in hearing directly from you, though, as to how you see things."

"We're a long way from that ideal, though. All the laws around cultivation and sale need to change and mature. That's going to take concerted effort. The State listens, but you still find gaps and outright conflicts, like between the State and the DOJ. Some growers in Denver got rousted just last week. Federal law enforcement came in and stomped all over everything, doing as much damage as they could get away with before they left."

She pressed her lips together in a defiant scowl. "And do you know how many convictions will come from those raids? Zero, that's how many. Zero. It's harassment, pure and simple. Nothing more."

We shoveled the last wheelbarrow of debris into the rent-a-Dumpster. "Thanks for your help, Russ," Sarah said. "I appreciate it."

"Glad to help." I checked my clothing to make sure I wasn't too messy to interview Stanford Sr. I was pretty dusty, but I figured a rancher would understand. "If banks aren't likely to make loans to businesses like yours, how are you going to manage getting back up to speed?"

"The lights are already on order and paid for. Most important, my cuttings, which are high quality strains, are undamaged." She smiled, hard and grim. "This would have been a real disaster if I'd lost them. The rest is just equipment, pretty easy to replace. Premium quality stock to clone, much harder to get."

"How did the vandal miss those?"

She smiled, almost smug. "They were somewhere else. Somewhere safe. And even you don't need to know where they are, no disrespect."

"I understand. And you can afford to replace the equipment?"

"I've tucked away enough cash over the last eight months to completely refurbish my grow." She laughed. "And no, the money's not on site either. It's somewhere safe, too. Not even Evan knows where or how much."

"Thanks, Sarah. I hope we can get to the bottom of this quickly."

"Again, no disrespect, Mr. Morgan—"

"Russ, please. I've shoveled your trash. You should call me by my first name."

She didn't think that was funny. "No disrespect to you, but I really don't care who did this. You can't change the past. You're here because Evan has his own agenda with the family. I doubt he actually cares about my business beyond his financial investment, which I'll pay off as soon as I'm up and running again."

Her aura flattened, steely, and dangerously cold. "I'll take...stronger precautions of my own to make sure something like this doesn't happen again."

It occurred to me that Sarah Landry might be quite capable of physical violence herself. I turned away and headed for the door, but she called out.

"Oh. One more thing. Whoever did this doesn't want the ranch to succeed. That's a useful clue for you, Mr. Morgan." Her aura said she believed that, all the way through.

"Russ, please."

She gave me her first truly friendly smile. "Okay. Russ."

Chapter Four

Stanford Ellis was still sitting at his desk when I knocked on the doorframe, since the door itself was ajar. He waved me to a wooden chair without a cushion. Maybe he was hoping that would shorten the interview.

"You ever live on a ranch, Morgan?" he asked wearily.

"I grew up on a farm near Hygiene," I said. "A lot of hard work for not much."

"Truer words never spoken." He scrubbed his face with a gnarled hand and gazed at me, his pale blue eyes steady, resigned. His aura radiated a sad fatigue that hurt me when I opened to it. He was a brokenhearted man.

"So what you want to know?" he asked.

"Do you think this could have been committed by someone outside the immediate family?"

His lips formed a thin line, and I suddenly understood why he was so resigned. He knew one of his family had done it. "We don't get casual visitors out here. It had to be someone who knew their way around the property. The barn was locked up tight. The dogs stay attached to Billy. If he hadn't been out in the fields, they would've announced a stranger immediately. The only person on the property who could've done it that isn't a family member is César Medina. He cooks dinner for the family six nights a week. He arrives at one, works through the afternoon to serve dinner, cleans up, and then heads back into town to work in his brother's restaurant. He's been doing that for fifteen, maybe sixteen years."

Ellis shook his head sadly, his eyes begging me not to force him to say the obvious. "César didn't do it."

"Anyone else on the property not family?"

"César's cousin Maria Isabel comes on Saturdays to do laundry and clean the house. It wasn't Saturday."

"Do you have any idea as to who might have done it?"

"You're not going to maneuver me into accusing one of my own children, Morgan," he said quietly. "It wasn't me, I don't think it was Sarah, and Evan says he was in Denver when it happened. Although I don't know that for a fact."

Stanford's three blood children were the only ones left, and we both knew it. He glared at me from inside his pain, defiant and ashamed. "You're going to have to work out the rest of it for yourself."

I nodded, letting it go. "Can you tell me about the ranch operation? How it's set up, how it's doing? Sarah told me the income from her grow was helping to keep the ranch afloat."

"It's all that's keeping us afloat. Billy works hard, but as bad as the money was in ranching thirty years ago, it's far worse now. All that's kept us going in recent years is tenacity and pride, and I have precious little of either left."

He snorted. "Marianne seems to have an unlimited supply of pride, but that's another story altogether. Besides, she hasn't put in a lick of actual work on this place in over twenty years."

"How is the business set up, and what will happen to it when you die?"

"You get right to it, don't you?" He stared at me for a while as if trying to decide how much to tell me. "For the last five years or so, the ranch has been held by a corporation with twenty-one shares. Don't ask me why twenty-one, but my lawyer thought it was a good number, and I didn't see any reason to argue. I own all the shares. When I die, the shares will be distributed among my children in a manner I haven't yet disclosed."

"All five, or just your biological children?"

He slumped back in his chair as if I'd struck him across the face. He swiveled away from me and sat silent a while, staring out the window. "Evan has obviously told you his version of our family story," he said with his back to me. He nodded as if he were in a silent conversation with someone I couldn't see. "I deserve that, I guess. But there's more to the story than he probably gave you."

He swiveled back around to face me, his eyes fierce, aura bright with truth. "I loved Carolyn Landry. Loved her more than my first wife. She was..."

His voice wandered away, but it came back in a little while. "I loved her. She begged me to adopt Evan and Sarah, saying that the Landry name meant nothing to her. It had belonged to a man who'd walked out on her when she needed him most, and she'd be glad to get rid of it completely, not just for her." He'd started rocking back and forth in his chair, tiny unconscious motions, and his aura flooded with dark regret.

"The biggest mistake I ever made was not doing that. And the worst part is that it's too late to do it now. The kids fight amongst each other all the time as it is." He chuckled, grim. "If I gave them all the Ellis name today, there'd be blood on the barroom floor before sunset. As it is, the minute I lose control of this place, it'll be torn apart. I was born on this land, lived my whole life here. Same for my father and grandfather before me. Born right here. My kids, too. I can't bear to see our home broken up, but I can't see how to leave it to the children and still prevent it from happening."

"What happened to Carolyn?"

"She died. Breast cancer, eleven years ago. After she died, the infighting really fired up. There'd always been sibling squabbles, but it turned mean then. And it's only gotten worse."

He sighed as his aura shifted from remorse to resignation again. "I know I haven't been a very good parent. Never knew how. Carolyn did. She was amazing. I know I've lost the love and respect of my own children, and I never had love or respect from Evan. He was the wild one. All he understood was the belt, and I used it to make him behave." He rubbed the back of his neck. "Looking back on it now, I should have used more of that discipline on Stan Jr."

He cleared his throat and tilted his head, as if his words were stuck in his throat. "Now they mostly ignore me, fighting over whatever they think they can get out of what's left of the ranch when I'm gone."

He started his tiny rocking motions again, squeaking his chair softly every time he pushed backward. He seemed oblivious to it. "You know what's really sad?" he asked, his voice far away, maybe even lost. "The only one of the kids who's affectionate with me is Sarah. Billy and I get along fine, but she's actually fond of me. It tears me up that someone in my family did this to her."

I waited for him to continue, but after a silent couple of minutes, I could tell the confession was over.

"Thank you, Mr. Ellis," I said, rising from the chair. The sun had gone behind Piñon Mesa, and with the exception of a small circle of light from a lamp on the desk, the room had darkened along with the sky. The saturnine gloom seemed perfectly appropriate to our conversation. I shook his hand and left him seated, staring out the window at the darkness falling across his domain.

*

I had no idea how formal dinner would be, so I showered and changed clothes before heading downstairs to the dining room just before six. I needn't have bothered. Sarah and Billy were both still in their work clothes. Marianne was still in her work clothes, too. She looked as if she'd just stepped off the broadcast set at the TV station.

The dining room was finished like the great room, with dark wood panel wainscoting, and yellow plaster walls with brass sconces. It, too, had been created to host large numbers. The table looked like it weighed a ton, made during the good times, no doubt, back when the cost of oak wasn't an issue. The seven places set for dinner looked apologetic, perched on one end of its dark gold expanse. Twenty, maybe more, could sit here, even when making space to avoid the four massive legs per side.

Evan introduced me to Stanford Jr.—Stan. Already drunk, Stan gave me a bleary stare and a slurred hello. He took a slug from his drink and yanked his chair from the table to park at his father's right. Marianne, still in public diva mode, deigned to shake my hand while delivering a look saying she considered me something she might step in by accident.

Billy's handshake was genuinely friendly, although it didn't give anything away. His aura was clear enough, but I got the impression his attention and energies were occupied elsewhere. Maybe he was so focused on ranch matters he had little interest in Sarah's business, apart from the income it provided.

I watched Stan empty his highball glass and pour himself a glass of wine. If you want insight into someone's relationship with alcohol, just ask an expert, like an alcoholic with a few years recovery under his belt. They've been there, so they know firsthand what the downhill road looks like. I figured Stan would soon be sitting in a meeting. If he was lucky.

When everybody had sat down, Stanford led us in a perfunctory little prayer, then rang a small silver bell. Its tinkle seemed almost silly, given the family's reality. Some vestige of the former Ellis grandeur, I guessed. César trundled dinner in on a cart, parked it next to Stanford, greeted him without even looking at anyone else at the table, and left the room.

It was telling to me that Ellis sat Stan, Marianne, and Billy in that order down the table on his right, and Evan, Sarah and me in that particular order on the left. Maybe that's the only way he could keep them all from coming to physical blows during the meal. Even so, the bickering began before the dinner dishes had made their first rounds.

Stanford raised his voice to cut across whoever else was speaking. "Listen up, now. I'll say this again. I expect everyone to give Mr. Morgan their full cooperation. And I mean full. He'll be around for a few days talking to each of you. You will answer all his questions fully. I intend to get to the bottom of this mess, and I won't take kindly to obstruction. Is that clear?"

Billy nodded cheerfully, lifting his glass to me in salute. Marianne glowered at me, refusing to offer any sign of consent. Stan took a big gulp from his glass of wine. "Riding to the rescue of Sarah's precious little weed factory," he muttered defiantly. "As if that's what this ranch needs."

Stanford Senior wheeled on him. "She's saved this ranch from bankruptcy, and you know it," he snapped.

"How much have your ideas brought in? They haven't made a single dollar for us. Altogether, they've cost us a small fortune."

"I've had plenty of good ideas. You've never given them a chance," Stan whined, keeping his eyes fixed on his plate. "It's not my fault one hasn't come through yet."

"Oh, yes it is," Evan jumped in. "You're the worst businessman I've ever met. Every one of your pathetic schemes has been a greased shortcut to catastrophe. Sarah's grow has made back your losses and much, much more."

Marianne leaned forward for a piece of bread. "Unlike you, Evan," she said icily, "who screwed your way into part ownership of a restaurant and then *really* fucked over your partners. You're the very model of a good businessman."

Evan lifted his wineglass to Marianne. "Is that how you landed your job at the TV station, sweetie? Because that's what *you* would do in a heartbeat. *If* you had a heart, and *if* you were attractive enough to make it work. Both, I'm afraid, embarrassingly big *ifs* in your case. Maybe if the room was really dark...no, I don't think even then."

That set off an angry racket that made my teeth ache. I felt a foot nudge my shin under the table. Across from me, Billy caught my eye and winked. "Should'a warned you, nobody's gonna hold back because of company," he said cheerfully. "I guess you figured that out by now."

I grinned, nodded. "Is it always like this?"

"Some nights nobody says nuthin' the whole meal. But when they do, they'll rag on about you like you're not even here," he said mildly. "Happens to me all the time. They go on and on about the ranch and almost never ask me what I think. It's kinda funny, really, since I'm the one who shovels the manure."

"Don't you get involved in the arguments sometimes?"

"Nah, that shit don't mean nothin' to me, and it don't change a thing where I work. Once in a while, I hafta give 'em a fact or two about the ranch, that's it. Other than that, I just let 'em go at each other. They think I'm too dumb to matter, anyway."

Now that was an interesting piece of information. I checked his aura. Mild and clear, nearly happy.

For most of the rest of the meal, I tamped down my sensitivity just to protect myself and kept my conversation focused on Sarah and Billy. Sarah handed me Rick Saxon's card and urged me to talk to him when I got back to Denver. I hoped by the time I got back to Denver, this problem would be cleared up, but I said thanks and tucked the card in my pocket.

Although I couldn't open too much to the energies in the room without getting nauseous, now and then I checked what was happening at the end of the table. Evan, Stan, and Marianne alternately lashed out at each other or ate in seething silence, their auras coiling and striking out like poisonous snakes. I caught Stanford's glance a couple of times. His eyes were dull, resigned, like a drowning man going down for the third time. A man trapped in a living hell.

As soon as I could, I said goodnight to Sarah and Billy and made my escape from the dining room. I don't think the others even noticed my departure. They were still snapping and snarling at each other like pit bulls chained to opposite walls, their tethers long enough for them to reach their food but short enough to keep them from drawing blood. It was a relief to retreat to my room to think about what I'd learned from Sarah and Stanford.

When I was finished, I pulled out my phone to call Colin, but saw I had a text from him, sent at seven p.m.

> *Missed you today. Trial prep going well, twelve-hour shifts for next few days so glad you aren't here to distract me :P Going for run, get something to eat and crash. xo*

I looked at my watch. Nine o'clock. He was probably already asleep. I decided to follow his example and turned out my light, but not before setting some antacids on the nightstand. The food itself had been just fine, but the family toxicity was already burning my gut.

Chapter Five

Tuesday

In his briefing the afternoon before, Evan had told me everyone was on their own for breakfast, so as soon as I was ready, I headed downstairs to fix something. Left to my own devices, I preferred to get up early, but by the time I got to the kitchen, Billy Ellis was just stepping out the door, thermos mug in his hand, dressed in scuffed boots, tan canvas overalls, and a frayed flannel shirt.

We exchanged good mornings, and I asked him if I could talk to him after I'd had some coffee and a piece of toast. He said sure, and if I hurried I could help him load the truck with hay bales. That sounded pretty attractive to me, so I hurried.

I got to the barn just as Billy was rolling the door shut. "You city folks seem to have a knack for showing up just when all the heavy lifting is over," he said, laughing good-naturedly. "That's a knack I purely never got. Seems I'm exactly the opposite." He gave a single sharp whistle, and two dogs shot from the barn and jumped into the truck bed. He slammed the tailgate shut.

"Let me ride with you," I said. "Maybe I can make up for some of that. Do you have an extra pair of gloves?" He pointed to the glove box, and we climbed in. The old pickup jounced down the dirt road, its suspension long ago defeated by countless potholes and ruts.

"One of our sources of income for the ranch," Billy said, "is boarding horses." He pointed to a fenced pasture on our left. "It's not a huge amount, but it's steady. We feed 'em, take care of their hooves, and generally keep an eye on their health. We don't provide vet services, but we'll call an owner if we see a problem, and they can send out somebody to take care of their animal."

It's probably not written down anywhere, but it seems universal etiquette on ranch land for the passenger in a vehicle to open and close gates. As soon as Billy stopped the pickup, I hopped out, unchained the gate, and pulled it open. He drove through, and I closed it behind us.

When I climbed back in, Billy looked at me sideways. "You been on a ranch before, haven't you?"

I nodded. "Spent my very miserable youth on the family farm," I said. "I didn't mind the work, but my dad and I... Well, let's just say we didn't get along very well once he found out I was gay." I smiled ruefully, feeling the old sadness like an ache. "He didn't kick me out because he needed the free labor. But he sure blasted me in his sermons."

"Good to know. Besides Evan, you're the only gay guy I've met." He chuckled. "That I know of anyway. Glad you guys aren't all like Evan."

I hadn't thought about being a goodwill ambassador for the rainbow flag. "You two don't get along?"

"The only person Evan Landry gets along with is Evan Landry," Billy said without a trace of malice in his voice. "He surely can be one selfish, mean son of a bitch. He fronted money for Sarah's business, I do give him that. Wouldn't be surprised if he charged her interest on the loan, though. I don't begrudge him his success with his restaurants and all, but if you have to be like him to succeed, then I'm for sure not interested." We pulled to a stop next to a water tank and climbed out. The dogs stayed in the back of the truck, happy, tongues lolling as Billy pulled down the tailgate.

The half dozen horses in the pasture had started ambling toward us as soon as we drove up. By the time we had the feed sack open, they were waiting, nickering, and shaking their heads, the most aggressive ones crowding the others for best position, teeth bared, and ears flat back. We poured the feed mix into wooden troughs on the ground, then broke up a couple of bales of hay and spread it around.

"Sarah seems to be headed toward business success in a kinder way," I said, resuming our other conversation.

"Yeah, she is. She's a much, much kinder person than her brother." He threw the empty sack and the baling twine in the back of the truck and climbed up behind the wheel.

"How did she get involved with growing marijuana?" I asked as I pulled my door shut. "Seems like an unusual job for a kind person."

Billy shook his head, grinning. "No, sir, you've got that one wrong. When the medical marijuana first became legal, years ago now, a provision in the law allowed someone to grow weed for people who needed it but couldn't grow it for themselves. Caregiver and patient, or something like that. Anyway, that's what Sarah did."

The truck slewed into a rut and bounced so hard I had to grab the door. Billy laughed. "Better hang on, this baby ain't had seat belts in forever. You okay?"

I nodded but decided to hang on to the door anyway. "So Sarah started with growing for others?"

"Word got around in a hurry, and soon she had folks with MS or doing chemo coming to her, and she grew it for them. She couldn't take money for her services, exactly, but she made a lot of friends that way. I think she had maybe a dozen people she was growing for."

He looked at me, calm and gentle. "She got a medical license, started growing for dispensaries in Denver, then got into retail as soon as she could. She says she has a larger vision, and I believe her." He laughed. "She has a ton of big ideas for the future, that's for sure."

So Sarah talked to Billy about her business. It would make sense to keep the ranchers informed and on her side.

"Who do you think trashed Sarah's grow?"

"That's a tough one. I know it wasn't me, and I don't think it was Pa." He shook his head. "If you put a gun to my head and made me choose just one person, I think I'd have to pick her brother Evan."

That really surprised me. "But you just said he had helped her get started. Why would he then sabotage the project?"

"I know you're here because he hired you, Mr. Morgan, so you may feel more loyalty to him than I do. But Evan Landry is a pretty tricky guy. I have no idea what his reasons might be, but I sure as shootin' wouldn't put it past him."

"You're not the first person to say something like that to me." Billy stopped the truck and I jumped out to perform my gate opening duties. When I climbed back in, I asked him if he had any suspicions about anyone else.

He put the truck in gear and got us rolling. After a while, he said, "Marianne could have. She's got a hair up her ass about the Ellis name being tarnished by the family allowing a marijuana grow on our property." He shook his head. "I have no idea where she gets that stuff from. Sure, our family has been here over a hundred years now, but that don't mean nothing. We barely have enough money to keep going. There sure as hell ain't no social register for broke ranchers around here. Besides," he said with a sad smile, "around here, that register would be full of broke ranchers."

We stopped at another gate, then headed toward another water tank.

Billy got out and looked around, took a deep breath, and let it out heavily. His aura expanded, flooded bright with contentment as if he could finally relax. "I tell you what, Mr. Morgan," he said firmly, hauling another sack of feed from the truck bed, "I will work this land until I die or the sheriff drags me off it, kickin' an' squealin'." He looked at me, his eyes and aura glowing with surprising intensity.

"I can't tell you how much I love this place. Sometimes I feel like just walking on the dirt of it is what keeps me alive, gives me meaning. I'm no good at explaining things like that, but I'd be a wreck if I couldn't live here. And I'll do absolutely everything I can, everything in my power to keep this place running."

"I think I understand that," I said, "even though I've never felt that way myself. I'm sure my father felt that way about our farm. He had a heart attack shoveling a path to the barn through snow one winter. He died where he belonged."

Billy nodded. "Good way to go."

I wanted to get back to Billy's list of suspects. "What about your older brother? Could he have done it?"

"Yeah, sure, he could'a. But he had no reason to that I know of." We broke up two more bales, spread the hay where it wouldn't get trampled.

"Stan's always got his head in the clouds about some fancy plan to make money," Billy said with a note of genuine sadness in his voice. "He never really pays much mind to what anyone else is doing. He can get pretty mean when he's drunk, though. Not just his daily dose, but soused. Maybe he got himself a snootful and wanted to lash out at the world. Apart from that, I don't see it."

After dropping off hay and feed in a third pasture, we headed back to the barn.

"I really appreciate our conversation," I said. "Will you be around today if I have more questions?"

"Sure. I'll probably be in the shop the rest of the day. There's something wrong with the power takeoff on the tractor. I gotta figure out what it is and how to fix it. Hope to god it's not the bearings."

I dropped my gloves on the seat of the pickup and nodded to Billy. "I enjoyed the feeding, too. Thanks."

He winked at me. "I do it every morning, Russ. You're welcome to join me any time."

I figured my best chance of cornering Marianne and Stan Jr. for interviews was in the kitchen. I pulled my courier bag with computer and valuables out of the pickup and headed toward the kitchen coffeepot to lie in wait.

*

Marianne was the first to appear. I wished her good morning.

"You don't belong here," she said, glaring at me. "In spite of Daddy making us talk to you, I'll make sure you're gone as soon as I can." She slammed the coffeepot back onto its plate. "The Landrys brought you here, and the day Daddy's gone, the Landrys will be out of here too. I'll make sure of it. They don't belong here either."

"Wow. I hope you're not eager for your father's death just so you can clean house."

She didn't break stride—or silence—as she headed for the fridge.

"So why don't the Landrys belong here?" I asked, goading her. "This has been their home for almost as long as it's been yours."

She stiffened and squared her shoulders, her posture proud, as if a brass ensemble softly played an anthem behind her. "This is the *Ellis* Ranch," she snapped. "It has been the Ellis Ranch for a hundred years. The Ellis name is important to this part of Colorado, part of its history. The Landry name means nothing here."

"Hmm." I wondered how far I should go and decided to push a little harder. "But now Landry money is saving the Ellis Ranch from bankruptcy. Is that an issue for you? Besides, your mother abandoned the Ellis name and the Ellis Ranch, it seems to me." I shifted my vision to check her aura, which for a moment was shocked flat before it began to boil. "Is that part of the reason you're so protective of the Ellis reputation?"

"You have no right," she sputtered. Apparently, she couldn't think of anything else to say at the moment, because she repeated herself. "You have no right to talk like that." Her aura showed not only anger but fear and shame. I'd hit a nerve.

"Carolyn Landry took care of you, mothered you into adulthood. Why would you hate her children so?" She looked as if she were about to burst into tears for a moment before the hard, bitter energy settled on her shoulders once again.

"That's got nothing to do with anything," she said, snatching a container of yogurt out of the fridge.

"I couldn't disagree more," I said. "Four nights ago, someone broke into Sarah's leased space and tried to put her out of business." I watched her carefully. "Was that someone you?" Nothing except more boiling anger.

"You think you're a hard-ass, don't you?" Her smile was condescending, but her aura was still scattered. She was shaken.

"If I do, I'm not the only one in the room who does. I prefer a friendlier approach, but you've never given me a chance to be anything but hard-ass. And you didn't answer my question."

"Evan is certain I did. He's accused me several times already. He hired you, so I'm assuming you share his opinion."

"You assume wrong," I said as calmly as I could. Her indignation had become tedious. "Look, I don't know the story behind why you and Evan hate each other so much, but the enmity between the two of you seems to be the core of the Ellis-Landry schism. One version I heard was that years ago you tried to straighten him out, and he turned you down. I know he can be cruel. Still, unless it becomes significant to my investigation, your shared past doesn't matter to me."

Marianne tucked into her yogurt as if I wasn't in the room, but her aura darkened into shame. Poor woman. Not the first to try to rescue a gay man and have it backfire. Hell hath no fury. I waited a couple of moments for her answer. None came.

"So did you do it?"

"I'd be proud to have done it," she said icily without looking up. "And that's as much of an answer as you're going to get from me." She favored me with a glare sharp as a knife. I deserved that, I decided. "You're just going to have to figure it out for yourself, Mr. Private *Dick.*"

Marianne snatched up her dishes and plopped them in the sink. Apparently, César was expected to take care of them when he arrived. "Sarah's nasty little operation does not belong on Ellis land," she declared with imperious certainty. "It's...*venal.* I'm not going to rule out any means, including illegal measures, to get it out of my home."

I swallowed my laughter at her word choice because her aura flared violently. Not a laughing matter. Sarah was wrong in her assessment of Marianne Ellis. She didn't lack the spine to commit violence. At all. Somehow, I didn't think she'd done it, but she was perfectly capable.

She strode to where I was nursing my coffee and glared down at me. "I don't care how much money the ranch makes off it. It doesn't belong here."

She stormed out, as much as anyone in stiletto heels can storm out across the uneven plank floor of an old ranch house kitchen. She was absurd. I felt a flash of pity for her, but it passed. She nearly ran down Stan on her way out. It was a good thing she missed, because he already looked like he'd been hit by a truck. Alcohol hadn't been kind to him or his night.

*

"Whatever you do, don't shout at me," he mumbled as he stepped gingerly to the coffeepot.

"Not my style," I said, surprised by the wave of sympathy I felt for him. "I recognize your condition all too well."

"What you mean?"

"I used to wake up sick and hungover all the time, before I got sick and tired of being sick and tired. For me, it was either keep drinking and die, or quit drinking and find another way to live."

"It's not a problem for me," he said bravely. "A little hair of the dog, and I'll be fine. I just need a cup of coffee first."

"You know best, of course." I waited until he looked at me. "But if you ever find that booze is making you give up too much of your life, people are waiting to help you give it up."

"Don't rag on me about my drinking, man." His hands shook so badly he had to park the mug on the counter and use both hands to pour the coffee.

He grinned at me, and I saw a flicker of the easy charm I'd heard he traded on all the time. "I suppose you're going to give me the third degree now, aren't you? Whatever you said to Marianne sure put her knickers in a knot. You might want to be more careful with her, bro." He tried to laugh, but it came out more as a wet cough. "She's the most dangerous member of our lovely little tribe."

I studied his aura, which was dull and muddy. Turgid. It had been a long time since I'd looked at the aura of someone that badly hungover. I probably wouldn't get much information from it.

"So I guess you understand I have to ask the big question—did you trash Sarah's greenhouse?"

He started to shake his head and apparently regretted it. He closed his eyes and gave a little groan. His aura curdled with nausea and spikes of pain. "I've got more important projects to concentrate on than her hippie co-op efforts to make America green."

His aura remained sullen, unresponsive. I'd ask him again another time. "Who do you think did it, then?"

"I don't care who did it, but don't rule out your employer, Mr. Evan fucking Landry. Take my word for it. He would put his own sister out of business without batting an eye." His aura cleared a little, just for a second. What he said was true, or at least he believed it to be true.

I decided to poke in a different direction. "Do you share Marianne's concern that the presence of a marijuana grow on the ranch is a stain on the Ellis name?"

"Nah, that's her own special little crusade. It's pathetic, really, the way she tries to make more of our history than it's worth." He sagged down into a chair across the table from me, but even that far away, his breath stank from last night's drinking. It took an effort not to turn my face away.

"Here's the deal, Russ," he said over a soft belch. "The Ellis family has one thing left, and it isn't our name. It's the land along with its water rights. One way or another, the ranch operation is doomed. I know nobody else wants to see that yet, but I do. I'm the visionary of this family, and I see it clear as day. The only real question we should be discussing is how to make the most money from what little we got left. I'll give you a clue—the land is only about half of the value. The water rights we hold, rights the family has owned for a hundred years, are pure gold, and they don't necessarily have to be sold along with the land. We can double the worth of this place if we do it right."

"That's very interesting," I said. "I take it your dad doesn't agree."

He grimaced, either in physical pain or frustration with his father. I couldn't tell which. "My dad belongs to a generation that doesn't see the real world clearly anymore," he said, pity lacing his voice. "He's a dinosaur. He just doesn't understand."

"But you do."

Stanford Ellis Jr. pulled himself out of his chair with slow, defiant effort. "Yes, I do. And you can take that all the way to the bank, Mr. Morgan." Once more or less vertical, he had to brace himself against the table for a moment. "It's a bitch of a job to get anyone else to see it, though."

He made his way to a sideboard laden with bottles, and pulled out the bourbon, already half-empty. He poured a few ounces into his coffee, smacking his lips at the gurgle, and marched unsteadily toward the stairs, leaving a drinker's vapor trail behind him.

The smell of alcohol in the morning wasn't a pleasant memory for me. I needed some fresh air to get my nostrils clear. I could ask Billy some clarifying questions about those water rights. I followed the path out toward the barn but stopped as I saw Billy slip out of Sarah's barn and close the door—not like a farmer doing his work, but like a thief sneaking away. Why would he not want to be seen there?

As he got farther from the barn, his posture lost its stealth. I watched him head toward the shop. In a moment, hammer-on-metal racket began in front of the shop as Billy tackled his tractor problem. I hoped Stan had earplugs. This din wasn't going to help his delicate condition.

Maybe Billy was more concerned with Sarah's business than he'd let on. I'd check with Sarah. Why hadn't I seen any intrigue in his aura earlier? Maybe when everyone has secrets to protect, their lies don't stand out so clearly. Or maybe he kept his aura walled against the constant squabbles. I'd have to think about that.

Those questions aside, I was certain the damage to Sarah's business was tied directly to long-standing sibling conflicts, and I wouldn't be able to identify the culprit without sorting out more of how those conflicts played. To that end, I needed to ask my client some questions that never would have occurred to me before I arrived. Would he really have sabotaged his own sister's business? I needed to find out.

Chapter Six

I caught up with Evan in the kitchen, where he was making himself an omelet and frying bacon. It smelled delicious.

He looked over his shoulder at me. "Do you want some breakfast? Or maybe brunch? There won't be any organized lunch, so this may be the best offer you get all day."

"Sure, thanks. I suppose it's impertinent of me to ask you if you need help in the kitchen."

He laughed. "This is probably the only aspect of my life where I don't need or want help. I'm making an omelet with Gruyere cheese, chives, and avocado. Will that do for you?"

"It'll do just fine," I said, scanning his aura. He seemed to be in a good mood. "Can I ask you a few clarifying questions while you work?"

"Sure. Are you getting any closer to proving it was Marianne?"

"I know that's what you would like to have happen, but I'm not at all convinced she did it. In fact, I've only eliminated two people, Sarah and Ellis Sr."

He made a displeased grunt. "Well, keep at it. One of the three remaining suspects did it, and I want to find out who it is even if it's not Marianne."

"Actually," I said, braced for his outrage, "I have three and a half suspects. My next job is to eliminate the half."

"You think César might've done it? I think you can get rid of that half pretty easily. He would never do something like that."

"Actually," I said, "you're the half. From some of the things I was told by the others, it seems like you might have had reason to do it yourself. Or at least would be willing to do it if you did have reason."

I focused on his aura while I spoke. The exploding rage I expected, but something else was behind it. Fear? Whatever it was, he was hiding something in his relationship to Sarah's operation. I hadn't expected that. Maybe he did have a conflicting agenda.

He turned around to face me, and a frying pan had never looked more like a weapon than it did right then. "How dare they?" He scowled at me. "And how dare you? I hire you to find out who did it. If it had been me, you wouldn't be here investigating."

"I had to ask, if only to make sure that my investigation is thorough. Over and over in my business, it's the details you accept without examination that end up being the key to understanding what goes on."

"Well, I didn't wreck Sarah's grow." He was angry but telling the truth. "I had no reason to." His aura flickered. That was a partial truth.

"I wasn't even on the property when it happened," he continued. "And I didn't hire someone else to do it." He turned back to the stove, and his aura cleared. "So now you can cross me off the list of people who wanted to scuttle Sarah's business," he said over his shoulder. "I didn't."

We ate without saying much after that. Just as I was gathering up the plates to put them in the sink, a woman screamed. We looked at each other. The woman screamed again.

"That's Sarah," Evan exclaimed, knocking his chair backward as he jumped up. "Sounds like it came from the barn."

We raced out the back door and toward the barn, toward a third scream. Sarah was standing at the open barn door, hands over her mouth, fixed on something large lying on the ground. In a few more strides, I saw it was Stanford Ellis Sr. He was lying on his back, eyes open, mouth agape and one arm flung out, as if reaching for the rifle that lay just beyond his open hand. A dead rabbit lay on the ground nearby. I looked at Stanford's aura, but he didn't have one anymore. He was dead.

I pulled out my cell phone to call 911, but Evan was already talking into his. I put my arm around Sarah's shoulders, wincing at the stabbing pain she radiated. I drew her head to my chest, looking past her at the body.

The side of Ellis's head nearest us was covered in blood, and more had pooled beside him. His face was smeared with mud, as if he or someone else had twisted his face in the dirt as he died. No, that didn't make sense. It took me a moment to comprehend the mouth was mounded full of...mud. It was hideous. No wonder Sarah had screamed more than once.

*

One by one, everyone in the family arrived, drawn by the screams. Marianne stormed down the path and tried to rush to the body, but Evan stopped her, grabbing her by the arm. She swung around and slapped him hard with her free hand, but to his credit, he didn't let go, telling her she'd just mess up the investigation if she stomped all around.

Billy arrived at a slower pace from the garage. Stan was the last to arrive, showered and shaved, but still looking hung over. Maybe he was full of enough medicine that he wasn't feeling any pain, but he looked terrible, and his aura was still an erratic mess. We managed to keep everyone a few yards away.

Together, we fell into an involuntary awestruck silence. I guessed none of them had seen the body of a family member come to a violent end before this. Evan gently peeled Sarah out of my arms and wrapped her in his, where she began to sob quietly. She'd obviously knelt over the body as soon as she'd found it. She had mud and blood on her hands, on her jeans and shoes. When she'd lifted her hands to her face, she'd left smears of blood and dirt on her cheeks.

Billy stood opposite Sarah, his face blank, hands stuffed in his pockets, staring at his father's body. His aura swirled with shock, grief, and something else I hadn't seen in him before. Fear.

Marianne and Stan stood close together between the body and the back of the house, whispering. Their auras were not at all grief-stricken, though they carried what looked like shock.

The late morning sun beat down on us, and I could feel someone get restless. After a few minutes, Billy said, "I'll be in the shop if anyone wants me." His face gave no sign of his feelings, but his aura was still swirling, uncertain, as he turned away. "I got work ain't gonna get done with me here."

Marianne looked down at her high heels, torn on the gravel. "These are ruined," she observed with detached disappointment. I don't think she even knew she'd said it aloud. "I'll be in the house," she said, picking her way to the back door.

"I'd better call Dad's lawyer. He'll need to dig out the will," Stan muttered as he started to walk toward the house.

"All ready to inherit your precious ranch land, Stanny?" Evan's voice had a vicious bite in it.

"Yeah, I am," Stan mumbled. His head snapped up as if he suddenly realized the implication of what he'd said. "But I wasn't that ready, if that's what you're getting at, asshole." He turned and stomped off toward the house. I figured his first stop inside would be at the bar.

Which left Sarah, Evan, and me. "They're going to eat me alive," Sarah said grimly, apparently referring to the remaining Ellises. "Well, I still have my lease, for whatever good that will do me."

"I'll help you set up in another place, if you have to," Evan said. "They may get their way, but they won't get you. I'll see to it."

Sarah just nodded, staring at the body. Her aura was busy, however. Probably thinking through half a dozen different possibilities for her business.

We didn't have to wait much longer for law enforcement to arrive. Two Mesa County Sheriff's Department cars pulled up behind the house. A tall, good-looking man, at least a couple inches over six feet, got out of the first car. He looked to be maybe forty or a little older. Handsomely weathered. Not artificially muscular, but lean and tough, without a trace of belly. He reached in to get his hat, which he planted over his graying blond crewcut, before he closed the door. Out of the other car came two men with arms full of equipment and a roll of yellow crime scene tape. One of them laid down his stuff, put on gloves, and walked gingerly to the body, put his head against Ellis's chest and fingers against his neck.

"No heartbeat, no pulse," he announced.

Evan greeted the tall officer. "Hello, Heath. It's been a while."

"Mr. Landry," the officer nodded. As he spoke, his aura rippled with something decidedly unpleasant. I couldn't tell what it was, but it looked like there was some kind of history between them. But then a tangle of history probably connected most everyone in rural Mesa County.

"Hello, Sarah," the officer said, touching the brim of his hat, his voice warming.

He turned to me, and his aura flushed warm for a second before it flattened into professional neutrality. "And you are?"

I stuck out my hand. "Russ Morgan. I'm a private investigator from Denver."

Suspicion and a tough kind of humor flickered across his eyes and animated his aura. "And why might a PI from Denver be here today, Mr. Morgan?" He took my hand and something pleasant sparked between us, something sexual. His eyes, however, were hard and flat. I glanced down at his left hand but couldn't see whether he wore a ring on it.

"He's here at my request," Landry cut in. "I hired him to investigate the vandalism to my sister's grow operation. He arrived yesterday afternoon."

"Did he indeed?" he said without taking his eyes off me, as if already evaluating how guilty of murder I might be. "I hadn't heard of that incident. And now this. I'm Deputy Sheriff Heath Baker," he said. "I'm afraid you're gonna have to step back for this new investigation."

"No problem, Deputy Baker. I'll be glad to help in any way I can."

Baker's eyes said he wasn't interested in my offer. He turned to Landry. "Who discovered the body?"

"I did," Sarah said, still fighting for control of her voice. "I came out of the barn and... And there he was. It was horrible. It *is* horrible."

Baker nodded at her over Landry's shoulder. "I'm sure it was." He turned to Evan and me. "Would you gentlemen please wait somewhere else? I need to talk to Sarah privately."

"Before you do, Deputy," I said, "may I have a word?"

"What is it, Morgan?" I didn't like that something in his manner felt like a threat.

"Russ, please." I didn't know why I felt so awkward disclosing my methods to him, but I did. I thought I'd left behind my fear of ridicule long ago, but something in him reactivated it. "I'd like to help if you'll let me. I... I'm psychic. An empath. I can give you extra information while you interview the family."

I watched him fight against a smile. He was not impressed. "Well, Mr. Morgan," he said, carefully polite, "that may be useful to you in your work, but I need to follow hard evidence. And right now, you're actually one of the people who might have done this. I couldn't possibly let you participate in my interviews." He grinned, and not kindly. "Tell you what, though. You can participate in my interview with you, when I get to that."

I could be disrespectful, too. "So how do I know that there's bad blood, probably quite long ago, between you and Evan Landry?"

That got his attention. He looked at me with renewed suspicion and a flicker of fear. "Easy. He could have told you."

"But he didn't." I decided to push harder. "I generally can tell what emotions a person is experiencing and am pretty accurate in telling whether a person is lying or not."

"Is that so?" He stared at me for a second. "Then, what did I have for breakfast this morning?"

"That's not how it works. Tell me you had some specific food for breakfast this morning, and I should be able to tell you whether you're telling the truth."

"Like a lie detector."

"Kind of. The stronger the emotion the easier it is to tell."

"Well, let's see about that. I have to warn you, I'm a pretty good poker player."

I searched his face, his aura, for some flicker about being gay, which I was sure he was. "I have no doubt about that."

I could feel him closing down further into his poker player mode. "I had pancakes for breakfast."

"This morning?"

He nodded. He was good, I had to admit. His aura was compact and almost colorless, and his face gave absolutely nothing away. A few little shadow-spikes popped in his aura. "Not true," I said.

"Sorry, wrong answer." This time his aura spiked more sharply.

I laughed. "That's two lies now. You're a very convincing liar, Deputy Baker. Remind me to never play poker with you."

"I don't think I'd want you to play poker with me, either." Heath's voice was easy, but his aura said his mind was racing. After a couple of minutes, it slowed down.

"Maybe I can take advantage of your very special skills," he admitted with a wry grin. "But you say nothing, okay? No questions, no comments. Just catch my eye, and I'll make a note of it. You can tell me about it later."

He stared at me hard. No doubt he'd got a lot of mileage out of that steely gaze in police work as well as poker games. "Agreed?"

"Agreed."

"Good. Then we're gonna start with you, instead of Sarah."

I shrugged. "Your call. I have no agenda in your investigation except we catch the killer."

He pulled a notepad from a carrier on his belt and took the pen from its loop. "Oh, we'll catch the killer, all right." He wasn't done giving me the steel eye, because he did it again. "Even if it was you."

In general terms, I understood his caution. It was probably a real stretch for him to give credence to my sensitivities. Still, it was a little irritating. I knew it showed on my face, too. I'm a terrible poker player.

"Well, when you do catch the killer, you'll know for sure it wasn't me."

He started writing, his attention on the pad. "So, Sarah discovered the body?"

"Yes."

"Where were you when that happened?"

"I was talking to Evan Landry in the kitchen. We heard her scream three times before we got to her."

"What were you talking about?"

"During my other interviews it'd been suggested to me that Evan might've had a motive to sabotage his sister's grow operation. I didn't think it likely and chalked most of it up to the internal conflict that this family harbors, but I needed to ask him directly so I could see whether he was lying or not."

"Using your special powers."

I wasn't going to let him make a joke of it. I stared at him hard. "Exactly. Using my special powers."

"I need you to account for your movements over the morning."

"I came down to get some coffee and breakfast before seven. Billy was just leaving to feed the horses, and he suggested that if I wanted to interview him, the best way would be for me to accompany him and help out. So I did. That took about an hour and a half, maybe a little longer. I got back to the kitchen after nine and interviewed Marianne."

"How did that go?"

I shrugged. "It went, and I survived intact."

A tiny ray of laughter shot through Heath's aura, but his face didn't even twitch. He didn't look up, so I carried on. "She's got some belief that the Landrys don't belong in their family even though Carolyn raised all five of them from childhood. Apparently, it was after Carolyn died that the animosity between the Ellises and the Landrys really broke surface."

"Well, the Landrys are recent arrivals in terms of the folks around here."

"I know," I said, not even trying to mask my impatience. "I've already heard the story. Several times. The Ellises have been here for over a hundred years. I'm not sure what status that gives them. After all, the Utes have been here several hundred years and look at their status."

Heath looked up at me for a moment, cautious. "You're mixing two different histories."

"Am I? I'm just trying to get the right timeframe in order to decide who the interlopers are."

Heath softened and chuckled. "Nice. I'll give you that one. But let me give you a smaller timeframe." He clicked his pen shut and shoved it in his pocket. "Stanford Ellis was a good man. A lot of people around here knew and respected him. My dad was a farrier, working on several ranches around here. Quite a few them were around in those days. Anyway, Stanford and his daddy Elias gave my dad plenty of work, even when times were hard for them. One year a horse kicked my dad, broke his leg. He was laid up for a long time, because you can't shoe a horse when you're wearing a leg cast."

He looked at me, challenging. "We would've gone hungry a lot during that time, but Stanford and his dad sent over food, including game that they'd shot, and kept food on our table. I was twelve and too young to fill in much, although that summer I mucked out barns and stalls to say thank you. Folks don't ever forget that kind of neighbor."

He pulled out his pen again and clicked it to ready. "So if you come across someone who gives more weight to what the Ellises say over what the Landrys say, don't be surprised. Landrys don't have the same roots here, and they've never given back to their ranching community like Stanford Senior and his daddy before him did."

I couldn't let that slide. "And have Stanford Jr. and Marianne given back to the ranching community?"

Heath's aura didn't even twitch. That was a nonissue for him. "Not much, but their daddy did, and that still counts for a whole hell of a lot."

"I understand." I pointed to the body, where the ME crouched, doing his thing. "Still, it kind of puts some pressure on you doesn't it, hoping that none of the Ellises did this?"

That got to him. His aura flashed anger, but he tamped it down in a hurry. "I can see how you might think that, but you don't know me. I'm not a grateful twelve-year-old boy anymore."

His hard-ass look put me in my place. "I'm a deputy sheriff in the Mesa County Complex Crimes Division. I'll be glad if the Ellises didn't do it, but I'll let the evidence lead me to the killer. And we will find him. Or her. On that you can depend."

"I get that," I said, conceding. "And I want to help."

Our interviews of everyone else who was on the property before Sarah started screaming were predictable and unfruitful. Nobody had heard the shot, but Billy had been making so much racket in the shop that it wasn't a surprise. Besides, Stanford often went out shooting rabbits because he liked the meat, so even on a quiet day nobody would have paid attention to a .22-caliber rifle being fired. While Heath's crew searched outward from the body past the tape, over the grounds and through the house, we talked to Billy.

I'd told Heath before we talked to Billy that I'd seen him leaving the grow barn in what I felt was a surreptitious manner, but he scowled at me and didn't raise it with Billy. Since I was constrained not to speak, I couldn't say anything or ask him. Right then, anyway.

Marianne was condescending to Heath and quite vocal about how sure she was one of the Landrys had killed her father. When the body was discovered, she'd been printing up research materials for a news feature she was working on for the station. I saw a ripple in her aura as she talked about that, but Heath didn't pursue, even though I caught his eye to indicate I felt something there. He seemed satisfied enough when he finished the routine questions about retracing her activities through the morning, including the breakfast argument with me. To her credit, Marianne was accurate in what she said about our exchange. Except for the part about straightening out Evan, of course.

Stan's interview held no surprise either, except that he seemed unfazed by his father's death. It was sad, yes, but he was ready to liquidate the ranch and move on. Between sips of bourbon, he said he'd gone upstairs after breakfast, laid down for a bit, must have dozed, then showered and shaved. He was just getting dressed when the screaming started. Again, I saw significant spikes in his aura, but Heath ignored my signals. I was just along for the ride as a courtesy, apparently.

Evan Landry was oddly personal to Heath during his interview, more flamboyantly gay in his expression than I'd ever seen him, as if he were rubbing his sexuality in Heath's face. In response, Heath closed down. His aura pinched, and his face went hard. Evan gave us no new information.

Sarah was still deeply shaken when we talked to her, and for some reason Heath's manner became more aggressive with her. He asked her, like he had all the others, if she had any idea who might have done this and why, but her answers were much less emphatic than all the others had been. He also grilled her about what might happen to her grow operation now that Ellis Senior was no longer here to protect her.

She still had her lease, she said defiantly. Stanford and she had made it a good one. She'd go to court to defend it. She was certain she would win. Sarah gave them an outline of her whereabouts throughout the morning. As we were finishing, one of Heath's men approached but stood at a slight distance signaling to Heath, who motioned him over.

"You'd better come see this," he said. "Someone's torn through Ellis's office. It's a mess."

Someone had indeed torn through Stanford's office. Stacks of files from the long table perpendicular to the desk had been rifled and dumped on the floor. The file drawer in the desk had been locked, apparently, but broken open because the wood above the lock showed bright gouges that hadn't been there yesterday. It was now empty. Strangely, the surface of the desk was relatively untouched. It seemed as though someone had been looking for something stored away.

Heath called the photographer in, and they took extensive photos. Others took fingerprints from around the desk drawer, although he acknowledged that since whoever had done this lived there, fingerprints weren't going to be much help.

"We're done with the interviews," Heath said, stating the obvious. "I'm going to confer with my team. I expect you to stay on the property and make yourself available to me in case I have other questions."

Was there some flirtatious energy in him when he said I needed to make myself available to him? It felt like it. I looked in his eye to see, and he winked. Yes, there was. "I expect your full cooperation in this investigation, Private Investigator Russ Morgan," he said with a quirk of his mouth I felt wanted to be a grin. "If you uncover any additional information here, you are to share it with me immediately. Is that understood?"

"Perfectly understood, Deputy Sheriff Heath Baker," I said, matching his almost playful tone. "You have my full cooperation. I'm hoping the same is true for you, that you'll share any information that may have a bearing on my investigation."

"Within reason," he said, nodding. "Or until you prove to be a more serious suspect." He rubbed a hand over his eyes. "Although my investigation takes precedence over yours, obviously."

"Of course. May I take a few pictures of my own?"

"Yes, but don't move anything. Don't even touch it." He went in search of the rest of his team, leaving me standing in the middle of the littered floor of Stanford Ellis's office. I crouched down to take pictures of what was on the floor first. I figured they were closest to whatever somebody had been looking for.

Stan appeared at the door. "Does Heath know you're here?"

"Yes, he was just here. He said I could take some photographs. Do you mind?"

He shook his head. "Knock yourself out. I have no idea what they were looking for or whether they found it. I'll clean up this mess later. Just leave everything where it is. I'm going to lie down for a little while."

I understood that problem. "Drink a lot of water," I called out to him as he trudged toward the stairs.

I was just taking my last photos when Marianne Ellis appeared at the door, looking angry as a boil ready to burst, and just as red. "What the hell do you think you're doing in here?"

"I'm taking photos of this mess. Your brother gave me permission, as did Heath."

"This house is as much mine as it is Stan's, and I say you're trespassing. Get the fuck out." Her aura was a scalding swirl of anger and...jealousy? Of what?

I nodded, not trusting myself to say anything. I tucked my phone in my pocket and started to walk past her out the door. She blocked me and held out her hand. "That camera. Give it to me. Those photos don't belong to you."

Astonished, I laughed before I could compose myself. "I don't know what demons you're struggling with that make you so stupid, but you don't get my phone or the photos on them. You've asked me to leave the office, and if you step aside, I will. But have you ever asked yourself if your high-handed temper tantrums might indicate an ability to commit a violent act? Maybe not a good strategy right now."

"You," she snarled, "have no right to interfere in this family's affairs. Get. Out."

While that wasn't exactly true, I got out anyway.

*

By six o'clock, the body of Stanford Ellis Sr., now covered, still lay in the dirt where he died. The rifle had been picked up and taken away, and each of us had been swabbed for gunshot residue. The officers had taken countless photographs of the body, of the water tap dripping into the water bucket next to the barn and the mud around it that had apparently been scooped up to be stuffed into Ellis's mouth.

I asked Heath why the body hadn't been removed, and he laughed, saying it wasn't like all the TV shows, that it wasn't unusual to leave the body where it had been discovered for twelve or more hours while they worked. He refused to say whether he'd found anything of significance in the house beyond the ransacked office. It seemed our semi-collaboration had run its short course.

One of the sheriff's cars had taken off but had returned an hour later, bringing a generator and half a dozen tripods with lights. Sarah had said they could use the power from the grow barn, but Heath insisted on the generator.

César had arrived at his usual time and made our dinner. At the usual time, we showed up in the dining room as if grateful for the comfort of any familiar routine. The table was set, except for Ellis Sr.'s place at the head, which remained empty. The little silver bell looked lonely without its familiar place setting next to it.

We each migrated to our regular places, except for Stan Jr. He casually slouched into his father's seat as if he'd been sitting there for years, pulling his place setting from his old spot and centering it in front of him. Everything stopped, as if we were in a snapshot.

Half seated, Marianne stood again. "Our father's body is still lying in the dirt outside, and you...you *presume* to sit in his chair? How dare you? Get back in your own place."

"Dad's dead, and someone needs to sit here. That someone," he said, lifting his glass in a toast to his sister, "is me."

"You pathetic little loser." Her voice had gone cold with disgust. "You don't even know how unworthy you are to sit at the head of this table. As if you were the head of anything in this house but booze consumption."

"This is how it's worked for generations, sis," Stan said. He sat up straight and put his fists on either side of his placemat. "It's tradition. You of all people should understand that."

"Tradition! If you don't—"

"Stanny." Evan's calm voice sliced through the bickering.

Stan's face darkened as he swung unsteadily to glare at Evan. "I told you not to call me that."

"Stanny," Evan repeated in the same dead calm voice. "Get out of that chair now, or I will break you in half, I promise. I'll give you a five-count. Five."

No one moved.

"Four."

"I'm not scared of you."

"Three. Shows how fucking stupid you are."

"I'm not—"

"Two." Smiling, Evan stood, elegant and menacing, laced his fingers together palms out, and stretched his arms forward, cracking his knuckles.

On the other side of the table, Billy spoke up. "He's right, Stan. Move it. Let's eat."

Stan's aura wilted, his sharp defiance shrinking into sullen retreat. He pushed back from the table and stood.

"We're not done with this," he muttered, glowering at Evan.

"Of course we're not. Stanny. Not by a long shot. Now go sit in your own chair like a good boy. You can ring the little bell for César if it makes you feel like a real man."

Evan sat and pulled his napkin from its ring, as if nothing out of the ordinary had happened. I'd heard he could be cruel. What I hadn't realized was how much he enjoyed it. His aura radiated satisfaction. I supposed he would have to have some kind of payoff, as with any other behavior.

His face still flushed with embarrassment, Stan rang the bell. In rolled dinner, pushed by a red-eyed César, who served it up in silence. In sharp contrast to the night before, we ate in almost complete silence, even after Stan's humiliation faded from the room. I looked for grief in the auras around the table. Only Billy and Sarah showed any.

It was as if Stanford's death had erased their license to squabble. Perhaps the impending prospect of having to run the ranch or dispose of it without his oversight lay before them, more intimidating than it might have seemed twenty-four hours earlier.

Halfway through dinner, Sarah asked if anyone had offered to feed the officers. Both Stan Jr. and Marianne had clearly never given it a thought and dismissed it out of hand as unnecessary. Billy said it was a good idea but was overruled by his two siblings and Evan.

Stan sulked his way upstairs with a fresh bottle right after dinner, but Marianne, Billy, Evan, Sarah, and I sat in the living room for a long time, watching the log fire burn down, not saying much of anything.

Finally, at about ten o'clock, the noise of the generator stopped. The sudden silence was uglier than the noise. I stood outside the back door and watched Heath and his men load the body into a van, disassemble the lights and take down the tape. I followed Heath back into the house, where he informed the group they were done and heading out. He gave me a brief nod as he passed me on the way to his car.

One by one, the others went upstairs to their rooms, but I wasn't ready to turn in just yet. I went back outside to the scene of the killing and stood there in the moonlight. I wasn't hoping for some psychic revelation. I just wanted fresh air as I pondered the tangled family relationships that had culminated today in murder.

I supposed it wasn't all that rare for someone to murder a family member, but it was the first time I'd encountered it. The questions about motive and who had done it gradually crumbled away in the quiet moonlight, leaving me with a sense of what could only be called desolation. A family toxic as this one was a desolate place.

Well, tomorrow would be another day, full of a new set of squabbles and intrigue, I had no doubt. It was getting old, the in-fighting. For a few seconds, it occurred to me that a nightcap might be comforting, a way to insulate myself from all the unhappiness, at least for the night. I laughed sadly at myself and went inside.

Chapter Seven

Wednesday

The next morning at nine o'clock, Lee Merriwether, Stanford Ellis's attorney, sat down on the Landry side of the dining room table. The three Ellis children and the two Landrys sat on the Ellis side, and I took the chair at the foot. Predictably, Marianne had been furious when both Billy and Evan had insisted that I be present.

Merriweather dug into his attaché case and pulled out five nine-by-twelve envelopes, each labeled, passing them out to each family member. He retrieved a manila folder, placed it carefully in front of him, and opened it.

He cleared his throat. "My condolences to each of you," he began, "at the loss of your father. I was not only his legal advisor but also a personal friend. I did not expect to perform this duty so soon, and deeply regret having to do so. Each of you must be in terrible shock. This is a dreadful event."

He seemed to ignore the likelihood one of the people sitting in front of him at this table was in fact his friend and client's murderer.

"William Ellis is named executor of Stanford Ellis's estate," Merriweather said, his voice becoming brisk and official. "Although you each have a copy of the will, I'll go through the salient provisions now and answer any questions you may have. I've already prepared the new issue of shares in Ellis Ranch, Inc. according to your father's wishes."

I heard rustling around the table as five envelopes were opened and the documents extracted. Stan thumbed through each page, scanning quickly for something, and scowled. That was interesting. What was he looking for?

Merriweather drew a clear plastic folio from the folder in front of him. "Since all the assets of the estate belong to the ranch corporation, the first order of business is to distribute the shares of said corporation as stipulated by the will."

He passed out the certificates. "As you probably already know, the ranch corporation issued twenty-one voting shares, which Stanford held in trust for you, his beneficiaries. On page two, article four, the distribution of these shares is specified: to Stanford Ellis Junior, five shares. To Marianne Ellis, five shares. To William Ellis, seven shares. To Sarah Landry, three shares. To Evan Landry, one share."

He looked across the table briefly, as if to make sure everyone was keeping up. "A shareholder can transfer her or his share to another shareholder through sale or bequest. If a shareholder dies intestate, the shares of the deceased will be divided among the remaining shareholders *pari passu.*"

Marianne was positively wriggling with anticipation. Merriweather seemed careful not to notice. "Your father, after a great deal of deliberation," he continued, "felt that this distribution provided for the greatest chance of continued operation of the ranch he loved so dearly."

Marianne didn't seem particularly concerned about her father's love for the ranch operation. She wheeled on Evan Landry. "Now," she sneered, "we can finally get rid of you two. Your four of twenty-one shares won't even keep you on this property."

"In point of fact," Merriweather interjected, "your father's will stipulates that both Landry children have the right to live on this property for the remainder of their lives should they so choose, either continuously or in periods of their own determination until their deaths, or until the dissolution of Ellis Ranch Corporation."

Marianne's aura went dark as a thunderhead about to let loose, and so did her face.

Stan was busy with the math in his own way. "This means," he grumbled, "that Billy has virtual control of the ranch. In combination with one or maybe two others, he can decide what happens to it, and he'll try to work the ranch forever. This is total bullshit."

Merriweather frowned at him. "I'm sorry to hear you say that Mr. Ellis, but you are correct as to fact. William proved to your father over many years that he cares about the ranch in a manner closest to his own values. After much soul-searching, he arrived at this distribution to ensure that everything possible would be done to preserve this enterprise as a functioning ranch."

He adjusted his glasses and turned a couple of pages. "I want to emphasize that these are voting shares. These shares can be transferred as I described earlier. However, should the ranch property be liquidated, all proceeds from such liquidation will be divided equally among surviving shareholders regardless of voting shares held."

Five auras exploded in surprise. Stan's and Marianne's twisted into fury.

"Wait a minute!" Stan's voice cracked as it rose in pitch. "You mean the Landrys each get a fifth of the ranch when it's sold? They'd get the same as me?"

"Yes," Merriweather said carefully. "Assuming all five of you were alive at the time of the sale." I wondered if he should have pointed that out, given the circumstances.

Stan waved his copy of the will at Merriweather. "You did this, didn't you?" he shouted, his aura blazing. "You interfering little bastard."

"*Mr. Ellis.*" Merriweather's aura hardened to a sharp edge, and his voice stilled the room. "This is your father's will. There isn't a single provision in it that wasn't his decision. I don't care what you think of me, but you insult your father with that accusation, and I won't stand for that."

Stan slammed his papers on the table, slumped back in his chair, and crossed his arms.

Evan smirked. "Don't pout, Stanny. It's so unseemly." Evan was enjoying this.

"Now don't you start, Evan," Billy said calmly. "We got enough trouble around this table already, dammit."

Merriweather took a deep breath, collecting himself. He resumed as if no unpleasant disruption had taken place at all. "Your father's instructions stipulate cremation of his body, no church services, and that his ashes be scattered on ranch property in a manner his executor deems appropriate."

Merriweather paused, looking oddly defiant. Nobody seemed to notice. His aura spread, ragged and bruise-dark with pain, not just grief. It occurred to me he might have some very private reasons to mourn the passing of Stanford Ellis Sr.

"Regardless of what each of you may have thought of him," he said, "I can tell you with certainty that he loved each of you. As best he knew how."

He looked down at the papers in front of him, and his shoulders sagged. "There are other minor provisions in his will, but the most significant ones relate to ownership of Ellis Ranch Corporation as I've already outlined. Do any of you have questions for me?"

"I have one," said Sarah. "Over the last six months, I had several conversations with Stanford. He assured me that he would leave me a legally subdivided section of the ranch, which would include the barn and a utility easement." She looked lost. "I'm guessing there's nothing actually in his will related to that. Is there?"

"No, there is not," Meriwether said crisply. "That provision does not exist in either this or any draft version."

"He would have never agreed to anything like that, and you know it," Stan growled at Sarah, his aura spiking violent red. "He was so goddam stubborn about not breaking the ranch up in any way. If he wouldn't do it for me, he sure as hell wasn't going to do it for you."

"Who knows, Sarah," Marianne added with a thin smile. "If you believed that's what he promised you, maybe you just decided to hurry things along a bit. You must've killed him."

Sarah's jaw dropped open, her aura shocked flat. And eyes wide. "You vicious bitch," she said quietly. "If anyone at this table possesses the heart of a murderer, it's you."

And then all hell broke loose.

Amidst the snarling and snapping, Merriweather closed his folder, packed it away and stood up. The furor stopped. "Your father's vision," he said with surprising sincerity, "was that you five, and in due time you and your families, could find a way to live peaceably together here on the land he loved so much. I'm painfully aware you have grudges and differences among you, as he was, but surely this is the best possible time to put those aside and fulfill your father's wishes."

Stan belched. "Thank you, Mr. Merriweather," he said, insolence dripping from his words. "I expect that in the near term, we'll continue to consult with you concerning the legal affairs of our ranch. But please be aware that we might just as easily retain the services of another firm should the need arise."

Merriweather looked at Stan for a moment, sadness wrapping his thin little body. He hugged his folder to his chest as if to protect himself from the dead man's son. "I understand perfectly, Mr. Ellis. Before you do anything rash, however, I think you should know that I have provided legal services for your father without charge for the last five years. With the contentiousness that you exhibit so freely amongst yourselves, I suspect the services of another firm will run you quite an expense. Out of respect for your father, I will continue to provide services to Ellis Ranch Corp. without charge. You choose whatever legal counsel you see fit. Good day, and I am more sorry for your loss than you are capable of understanding."

Billy walked out with Merriweather. Stan, Marianne, and Sarah headed in different directions, leaving Evan Landry and me sitting at the deserted table.

"Well. So what do you make of all this?" Evan asked. "I hired you to find out who trashed my sister's barn, but I can't help but think that Stanford's murder and the damage to Sarah's business are connected."

"I'm certain of that, but I'm not really part of the investigation of the murder," I said. "Heath is in charge of that, and I've offered to help him as much as he wants. But he doesn't know me from Adam and he is, rightly, cautious about who he allows into his investigation. He certainly hasn't shared much information about the evidence he's gathered."

Evan laughed, and it wasn't friendly. "I wouldn't worry about Heath's caution too much. If need be, we can apply a little pressure on him to let you get more involved. After all the times he and I fooled around, starting in high school, and since. He's as gay as you or me."

I stared at Landry, stunned at having my suspicion so crudely confirmed. In that case, Heath's sexuality must've been a kind of open secret in the area, but gossip like that could really do some damage. Was Landry really so ready to use his private knowledge to pressure a public officer? A wave of disgust rose up through me.

"That's pretty low," I said. "Trading on that knowledge is more than just nasty. It's blackmail of a police officer. His standing in the community might be at risk, maybe even his livelihood."

Evan shrugged, unperturbed. "You can see it that way if you like. But it's history. It's fact. And in a relatively small community, knowledge of your history is used against you all the time. You don't think that my history here hasn't been used against me? Think again." His aura flashed red, I assumed at some memory of what he was saying. "Besides, I've already told you I'm not necessarily a nice guy."

I nodded. I understood that better all the time. "I figured he might be gay just from some of the flickers I got from him."

"Wouldn't that mean he likes you? If he's attracted to you, that's to your advantage, however you might want to use it." He grinned. "Heath's a great lay, even though it's been a few years since we went at it. Not because I didn't want it, but because he said no. It's always good to have a stud in every port, I say. And he was a fine one."

"Well, whatever your history with him might be," I said, "it's completely unethical for me to trade on it."

"Sorry to hear you say that. Me, I'm just interested in results." He stood up. "Are you going to keep working with Heath on the murder investigation?"

"As much as he'll let me. I've still got my own assignment, and I intend to finish it. As soon as I do, you'll have my report and I'll be on my way."

I wandered outside into the yard between the house and the barn. While it was true my investigation was now overtaken by Ellis's murder, I knew in my gut that solving one was likely to solve the other. I decided to talk to Heath about that connection and left a message on his cell phone to let him know.

Chapter Eight

Just as I was putting my phone back in my pocket, a car bearing the markings of the Mesa County Sheriff rolled up the drive. It wasn't Heath. An officer who hadn't been at the scene of the murder yesterday got out and marched toward me.

"Are you Russ Morgan?" he asked.

"That's me." Something was off-key. His greeting was too formal, and the man held his energy flat and hard. "What can I do for you?"

"Sir, I have a restraining order," he said, handing me an envelope. "It prohibits you from being within a hundred feet of Ellis Ranch property. I need to escort you off the property now. Sir."

I would have been offended at being called sir twice in the same breath by someone booting me off the property, except I was too stunned to be offended. Only one person would've arranged this, and that was Marianne Ellis. It was a petty gesture, of course. It was old news that she didn't want me around, but this was still a blow to the gut.

"Very well, officer, but you're going to have to give me some time to collect my belongings. I'm not leaving them behind."

"Yes, sir, but I'll need to accompany you."

I shrugged. "Suit yourself, I won't be long." As we headed up the stairs to my room, Evan Landry started down. He stopped when he saw my escort.

"I have to leave," I said. "I've been slapped with a restraining order keeping me off Ellis Ranch property."

Evan's eyes went wide, his mouth slack with surprise. It took a moment before he said, "That bitch. Don't worry about it, Russ," he said, staring directly at the officer. "I'll take care of it. This will be cleared up by tomorrow, next day at the latest. In the meantime, I'll put you up in a motel nearby."

"No," I said. "If I can't do my work here, I may as well go back to Denver. I want to check out some things there anyway. Just let me know when I'm allowed back."

I stuffed my things into my bag. I would've normally stripped the bed and collected my towels like a good guest should, but in this case, it neither seemed necessary or even appropriate, with a stone-faced deputy sheriff standing in the doorway.

I picked up my duffel and backpack. "Okay, officer. I'm ready." The deputy followed me to my car and waited for me to get in, then drove behind me to the property line, where he parked. I could see his car in my rearview, until a bend in the road cut my line of sight.

A restraining order. I had to give Marianne full marks for originality. Adrenaline from the shock of being evicted had made me jittery, so I put on some music and began my long drive back to Denver. I stopped in Glenwood Springs for gas and sent Colin a text. He'd be at work, and I knew personal calls were forbidden, but I wanted him to know that I'd be home and that I hoped to see him.

That was a pleasant discovery—I did want to see him. It wasn't that I was in serious need of some sane and civilized company, although I certainly was. It was him I wanted to be with. I wanted to share his stories of how he'd been, what he'd done since we were together. I had his clean hiking clothes to return. I blushed, remembering how I'd put them in the washer. I felt a lot better at the thought of dinner with him.

By the time I'd gone through the Eisenhower Tunnel, Evan had called twice, the most recent call confirming that he had arranged an expedited hearing to revoke the restraining order tomorrow. I reminded him I wanted to do some research anyway, so it wasn't entirely wasted time, but I would have to bill him for the extra mileage and time, which I would try to keep reasonable. He seemed unconcerned.

His voice seethed with anger so intense, I had a fleeting thought about Marianne Ellis's physical safety. Which I dismissed. While I didn't wish her harm, she'd declared herself my enemy in a way that relieved me of any responsibility to warn her Evan was angrier at her than usual. The cynic in me said getting to Evan with the restraining order was her goal in the first place, and I didn't need to inform her how well she'd succeeded.

As I was passing through Idaho Springs, my phone clinked with a reply from Colin. He was still pulling the extra hours in trial prep but would be free by seven. He'd see me at my place. I pulled off the road and sent him a reply, saying I'd have dinner ready, and started imagining a meal without petty in-fighting. Bliss. I would light candles. We would talk without rancor. The thought of his face in candlelight brightened my body as well as my spirits all the way home.

*

When I got home, I took a shower, threw my laundry in the washing machine, and settled down to do more research on cannabis law. I made a note of the address for

Marijuana Enforcement Division and gave them a call to see where I could track licensing activity and requirements. The woman on the phone directed me to their website where I browsed through much more than I could absorb. I made coffee, and that helped for a little while.

I don't like Internet research much at the best of times, but it's pretty straightforward if you know where to go and what terms to use in your search. When I don't really know what I'm looking for, though, I usually get overwhelmed and discouraged at page after page of almost relevant information with no real answers.

After a couple of hours of wading through exhaustively detailed government pages that told me how to apply for a license or file a complaint, or the location of the next public hearing, plus a bunch of out of date private pages, that was me. Overwhelmed and discouraged.

Mercifully, I remembered the business card Sarah had given me. I called Rick Saxon. Sarah's name worked magic on him, and he gladly set a breakfast appointment for the morning.

I went back to my frustrating research. The rest of the afternoon slipped away, and when I looked at the clock, I had just enough time to tidy up and make a quick run to the supermarket to pick up some fresh produce, a tub of my favorite salad mix and a roasted chicken. Colin rang the bell promptly at seven.

My heart jumped when I opened the door and saw him standing there, worn but happy and hopeful. Before I had a chance to overthink, he closed in for a kiss, pulling my head down to his. My arms had no chance to overthink either, they just wrapped around him tight. He felt so good.

When we unwrapped, we both were grinning, playful and happy in our arousal. Colin trotted upstairs to shower, and I made myself stay in the kitchen. I threw together a salad with the greens, the still-warm chicken, feta cheese, and some dried cranberries I found hiding in the fridge. A little raspberry vinaigrette, and we were all set. I was setting the table when I heard my creaky stairs announce Colin's return. I turned, and there he was, looking scrubbed and far more delicious than dinner.

"I don't even know what kind of beverage you like to drink with your meal," I said in apology. "I have some sparkling water and a couple cans of ginger ale—we can mix the two of you like. I did buy a lime. If you want a beer or wine, I don't mind serving it. I can lay some in for next time." *Next time.* It was a little scary how much I liked the sound of that.

"Plain water with a slice of lime for me, thanks. I don't really enjoy alcohol much," he said. "I'll have a glass of wine once in a while, but that's it." He looked at me as we sat. "I like it that you don't drink."

"I'm glad you like that. I like it, too. I wasn't much fun to be around when I did." That was in the past. Tonight, I was sober and having dinner with Colin. A mild euphoria washed through me as I shook out my napkin.

"Ooh. Cloth napkins and everything. Classy."

I shrugged, instead of examining how dangerous my happiness felt. "Just trying to do right by the quality of the company."

He blushed, enchanting me. I filled him in on the case, the characters, the toxicity, including the restraining order. Technically, I wasn't investigating the murder but energetically they were certainly connected.

"Have you ever been involved in a murder investigation before?" he asked.

"No, first time. And I'm not fond of the difference it makes. All indications are that one family member has killed another. While I hated my father, I don't think I could have ever killed him, even at the worst of times." I was sick of thinking about the Ellises and Landrys—my Hatfields and McCoys—so I changed the subject. "Tell me about your family. I don't even know where you were born."

"I'm a local," he said with a note of pride. "My folks live just west of Fort Collins, on Horsetooth Reservoir. I was born in Loveland, but we moved to Fort Collins soon after. They're pretty easygoing, very liberal folks, who taught me to love the outdoors. Our summer camping trips to Red Feather Lakes were magical."

I made a mental note. We'd go camping up there sometime soon.

"I was the last of the litter," he went on. "My parents were both in their forties when I came along. My next youngest sibling is twelve years older than I am."

He looked at me sideways. "I can guess what you're thinking. And it's true. I've lived my whole life surrounded by people older than I am. They always treated me as an equal. There were none of the competitive bullshit games at home, everything was handled pretty rationally. I had to go to school to learn the competition thing." A sharp red streak shot through his aura. An old pain, and its story. I wanted to learn it and make it go away forever.

"What about you?" he asked, drizzling a little more vinaigrette on his salad.

"I'm a Colorado native, too. Grew up in a tiny farming community. Hygiene, west of Longmont. Well, it was tiny when I was a kid. It's hardly recognizable now. My folks had a farm and just scraped by, economically speaking, like most small farmers in the area. Like most small farmers anywhere, I guess.

"They were anything but liberal. My father was a church-going fire breather, straight from the 'spare the rod and spoil the child' school of thought, and he certainly did not want his youngest son to be spoiled. My mother was kinder by nature, but she never challenged my dad about the way he treated me and my two older brothers. My parents are dead, my oldest brother, too. He was killed in Vietnam. My other brother and I..."

I thought about the stranger who shared a family name with me. "My brother and I are on divergent paths. We're civil, but we have nothing in common except some DNA. We don't see each other much. He has the farm, or at least the land."

Colin looked up at me, happy mischief in his eyes. "I'd like to share more DNA with you tonight. As soon as we clean up the dishes."

I laughed. "You're going to wear me out, young man. When you're old like me, pacing is everything."

He licked his lips. "I intend to wear you out every chance I get."

In a pleasant cloud of anticipation, we cleaned up the kitchen and headed upstairs.

*

"I love being with you, Russ," Colin said. His head was a delicious weight on my chest, and the weight of his leg hooked over my thighs grounded me.

"I'm glad you do. I love being with you, too," I said, stroking his head. "It's probably going to take me a while before I stop feeling like the other shoe is about to drop, though."

Colin pushed up and away from me. His face hovered over mine, eyebrows knit. "Eventually you're going to have to take me at my word, like adults should."

He started to say something and stopped. The silence was terrifying. "I love being with you, Russ Morgan," he breathed down on to me. "Please don't hang onto that old pain just out of habit. It will get in the way of what we could have now."

"How did you get to be so wise about these things?" I smiled up at him in wonder. "Here I am stumbling around trying to be brave, and you, you're so clear about what you want. That's a little scary."

"I've been told I'm an old soul." He kissed my nose. "Whether that's true or not, I'm very clear about what I want. I want you. You're a good man. You have some sort of kindness that is very rare. I feel it in everything you do."

"Kindness? Kind is not something I'm usually called."

"Maybe not professionally." I could hear his grin in his voice. "I'm sure you can be a hard-ass when you need to be, but even so there's a gentleness or kindness, something, maybe it's compassion that just radiates out of you. I love that. You care about things. You think about things, and I love that thoughtfulness." He licked my nipple. "It's very sexy to me."

I laughed, mostly because I could tell I was blushing. "That's probably the kindest, most flattering thing anyone has said to me in the last twenty years." I pulled him up to kiss him thank you.

"After you're back from your work on the western slope, I want you to meet some of my friends. I don't have that many, but I hang out with a pod of maybe half a dozen or so. They need to meet you."

"Do you really want to do that? They'll think we're serious."

Colin frowned. "What are you afraid of? That they'll think we are?"

I had to think about that. "I'm afraid they'll think I'm a predator, and think less of you, too."

"Stop that," he snapped, sitting up and scowling at me. "I'm not going to say it again." The frustration in his voice made me ashamed. "Russ, I'm not a fucking minor. I'm twenty-six years old, and I do have the capacity to make my own choices. My friends already know about my taste in men. For God's sake, they're my friends. Why wouldn't they know?"

I stared at him, suddenly so far away.

"Think of it as another kind of coming out," he said. "Are you afraid one of my friends is going to squeal, 'Eeew, Colin, he's OLD. Omigod, that's like, totally disgusting!' and drama-prance out of the room in his glitter T-shirt, skinny jeans, and turquoise high tops?"

I had to close my eyes. That was exactly what I was afraid of. I was astonished at how afraid I was of letting the world know I was dating a man in his twenties. It seemed so...so worthy of suspicion, if not condemnation.

"You know what?" The anger in his voice made me open my eyes. His face showed his anger, too. "I'm insulted you think I might have friends like that." I reached to stroke his cheek, but he pushed my hand away. "No. You pretend it's other people's ageism you're afraid of when it's really your own. This is your stuff."

And there it was, the ugly, humiliating truth. "You're right," I said, staring up at him. I had to swallow before I said the words. "I'm afraid."

"Maybe there's nothing you can do about what other people think, but you've gotta take care of your own shit. You *can* do something about that." Colin's energy shifted, no longer angry. Afraid. "You've got to, because you're the only one who can. And I'm afraid, too—afraid you might not."

I looked up into his amazing green eyes, almost black in the dim light of the bedroom, and surrendered. "Okay. I promise," I said, reaching up to wrap my arms around him and pull him to me. He resisted, and I let go. The last thing I wanted to do was force an embrace.

As soon as I dropped my arm, he snuggled down beside me and kissed my neck.

I kissed the top of his head as he burrowed in. "But for God's sake, don't ask me to come meet your parents yet. I'm really not ready for that yet."

"Come out, come out, wherever you are, come out," Colin crooned against my chest in a singsong voice. "You know, you can't just say no until I get tired of trying to drag you into my world, give up, and go away. I'm not going to make that choice for you. All I ask is that you don't be all passive-aggressive about it while you blame everyone else for being ageist. Not choosing is a choice, too."

"Wow. You really are a lot wiser than I am. I don't know what I did to deserve a gift like you, but thank you."

Chapter Nine

Thursday

Even though Colin had to be at work early, I insisted on getting up with him and fixing breakfast for him as the sky got bright. I fussed over him, I admit it. It felt good to fuss.

"You're sure I can't fix you a lunch?" I asked, refilling his coffee cup.

He laughed. "No, and you can't pin my address to my shirt for the bus driver, either."

"Hey, this isn't the age thing. We struggled through some of that last night. You have to let me do things for you simply because I'm in..." It was too early to realistically say *that* word, so I just confessed the truth. "I'm getting crazy about you. I can't help it."

Suddenly serious, he stared at me. "Good to hear. Me, too, and I'd hate to be the only one. That would be bad." He kissed me, soft, intense, deliberate. A message kiss, saying we were in this together. I got the message.

It was just after eight when I got to Sam's Number 3 on 15th Street. The place was already busy, but then I'd never seen it when it wasn't. People of every stripe ate there every day—suits, tourists, grunge, dull and ordinary, folks out all night.

"Are you Russ Morgan?" a voice behind me asked. A thin, pale man no more than thirty, sporting a buzzed head and fashionable scruff waited for my nod before closing the distance. "I'm Rick Saxon."

We shook hands and traded cards. His energy was like a horse at full gallop. "Thanks for meeting with me," I said. "I can tell you're a busy man."

"Anything for Sarah. She's good people." We followed a waiter to our table and sat. He glanced at the menu for all of ten seconds and set it aside. "I heard someone did serious damage to her operation."

"Yeah, it's not good. Basically, she's starting over." I felt bombarded by his intense urgency, as if I needed to keep up but didn't know where we were going. I could tell he was bouncing one knee up and down like a jackhammer. His sparking aura looked like he was a ten-amp wire carrying a fifteen-amp current.

I forced myself to take a deep breath and study the menu. When I'd managed to restore my own calm, I looked up. "I have to say I expected someone older. You sounded older on the phone."

"I get that a lot," he said, drumming his fingers on the table. "I'm young, but I know my stuff. I'm a botanist by education." He made a half smile. "I've been involved with cannabis research since forever. I did my master's on developing medical strains for anxiety."

"Indica."

He grinned. "Exactly. You should see me after a couple of days without it." He guffawed. "No, maybe you shouldn't. For the last three years, I've been working on a new hybrid specifically for PTSD. I'm nearly there."

"Impressive."

We stopped as our waiter appeared. We gave him our order and chatted about the medicinal and economic potentials of the marijuana industry until our food arrived. Saxon was even more excited about the possibilities than Sarah. An evangelist spreading his gospel of a golden age coming, its possibilities barely imagined.

Before my plate landed, Rick had peppered his eggs. "So what do you want to know?" he asked as he attacked his bacon.

"I've been struggling with the motive behind what happened to Sarah. I've got two basic possibilities, family animosity and business competition, but I'm not satisfied with either as I currently understand them."

"I only know what little Sarah told me about her family situation. It strikes me that it would be more likely business related."

I wondered how much of Sarah's story he knew but decided it was less than I did. "Is competitive sabotage a common occurrence in your industry?"

"No, but there's more than a trace of the Wild West in the air we breathe, with all the cash circulating and very little in the way of a uniform legal safety net. Especially when it comes to unpredictable incursions from the Feds. No shortage of guns lying around, either."

Guns. "What are you saying?"

"I don't think," he said, mopping up egg yolk with a piece of toast and popping it in his mouth, "the industry is mature enough to see organized competition yet. Right now, it's kind of a gold rush stage—plenty of room to stake your claim."

"I see. Everyone's working their own claim without hindrance?"

He shrugged. "We have two main professional organizations to help in terms of standards and best practices, as well as having a stronger voice on policy and legislation issues, but yeah. There's plenty of opportunity for everyone at this point."

"Which says to me Sarah's situation is probably more than simple business rivalry. I think someone is now trying to frame her for her stepfather's murder, which happened after the vandalism."

Rick looked up from his food. "Jesus. I didn't know. That would be one sure way to put her out of business."

I shook my head. "Not if someone's willing to kill. Why not just kill Sarah then, instead of Stanford Ellis, if the goal was only to put her out of business?"

He didn't answer, and I didn't really expect him to, so I trudged on. "I've asked around as much as I could down at Enforcement, but didn't come up with anything useful. Do you know anything that might make business competition a more compelling motive for me to follow?"

Rick put down his fork and became still. Even his knee stopped bouncing. "Who hired you to investigate what happened to Sarah?"

Now that was an interesting question. I opened to watch his aura. "Her brother Evan. Why?"

Rick didn't say anything at first, but his aura churned. He was deciding something important. "If it came down to choosing sides between Evan and Sarah, what would you do?"

"Ah." Something clicked into place in the back of my head that I would have to examine later. Right then this was too important to miss. "I've been hired to find out who sabotaged Sarah's grow, and that's what I'm going to do. Evan wants the culprit to be his stepsister. Badly." I gazed at him, hoping he could feel my sincerity. "I intend to fulfill my assignment. I want the truth. It doesn't matter to me who did it."

"Regardless of who signs your paycheck."

"I hope I'll always pick truth over a paycheck. My integrity is too battered and precious not to." I held eye contact as I took a swig of my tepid coffee. "If my employer turns out to be involved, and this isn't the first time that possibility has been raised, I'm not going to bail on Sarah."

Saxon nodded, apparently satisfied. "Has he told you much about his own plans?"

"He has plans?"

"You didn't hear this from me, right?"

"I'll keep your secret unless I have to testify in court."

"Nobody but Enforcement actually knows who's applied for licenses. That's confidential until the licenses are awarded. But Evan Landry has been showing up all over the place. Public hearings, industry gatherings, he's even asked colleagues for clones to grow. He bought a used hydroponics system from people I know. His interest is way more serious than casual curiosity. I'd bet a lot of money he's got an application in for his own grow, but it hasn't been approved yet."

I didn't have to wait to examine what fell into place in the back of my head. It came charging to the forefront all by itself. When I'd first asked Evan if he was involved in the vandalism, he'd said no, and his aura said he was telling the truth. But at the time, he'd also said he had no reason to, and his aura gave that away as a lie. He did have a reason, and this was probably it.

"That's a very useful piece of information, Rick. Thanks."

"It's only an opinion."

"It's a very useful opinion, then. It shines light on motive for me."

"And you'll keep this confidential? From what I've heard, he's got a rep for revenge." His knee was bouncing again.

I nodded. "I've already promised. That won't change."

We finished up, and I took the bill when it arrived. "I appreciate your time, Rick. You've given me an important piece of the puzzle."

"Glad to help, if it helps Sarah."

Outside, morning rush hour traffic clogged 15th Street. We shook hands, and his high-strung energy hit my solar plexus before I could shield myself. "May I call you again if I need to?"

"Sure," he said with a grin. "I'm eager to know how this turns out." He took off down the street before I had a chance to reply.

It felt good to slow myself down to normal, although it took a while to do. As I walked up the hill toward home, I pondered the phone call I needed to make to Evan Landry. I decided a direct confrontation was best.

*

When I got home, I made a few notes and got myself settled at my desk before I called Landry.

He answered on the first ring. "I was just about to call you," he said. He sounded jubilant, "I'm just outside the courtroom. The restraining order against you has been dismissed. If you leave now, you can be here before two o'clock. I want to get this wrapped up and take care of that sorry bitch."

"I'll leave as soon as I can. Before I do—"

"When can you leave?"

I pushed down my irritation. "Soon, and let me finish. When were you going to tell me about your own cannabis project?"

The silence was short, but it was absolute. "How did you find out about that?"

"It doesn't matter. It's true, isn't it? You were going into business for yourself."

"So?"

"It shouldn't come as a surprise to you that might serve as a motive for trashing your sister's operation. Is that what this is about?"

"No!" His vehemence rang true, even over the phone. "She couldn't get a conventional loan because banks can't be involved in the business. I loaned her money to get started. Why would I burn my own money?"

"You tell me. Because you thought you could make more on your own?"

Silence. *Paydirt.*

"So why are you going into business for yourself, Evan? Why not just partner with Sarah?"

"She didn't want me as a partner." His voice was petulant, a victim's whine. "Which was just as well. You don't know my sister," he went on. "She'll fail, and I don't want to fail with her. There's a staggering amount of money to be made in this business for those who can get going now. Sarah's constantly distracted by her altruistic vision."

He drew breath and plunged on. "She wants her damned business to morph into a co-op making hemp shirts and macramé flowerpot holders, for god's sake. To really make money, you have to be agile and focused. She's not agile, but I am."

Coming out of Landry's mouth, 'agile' sounded ugly, like 'ruthless and utterly pragmatic.' "What do you mean by agile?"

"Everything hinges on highly efficient vertical integration. Sarah is co-owner in her retail and medical outlets. Even if she wanted to, she couldn't make the kind of quick decisions I might need to make. She doesn't mind taking her time making decisions that need to be made on the fly. I'm going to have my own licenses so I can do things my way."

Maybe Evan's plans to build his own business weren't as sinister as I'd first thought. He and his sister had incompatible ways of doing business, that was certain.

"So where are you going to set up shop?"

There was a slight pause. "On the ranch. Stan and I have a business agreement."

Now there was a partnership made in a dark alley. "You don't want to be in business with Sarah, but it's going to be fine with Stan?" I heard the amazement in my voice and didn't care.

"Sarah's too strong-willed. Stanny will do what he's told. He's very eager to get going."

Yeah. Because Stan always did what he was told. "I can see your point. I'll be there as soon as I can."

"Good," he said as if we were perfectly on the same page, and hung up.

While I was packing, I decided I should let Heath know what I'd uncovered. I dug out his card and called his cell.

"Baker. I'm busy, Russ." He sounded tired and peeved.

"I'll make it short. I'm on my way back to the ranch. I found out today that Evan Landry and Stan Ellis have plans to start their own marijuana operation, also based on the ranch. That easily raises questions about their involvement with Stanford Sr.'s death."

"It might. But I'm on my way to the ranch right now to arrest Sarah for Stanford's murder, and don't you dare warn anyone. The evidence we have points squarely to her. Her boot prints are all around the bucket, she had mud under her fingernails, and bits of her marijuana crop were found on Stanford's clothing."

"She was first on scene. She'd been working in her barn. Her screams were not those of someone who had just killed another human being, I promise you."

"Now, Russ, we can talk about this when you get here, but I'm about to turn up the ranch drive. She has no verifiable alibi. We found some papers from Ellis's office in her barn."

"Which weren't there when you looked the first time."

"No."

"That stinks like rotten fish."

"Maybe. When you get here, you can set me straight."

I knew better than to make a joke of that. "Will do. See you in a few hours."

"I'll still be here. We'll be doing another sweep of the grounds. Talk later." He hung up.

As I returned to my packing, the situation I was headed back into felt darker to me, as if some wrong was being done that could never be fully set right. I knew Sarah was innocent. Even if I could prove it, she would carry the experience of being arrested and charged forever.

I opened the locked drawer where I kept my gun in its plastic box. I didn't hate guns. I'd grown up around them just like any Colorado farm boy. But a few years ago, when I'd bought this Browning Mark III 9mm pistol, it had felt different. It was nothing too snazzy, not a prestige item for the militia fetish folks, but it had proven effective, specifically for use against humans, not animals.

I'd taken the safety courses and got my carry permit. I went to the range twice a year to practice, but I'd never carried it on an assignment. Never felt the urge to. I stared at the box for a moment, feeling the urge. It didn't go away. I took out my box of cartridges, the gun, and my permit, and locked the drawer again. I packed them in my duffel, feeling oddly sad.

I sent a message to Colin saying there had been developments in the investigation, and I had to head back right away, that I missed him already.

I locked up, put my backpack and bag in the car, and headed for Grand Junction.

Chapter Ten

I was passing the town of Eagle when my phone clinked. I took a quick glance down to see a message from Evan asking me where I was and that Sarah had been arrested. I drove to the next exit and sent him a reply, saying I was still a couple of hours away.

His response was two words: *Please hurry.* That was a first in our communication, the word 'please.' I figured Evan Landry was frantic.

I got back on I-70 and headed west with "Marriage of Figaro" filling my little Subaru. I was going to have a busy afternoon once I arrived, and spectacular music with an impossible but happy ending would give me a little extra energy.

When I pulled up behind the ranch house, Heath was leaning on his squad car talking into its radio. I went to say hello, but Evan intercepted me just as Heath and I shook hands. I'd never seen Evan so frightened.

He scowled at Heath. "I need to talk to you right away, Russ. You can talk to the *arresting officer* later." He spat out his description of Heath.

"Mr. Landry," Heath said in a steel-hard voice with posture to match, "I took no pleasure in arresting your sister. I'll take a great deal of pleasure releasing her when we know she's innocent."

"She's innocent until proven guilty, Deputy Baker. That's how it's supposed to work."

"At the trial, you're exactly right. In the steps leading up to trial, not so much. I promise she will get the benefit of every aspect of due process."

I needed to get Evan away from Heath before he said something that would make things even worse. I took hold of his elbow. "Let's go talk, Evan. You're not helping here."

I looked over my shoulder at Heath. "I'd like to report to you as soon as Evan and I are done. How long will you be around today?"

"We're searching as much of the grounds as we have manpower for, and going through the outbuildings again. We'll be here until dark, and then again tomorrow morning." He cracked a smile at me, grateful and grim. "We can talk any time."

I nodded and steered Evan toward the house. We ended up on the front veranda, sitting side by side on Adirondack chairs. Evan's hands shook as he massaged his face.

"Things are not going well," he said.

That struck me as an odd understatement. What things had he expected to go well? His bid for a marijuana business? His sister's resumption of business? I decided not to ask, but to let him steer the conversation.

"I want you to clear Sarah of suspicion. Find out who killed Stanford."

"A couple of clarifications first. You need to know I've never taken on a murder investigation before, so I'll be learning as I go."

Landry nodded, so I continued. "I need to make clear that I can't eliminate you as a suspect. The only person I'm certain didn't kill Ellis is Sarah."

He closed his eyes and nodded. "Believe it or not, I didn't kill Ellis, so I'm not that concerned. Just clear my sister."

"I don't have any idea what your motive for killing him might be, so you're not first on my list, that's for sure."

"For years, I've expected nothing from his will, and expected nothing but trouble from any of the Ellises. I'm stunned I got the single voting share and twenty percent of the value of the ranch upon sale." He blew out an exasperated breath and twisted to face me directly. "I wanted nothing from any of them. I did not expect this. Not in a million years."

"Do you have anything more you want to say about starting your own grow in league with Stan Jr.?"

He gave a weary sigh. "Not really."

"Does Stanford's death affect your plans at all?"

"I don't think so. I hope not. My application isn't likely to be approved for another three or four months. By then, you'll have cleared Sarah and our lives will be back to some sort of normal. Marianne will object to another grow on the property, Sarah probably won't care. She doesn't have a competitive bone in her body, which as I see it, is part of her problem. Billy will go along because the ranch will get more money. He's not very bright, I'm sure you've already noticed. He'll be easy to persuade, and with him and Stan, I'll have all the votes I need."

I wondered if I should disagree. I decided no. My client had enjoyed decades of opportunity to learn otherwise and hadn't. If he wanted to believe Billy was not very bright, he was entitled to his mistake.

I got up and stretched. The car ride still sat in a twisted knot in my lower back. "Well, good luck with your plans. I should be able to finish my investigation of the vandalism today." That got his attention. He sat up, eyes hungry for revenge.

"You know who did it? Who?"

I shook my head. "By the time I give you my report, I'll know for certain." He frowned and slumped down in the chair, staring at the cottonwoods as their leathery leaves clatter-chatted with each other in the afternoon breeze.

I left Evan brooding in his chair on the veranda and headed back to find Heath, who was still standing next to his car, talking with a couple of his men. When they left, I moved in.

"Evan all done with you?" he asked with a smirk.

I shook my head. "Not yet. He wants me to help clear Sarah of suspicion."

Heath's face tightened. "I figured he might."

I waited for more, but apparently he was done commenting on that.

"What do you think about the two of us talking with Lee Merriweather about Stanford's will? We'd need clearance from Billy, of course."

Heath stared at me for a moment, surprised, tired, frustrated. I waited while he thought about it, prepared for the worst. But slowly his aura warmed, smoothed out. "That might be a good idea. What are you thinking?"

"I'm wondering about Stanford's will and the way it apportioned ownership to the children. What if the problem is not something that's in the will, but something that isn't? When the will was distributed, Sarah said something about expecting a provision allowing subdivision of the property. Who knows what we might uncover?"

"Worth following up. You can use your aura woo-woo on him. I'll talk to Billy about it."

I laughed. "I'll be glad to provide my aura woo-woo for whatever good it might do, although Merriweather doesn't strike me as likely to lie."

"Hey, Russ!" Billy called across the yard. We looked over to see him approach, dogs trotting close behind.

Heath leaned against his car and grinned. "Well, speak of the devil."

"My ears started burning," Billy said with a laugh. "I figured I'd better come see what you guys were sayin' about me. Plus, I want to talk to Russ when you're done givin' him a hard time."

"That's not gonna stop any time soon, so don't hold your breath," Heath said amiably. "In the meantime, we want your permission to talk to Merriweather about how your dad's will came to be like it is." He cocked his head at me. "Big city PI here thinks there might be a clue or two in that."

"Merriweather? Sure, I'll give him a call. I assume that'll be enough." He looked at Heath. "Anything else?"

"Nope, that's it." Heath winked at me. "You can have him for a while now, but I'll want him back eventually." His radio scratched to life, and he reached for his shoulder mic.

Billy poked me on the shoulder. "So, Russ, you got a minute?"

"Sure."

Billy pointed a finger at the shop he'd come from, and we strolled over. He looked around before speaking, maybe making sure we were out of earshot. I waited for him to start.

He stared straight at me, the good-natured banter gone. "I want to hire you to get Sarah out of trouble. I've got some money put aside, not much, but I could pay you in pieces. I'm good for it."

"I have no doubt you are, but there's no need. Evan's already hired me to do exactly that."

"I don't trust him to clear Sarah. Come to that, I don't trust Stan or Marianne, either. I know Sarah didn't do it, but anyone else could have."

"What about you, Billy? Are you on that list, too?"

He looked at me, head cocked as if he was deciding whether to take offense. "You can keep me on that list if it suits you," he said calmly. "But I surely didn't kill my dad."

"That leaves a very short list of suspects, then, doesn't it? Evan, Stan, and Marianne. Are you comfortable with finding the killer on that list?"

Billy looked out toward the pastures, over the tractor he leaned on. "Hell, I'm not comfortable with any of this shit. Somebody killed my dad, and that somebody is turning out to be a family member. I hate that. But I am one thousand percent sure it wasn't Sarah." He thumped the top of the tractor. "So just remember, I've got some money tucked away if it turns out Evan is part of the problem."

"Why are you so committed to helping Sarah?"

"I could give you a bunch of reasons, but I'm gonna give you just two. First, with Sarah in jail, the real killer's still free. That ain't right. Second, I love this ranch more'n I can say, and Sarah's business is gonna save it."

He stared at me hard and held it. He meant it. "That's my deal. Nothin' fancy."

"Good enough for me," I said quietly. "I'll let you know if I run into a wall with Evan."

Billy smiled. "Attaboy. I feel a whole lot better now." He gestured toward the shop. "You wanna get your hands dirty?"

I laughed. "Another time. I've got a couple more things to do before dinner. And thanks for arranging us to talk to your attorney."

"Oh, yeah," he said, reaching into his pocket. "I better call him before I get grease all over. Thanks for the reminder."

*

The great room smelled of cooking dinner, and I realized I was hungry. My short stop on the road seemed a long time ago. I stood in the middle of the room taking deep sniffs, as if that was going to make me less hungry. Maybe I'd sneak into the kitchen and grab something from the fridge. My stomach growled, and that's when I noticed the music.

It was the first time I'd heard music here. It was only mindless easy listening, but still. It was coming from Stanford's office. The door was open, so I stuck my head in. Stan sat at the desk, papers spread in front of him and a tumbler of booze nearby. Just the person I wanted to see.

"Hello, Stan," I said. His head jerked up in a hurry, but his eyes were slower to find me.

"Back so soon. Too bad." He took a slurp.

"Yeah, back from the big city. It wasn't wasted time, though. I found out you and Evan were going into the growing business yourselves. And I think that means you were the one who trashed Sarah's operation." I don't really know what kind of response I was expecting, maybe more hostility or defensiveness. It certainly wasn't laughter.

"That took you long enough. You must be a really shitty PI." He burped proudly. "Yeah, it was me. I figured she'd gotten too far ahead of us and needed to be slowed down some. So I slowed her down."

My stomach rumbled, but I wasn't hungry anymore. "Nice. What a prince."

"Whatever. Anyway, I'm not going to get into any trouble for it. Sarah killed Daddy, and nobody is going to care that her grow was trashed." He picked up his tumbler and lifted it to me in a jeering toast. "Good reason for me to celebrate, don't you think?"

Disgusted, I stared at him while the radio played a sappy string version of "Bring Him Home." He sat there grinning, triumphant. Poor guy. He had no clue how pathetic he was. I could think of nothing more to say, so I turned around and left. I needed to find out if Evan had known of his business partner's actions. Maybe I'd end up working for Billy after all.

I found Evan next to his Mercedes behind the house, talking on his phone. I waited until he'd finished.

"Well, I'm ready to make my report," I said, "but first I have to ask you once more about your involvement in the vandalism."

"What the hell, Russ—"

"I know you didn't do it yourself. But I'm wondering now if you've known all along who did do it."

"Stop being an asshole." I watched his curiosity overcome his anger. "Why would I already know?"

"Because it was your business partner, Stanford Ellis Jr. He decided Sarah was too far ahead of your project and needed slowing down." I shook my head, still disgusted at the mean-spiritedness of it all. "You go into business with some nice folks."

Evan's face had gone slack, his aura shocked flat. So he hadn't known. That was something to his credit, anyway.

"That little shit." His eyes had gone dark and cold. "I should have guessed." He stomped away, headed, I supposed, for an unscheduled partners' meeting. At that moment, I didn't really care.

I was exhausted. Upstairs in my room, I found fresh linens placed on the foot of the bed. I settled in, made the bed, and laid down, with just enough time before dinner for a power nap.

*

The atmosphere in the dining room was unnervingly civilized when I arrived downstairs. Evan was in his polished restaurateur persona, witty and affable about nothing in particular. I became even more wary when Marianne greeted me courteously. She seemed positively euphoric. I braced for the drop of the other shoe.

Stan seemed to be avoiding eye contact, and when he finally looked across the table, I saw why. He was sporting an enormous black eye. It was purple, actually, and still puffy, half closed. I figured it was a result of his partners' meeting with Evan.

César wheeled in dinner, and the five of us tucked into our food.

Halfway through the meal, Billy cleared his throat. "Dad's ashes are coming back from the cremation folks tomorrow morning. I'm hoping everyone can meet up at two o'clock tomorrow behind the barns. Everyone except Sarah, that is. We can go up the hill a ways and spread them in the trees. That work for everybody?"

The room became somber as everyone confirmed.

"You're welcome to join us, Russ, if you'd like. You didn't know him long, but you were here when he died. I think he'd like you there."

"Thank you," I said. "I'd be honored."

Marianne gave her younger brother the fisheye, but said nothing. Billy seemed oblivious.

The rest of the meal passed in almost complete silence, as if each of them was pondering the ritual they would perform the next day. I excused myself as soon as I could and went to my room.

I called Colin, and when he answered, a happiness that felt distinctly ours washed through me. It felt like ages since I'd seen him, even though it had only been since that morning. I missed him and told him so again. We laughed about nothing much, murmuring aimlessly to each other, stretching the conversation even with details of food we'd eaten. Eventually we hung up, blowing kisses.

I stared at my phone. I couldn't remember the last time I'd happily talked to anyone on the phone for thirty-four minutes. Apparently, I'd fallen hard, and at that moment, content and fuzzy, I didn't mind at all. When I turned out the light, I imagined he was lying next to me. I could almost feel his soft sleeping-breath against my skin. It was wonderful.

Chapter Eleven

Friday

By the time Billy and I got back from feeding the horses, Heath's car and a Mesa County van were parked behind the house. Heath stood with a group of men, pointing to a map, then up toward the pine woods and sweeping his arm out toward the fields. Another day of search.

"Well," I said to Billy. "It looks like my recreation is over. Time to go to work."

"Better you than me, Russ," he said. "I've got a baler to coax back to life. It hasn't even coughed since last fall."

I shook my head with a grin. "In your own words, better you than me." I lifted my hand in salute and headed to where Heath was handing out marching orders.

He saw me coming, said something to his crew, and strode toward me. "We're due at Merriweather's office in half an hour. You ready to go?"

"All ready, although I wouldn't mind washing my hands."

He nodded. "Meet me at my car in five."

As we drove down the hill to the road, I figured it was a good time to bring him up to date. "I don't know if you've heard, but it turns out Stan Jr. was the one who trashed Sarah's grow. I told you yesterday he and Evan plan to start their own marijuana operation. Turns out their license applications are still pending. Stan decided Sarah was too far ahead of him, so he took a baseball bat to her shop."

I looked at Heath for some reaction, but he had his poker face on. I didn't bother opening to his aura. "Oh. And I brought my handgun with me. I feel more trouble coming." That got his attention.

"Don't care about the handgun as long as you've got a permit." I nodded. "We don't look at guns the same way some of you bleeding heart liberal city folk do," he said with a playful smile. It felt like he was only half joking. Then he stopped joking altogether. "So you don't think this is over?"

"I'm certain it's not. Feels to me we're a long way from being done."

"Hmm." We drove in silence for a few minutes.

"So what charges are you going to file against Stan Jr.?" I asked. "He's confessed to the crime. Proudly, I might add."

"If Evan or Sarah want to file a complaint, then we'll have to act. Otherwise, it's a family squabble as far as we're concerned."

"Even though he did enough damage to warrant a hefty felony charge?"

"Even though. You have to understand not everyone is as enthusiastic about the cultivation of marijuana as Sarah. Or Evan and Stan, I guess."

It took effort to control my anger. "I daresay if Sarah Landry had destroyed thirty or forty thousand dollars' worth of Ellis property, your official response would be a little different."

Heath shrugged, unmoved. "Maybe. But that's the way things are. Like I said before, the Ellises have been here for four generations. My family's been here for three.

The Landrys arrived twenty-five years ago by marriage. It's not the same."

I wasn't going to let him get away with that. "On the contrary. In the eyes of the law, it's supposed to be exactly the same. That's what the law is for, to erase inequality of position and power."

"That looks good on paper." Heath's jaw tightened. "But the realities of small community life are more complicated than the theory."

I was stunned. "How can you even say that?"

"Look. You don't owe this community anything, and it doesn't owe you anything. That's the big city way."

He hunched over the wheel to shift his weight. "You can breeze in here, do your thing carrying that kind of theoretical flag, but I'll be living here the rest of my life. I uphold the law, but I also have to be a realist."

His aura flickered with something that looked like regret. *Oh. That looked like something deeper.*

"Do you not want to live here for the rest of your life?"

Heath snorted. "Is that part of your aura reading stuff?"

I nodded.

He started to say something and stopped. "That's a longer conversation than we can have right now." He grinned, full of country boy charm. "Why don't you swing by my place this evening around seven? I'll draw you a map, but just ask anybody where the old Baker place is, and they'll point you in the right direction."

More was behind the invitation than conversation. Heath's aura had warmed up with sexual energy.

He must have felt my hesitation. "I got the coroner's report from Ellis's autopsy today, and I can fill you in on that, too."

"Sounds like a plan."

"So," he said, all official business again. "How do you want to do this interview?"

*

It took me a moment to understand that Lee Merriweather and Andrew Kommen, Colin's boss at Stelnach, Breyer and Kommen, were in the same profession. This modest suite above a dentist didn't even have a receptionist. We stood in a small waiting room, sparsely furnished, that looked like it served two other professionals besides Merriweather—an accountant and a therapist with an impressive string of letters after her name. Atop a coffee table in the corner, next to a lamp and a magazine with a smiling and well-dressed white middle-class couple enjoying life on the cover, a small portable fountain burbled a happy trickle over plastic rocks and bamboo.

Merriweather opened the door to his office, ushered us in, and sat us down in comfy but utilitarian chairs in front of a scarred oak table. I did a quick estimate from memory. Andrew Kommen's desk was nearly as large as this entire room.

"You understand, I'm sure, the only reason we can have this conversation is because William Ellis—Billy—has authorized it," he said, opening a file sitting on a beige metal filing cabinet to his right.

"I appreciate that," said Heath, his voice affable and courteous. "We sure don't want to apply any inappropriate pressure on you. If you have any concerns at all about that, you speak up, okay?"

"No, no," Merriweather said with a heavy sigh, shaking his head. "I'm not really sure why I even said that.

It's just that..." His aura swirled dark with grief. "This is such a terrible business."

I caught Heath's eye and raised my brow, hoping he recognized my signal as wanting to speak. He nodded. "This certainly is a terrible business," I said. "We're hoping this conversation will help put it to rest as quickly and decently as possible."

Merriweather swallowed and looked at Heath. "What do you want to know?" He obviously felt better with Heath in charge of the conversation.

Heath looked at me. "You've got some questions, Mr. Morgan?" I tried not to smile at the formality.

"It seems to me," I began, looking for a way to reassure Merriweather I was an ally of the family, "that the discord among the family arises from the ranch itself—its history, its role in the ranching community, its potential for real estate development, and its current use, which includes Sarah Landry's cannabis grow op." I opened my vision to watch Merriweather's aura. "From everything I've heard, Stanford Senior was very much in favor of Sarah's project and gave her all the support he could." Merriweather's aura flickered but there was no major reaction.

"Yes," he said. "Stanford wanted more than anything to see the ranch continue operating as a ranch. He was very aware that the income from Sarah's operation was going to allow it to continue in that capacity."

"I assume you drew up the lease for Sarah's business?"

"Certainly. I'm intimately aware of every provision."

Out of the corner of my eye, I saw Heath lift his hand off his thigh, a motion too small for Merriweather to see from his side of the table. I waited for Heath to speak up.

When he did, he sounded almost nonchalant. "Was there any disagreement between Stanford and Sarah as they drew up those terms? Anything to indicate that either side was unhappy with the final version?"

"Not at all," Merriweather said emphatically. "It was a very simple process. Stanford asked Sarah what she needed. She drew up a list of bullet points—" The little man blanched. "Oh. That was wrong. Anyway, together they arrived at their business terms. They did that here in this office. I watched them. Everything went forward without a shadow of disagreement."

I wasn't sure Heath would frame the most important question neutrally, so I jumped in. "You'll recall that when you distributed Stanford's will the day after he died, Sarah spoke up asking about a provision she expected to be in that will. About deeding the barn and an easement to her."

"Yes?" Merriweather said, as if reluctant to say anything more.

I kept going. "Was that a provision you and Stanford ever discussed, or was Sarah just making that up?"

Merriweather glanced at Heath, as if asking permission to continue. He nodded. "That's very important information for us to know," he said.

"Very well." His aura flooded with relief. Interesting. "Stanford and I discussed both the provision and its legal ramifications over a number of months. Probably the last six. There were many technical difficulties involved, since the portion of the property in question was situated in the middle of the ranch buildings proper."

Merriweather's voice softened, as if with nostalgia. "Stanford was very concerned about making any change to the ranch because of the...discord among his children. That, combined with the technical difficulties of such a subdivision, made him reluctant to take action." He looked at Heath. "He very much wanted to take care of Sarah and her fledgling business. He told me more than once Sarah was the only one of his children who was actually fond of him. And he was fond of her."

"And?" Heath's nudge was kind, firm.

"A week before his death, Stanford came to my office, asking me to draw up that provision to be included in his will. There were many steps, of course, including a new survey of the land and, of course regional district approval, even though both portions of the ranch would be retained to agricultural use. It would take months, maybe years."

Merriweather's wistful little smile was heartbreaking. "He was concerned about the reaction that might arise, especially from his older son when the surveyors arrived at the ranch to do their job."

"But he had decided to proceed with the project, I hear you saying," Heath said.

Meriwether nodded, looking close to tears. "Yes." He cleared his throat. "He didn't mind it was going to take a long time, because he felt he needed that time to get his family on board with his decision."

"And he was most concerned about Stanford Junior's reaction to this decision?" I asked.

"Yes." Merriweather's voice was barely a whisper, as if confessing a terrible secret. His aura showed all kinds of conflict, and I realized he was at the edge of disclosing his own suspicion of his friend's murderer.

"Knowing the family as well as you do," I said carefully, "do you think it's possible Stanford's death might be connected directly to this new provision in his will?"

Merriweather looked down at the folder in front of them. "Yes, I do."

"Do you think," I pressed, "Stanford Junior, in learning of this provision, might've killed his father?"

The little man stiffened, and his eyes took on a harder light. "That's not for me to say, and my opinion is hardly relevant." He paused. "I can tell you, however, his older son's behavior was a frequent source of pain and disappointment for Stanford."

I looked at Heath, who shrugged lightly. He wasn't impressed. He shifted in his chair. "Is there any other information about the family's legal affairs you feel might have a bearing on this case?"

"Not that I can think of."

"Well, you've been very helpful," Heath said. He stuck out his big hand, which engulfed the lawyer's much smaller one.

Merriweather nodded, looking desolate. He showed us out.

*

On the street, Heath turned to me. "What do you make of all that?"

"It confirms my suspicion that Stan killed his father. My scenario is he found out about his father's plans to subdivide the property and went nuts. And now you know that even Stanford Sr. was most concerned about Stan's reaction to the decision he was making. I realize you don't have any hard evidence, but surely you see these facts can be interpreted this way."

Heath nodded slowly, disagreeing. "Yes, they can. They could also be interpreted that Sarah Landry knew Stanford Senior was going to change the terms of his will and killed him, assuming it was a done deal in order to get hold of the land sooner."

"But that makes no sense at all." I tried to sound like I wasn't peeved at his obstinate refusal to see things my way, but I was. "Merriweather said it would take a long time, and Sarah would've known that, starting with whatever zoning issues might be involved. Then a survey team. None of that had happened. She for sure did not kill Stanford assuming it was a done deal. She'd be shooting herself in the foot. So to speak."

Heath smiled, as if gratified he'd gotten to me. "Then why did she ask about it when the will was distributed? She was expecting it to be there."

"I think she expected it to be there, true enough. But she'd been told it was going to happen. It could easily have been that shock made her blurt out a question she didn't really want to raise in that company." I caught Heath's eye and held it. "I'm convinced that Stan is our killer. I'd bet a dollar on that, which is as high as I go."

"I knew you'd be no fun at poker," Heath said with a chuckle. He got dead serious again. "We're still looking for more evidence. Do you know how many places you could hide bloody clothes on a ranch? We're not even looking for the murder weapon. We've always had that. We tried to use dogs, but we just don't have the resources to search every damn inch of that ranch."

We got in his car, and I rolled the window down.

"Do you want the AC?" Heath asked.

"Not unless you do. I prefer the fresh air."

Heath took off his hat and ran a hand through his crewcut. "Me, too."

The air blowing through the car rumbled and thumped around us as we picked up speed, making conversation difficult. I didn't mind. I'd already talked more than felt good. Heath evidently didn't mind, either. We drove in silence.

"Well, that was time well spent," Heath said as he parked the car behind the ranch house. "I'm not so ready to drop charges against Sarah as you are, and I'm nowhere near as ready to file them against Stan, but what Merriweather said gave me a lot to think about. Good idea."

He got out and stretched. He had a very nice frame. "If you believe in luck and faith," he said gravely across the roof of the car, "then wish me the luck in finding something I can use in this case. And keep the faith that justice will be served."

"Absolutely," I said. "On both counts."

He squeezed his shoulder mic and called for status reports from the field.

As I headed toward the house, my phone rang. It was Evan. I got a hello out before he started.

"This has to be quick, I'm at the courthouse with my attorney. Sarah's going to be arraigned this afternoon on a charge of manslaughter. My attorney, Arvind Fletcher, will be here for that, since I've got to be back on the ranch by two for spreading the ashes. We're trying to schedule a hearing for her bail this evening. I don't want her spending the weekend in jail if I can help it."

"Do you want me to do anything?"

"No, just don't let them do the ashes without me there. I should be back in plenty of time. Oh. Gotta go."

Chapter Twelve

I went into the house, heading for my room. I wanted some time alone, to think about what Merriweather had told us and what to do next. As I headed up the stairs, I met Stan coming down. In that moment, I knew exactly what to do next.

"You going to have lunch?" I asked him.

He looked at me with a flash of irritation, which he managed to stuff down. He didn't look like he was feeling all that well. "Yeah, I am." He passed me at close range, and the reek of booze coming off his skin made me regret I'd been breathing in right then.

"I think I'll do the same," I said, cheerful as if I'd just found a twenty in slacks I hadn't worn for a long time. I turned around and followed him down.

Over his shoulder, he said, "I'd rather you didn't. I'd like to eat alone."

"Heck, a man's got to eat." I tried to make my voice sound light.

He didn't object again, so I followed him into the kitchen. He headed to the sideboard for a drink, and I headed for the fridge. "I'm guessing Evan gave you that black eye," I said as if it were a nothing but a joke. "It's a beauty."

"That asshole."

"Did that happen when he found out you had sabotaged Sarah's business?"

He grunted. "Yeah, we had a little disagreement over implementation of our business plan."

"He'd be a tough one to be in business with, I'm sure. Heck, he was in business with Sarah, at least as an investor, and he was ready to throw her under the bus in favor of the project you guys have going. Think he might do the same to you?"

"Maybe. I can take care of myself."

Somehow I doubted that, especially against Evan. "Here's some leftover stew from the other night. Shall I heat some of that up?"

"Whatever. Just not too much for me," he said. "I don't think I can eat a lot right now."

"I understand. Toast will help." I cut three slices of bread from the loaf and threw two of them in the toaster, then put enough stew for the two of us into the microwave.

While it was running, I watched Stan slumped at the kitchen table, both hands cradling his drink as if it were the most precious thing in the world. I could relate. I remembered the posture very well, and the defiant hopelessness that went with it. So angry. So empty.

"I know Sarah didn't kill your father," I said calmly.

Stan's head snapped up. I was looking for fear, and I found plenty. "Why are you telling me that?" he said with his standard truculence.

"I just thought you'd like to know. Somebody's framing her. I know now that she couldn't possibly have placed those papers from your dad's office in the barn. Funny how an attempt to frame her is actually going to prove her innocence."

His aura flooded with something close to terror. "Don't talk to me about that shit right now. I'm not in the mood."

I shrugged. "No problem, I just felt you should know I'm making progress on the case. I know it wasn't Sarah, and I know it wasn't Evan." I stared at him hard. "That means," I said, putting a lot of weight into my words, "that your father's death was patricide."

His guffaw wasn't convincing. "Is that significant? Really?"

"Oh, yes. The ancient Greeks knew all about shedding family blood. They even had special deities, called the Furies, who avenged the crime when one family member killed another. They were an especially nasty lot, and they never stopped—"

"Jesus fuckin' Christ, just shut up with all that shit!" Stan exploded. "I'm not in the mood to hear your fairy tales. And I'm not eating with you, you jerk." He said that as if I should be crushed, deprived of his company.

Well. This was more progress than I'd hoped. The fear I'd seen in his eyes and his aura was enough for me, even if it wouldn't be enough for the Mesa County DA.

"Sure, whatever you say. I'll leave some of the stew out for you."

"Don't bother," he shouted over his shoulder on his way out. "I've had my lunch."

I watched him weave toward the stairs. Yup, he'd already drunk his lunch.

It wasn't really my place to remind him, but in his condition, he could easily sleep through the meain event of the afternoon. I called out after him, "Don't forget we need to be on the hill at two o'clock to spread your dad's ashes."

I ate lunch on my own. César was a good cook, and stew always tastes better a day or two after it's made. This was delicious.

By the time I was finished, César had arrived and was prepping the kitchen for the evening meal. I complimented him on his stew, filled my water bottle, and grabbed my backpack, heavy with computer and gun.

I didn't want to go upstairs. I had just enough time to find a quiet place outdoors where I could let my thoughts wander for a while, at their own pace and without interruption.

*

Billy looked like a stranger standing in front of the barn, holding the bright gold urn and a paper bag. He'd changed out of his work clothes into clean jeans, a checked sport shirt, and cowboy boots. Evan and Marianne were already there when I joined them. We stood around in restless silence for about ten minutes, waiting for Stan to show up.

Evan looked at his watch. "Should I go see what's keeping him?"

"Yeah, why don't you," Billy said. "He should be here."

Evan sighed, a little too dramatically it seemed to me, and turned toward the house. Before Evan reached the back door, Stan emerged, putting on his sunglasses. They walked back to us at Evan's pace, Stan hurrying to keep up.

Once we were assembled, Billy said, "I figure the hill up behind the barn is as good a place as any for Dad's ashes. Anyone have another suggestion?"

No one spoke.

"Well, if anyone wants to spread some in another place, I have a couple of plastic cups here. We can split up the ashes if need be."

At the edge of my vision, I saw Evan roll his eyes. If Billy noticed, he didn't react. "I want everyone to feel right about this," he said.

"Sarah murdered our father just a few yards from where we're standing," Marianne said, her voice acid. "How can anyone feel right about that?"

Billy shook his head. "We're not gonna get into that right now, sis. This here is about Dad, not anybody else. Just give that a rest." The firmness of his tone must have surprised her, because Marianne did what she was told. I could easily imagine Marianne and Stan were struggling with the change in Billy's status in the family. Maybe they didn't even know how to talk nicely to him in his new role, and I felt a pang of pity for them. It passed.

"Okay then, let's go." Billy turned and started off, with the rest of us following. When we got to a rocky outcrop surrounded by pine and juniper, he stopped. "This is where I had in mind. This okay with everyone?"

No one said a word, but the air flowed through the trees in a long, soft song in answer.

"Stan, Marianne, you might come around here and stand upwind."

I suppressed a very inappropriate laugh. Billy was nothing if not practical.

When we were reorganized, Billy resumed. "If anyone wants to say something, this is the time."

I was surprised when no one spoke. I opened to look at their auras. Billy's was businesslike and rather flat. I guessed he was as unused to taking charge as the others were in having him lead. Evan's showed some kind of freedom. Marianne's was angry and frightened; Stan's aura showed the saddest of them all.

A flood of compassion dislodged me from my observer role, sweeping me up into the pain and confusion of the human beings gathered around a can of ashes once the body of a man they had lived with for decades in pain and rage and grief and longing. I lost my balance and nearly fell, caught in the swirl of lives that had drifted apart for all the wrong reasons.

A few deep breaths, and I was okay again, but I'd become more vulnerable to the pain of these people. I saw this family not just as some dysfunctional entity, but as a group of adult children who'd been bound together by decisions made by others, who had never accepted each other as friends. Perhaps that wasn't as great a tragedy as Ellis's murder, but it suddenly loomed large on this hillside, hovering sad and dark in my heart.

Why did I even do this work? I knew the answer before the familiar question had finished forming. Because as much as I hated the pain and poison I had to enter when I took a case, I loved the truth more. A wave of sad fatigue washed through me and kept on going. It would probably come back soon. It usually did. I set my introspection aside.

"…so thank you for doing the very best you could, Dad, 'cause like it or not, each of us knows how hard you tried." Billy's voice rang tight and passionate, and his knuckles had turned white as he gripped the urn.

"Maybe we could have been an easier bunch to manage, but you did a good job with what you had to work with, and that's about the best thing anyone could say about a man." Billy undid the lid of the urn and held it upside down. A feathery plume of gray and black poured out, made broad and elegant by the breeze. "You loved this land, Dad, and I'm glad—we're glad—you decided your ashes belong on it. Rest in peace."

Billy put the lid on the empty urn and pulled in a deep breath. "Well," he said. "We've done it. Unless somebody wants to say something now." Nobody did.

We walked back to the house in silence.

Chapter Thirteen

The somber mood of the afternoon carried through to dinner. On the rare occasion someone spoke at all, weary resignation colored every exchange a polite, dull gray as if fighting wasn't worth the effort at the moment.

I hurried through my meal and excused myself, saying I'd be at Heath Baker's place for a couple of hours. Evan's head snapped to attention at that information. He kept his lecherous smirk in check, but his eyebrows lifted in a question only he would ask. I shook my head and when he saw my answer, so did he. He obviously felt I was passing up an opportunity I shouldn't.

Once settled in the car, I pulled out the map Heath had left for me and spread it on the passenger seat. It wasn't complicated, just a few turns leading to a square marked OLD BAKER PLACE in block letters, but my night vision was not what it once was. In fading light, strange roads, probably without much signage, were not fun for me.

I turned the key. The faster I got there, the lighter it would be when I arrived. Finding my way back would be easier.

*

The directions were simpler to follow than I expected. In twenty minutes, I parked outside a sprawling wood frame house that had clearly begun as a cabin, with extensions added as needed. I guessed it must have had close to ten rooms, but somehow it retained its cabin feel, perched on the crest of a forested hill, cozy and welcoming.

Heath was sitting on the front porch, definitely not in uniform. His bare feet were crossed at the ankle, resting on the porch rail. "C'mon up," he called. "I wasn't sure you were going to come."

"Hey, I was promised a longer conversation about an interesting topic plus a briefing on the coroner's report on Ellis. How could I not come?" I took the three wooden steps up to the porch. In the twilight, I could see he was dressed in a worn sweatshirt and jeans. Feet weren't a fetish for me, but his were fine. Big strong, lean feet with impressive toes. Nice and manly, with a strong, high arch.

He must have caught me looking. "You a foot man, Russ?"

"Not really," I laughed, and hoped the gloaming hid my blush. "Can't say I didn't notice, though."

He tilted his head toward the front door. "Chili is still on the stove if you haven't eaten yet, but as I recall César serves up dinner right at six o'clock on the ranch. Plus, I've got beer and bourbon. Can I get you a beverage?"

"I'll take water, thanks. I don't drink alcohol."

Heath's eyebrows went up. "I never took you for a teetotaler, Russ. I must say I'm a little disappointed."

He got up and strolled to the screen door. "Kitchen's this way."

"Thanks. It wasn't always so," I said, following him in. "But I consumed far more than my share during the years I drank. I figure it's only fair to let others try to catch up if they can."

He grunted in understanding. "How long has it been?"

"Sixteen years," I said. "I'm one of the lucky ones."

"Good for you," he said quietly. "I had a cousin who would've lived longer if he'd done that. Got drunk one night, like most nights, and drove into the river. He must've hit his head, because he was still slumped over the wheel when we found him the next day. He never even undid his seat belt." He handed me a glass. "Good spring water, just up the hill," he said proudly. He poured himself a finger of scotch and dropped in more ice.

I followed him back outside and sat next to him, gazing into the night.

Heath scratched his jaw slowly, his aura shimmered pliant, reflective. "I do believe Stanford Junior would do well to take a page out of your book on that count."

"I've never actually seen him sober, so I wouldn't know whether it would be an improvement. He's not a pleasant person to be around the way he is. I've already told you I think he's the one who killed Ellis. I'm certain it's not Sarah."

Heath grunted. "As circumstantial as the evidence we've gathered against Sarah might be, we have even less against Stan. We have nothing to link him to the crime." He lifted his drink to me. "You find his clothes with his father's blood on it, or even a viable motive, and I'll reconsider. I told you before, I've got to let the evidence lead me. The DA knows the case against Sarah is weak, which is why she was charged with only manslaughter this afternoon. Evan's attorney has already got a hearing tonight to set bail."

"You got a viable motive for Stan from Merriweather. Don't pretend otherwise."

Heath took a sip of his drink and stared out across the darkening valley.

I pushed. "Even with the evidence you have against Sarah, you know in your gut she didn't do it."

Heath shrugged. I took the gesture as a confession.

"You said you brought a firearm with you this time," he said, "like you're expecting more trouble."

"Yes," I said, feeling sad. "This thing is far from over, I can feel it. I don't like carrying a gun, but it seems necessary right now."

"Guns aren't so bad," he said. "When you grow up around them, it's different."

"Oh, I grew up around them, too," I said. "I'm a red-blooded Colorado boy. I learned to shoot. I even learned to hunt, although I'm proud to say I never killed anything."

"My daddy taught me to hunt," he said. "And we would've starved if we hadn't taken an elk or deer every autumn. We shared with our neighbors, and they shared with us. That's part of his legacy to me, and I don't plan to let it slide."

"My daddy taught me to shoot with a bolt action thirty ought six," I said. "Damn thing weighed a ton. I don't want to turn this into a gun-control argument, but I daresay your daddy probably didn't teach you to hunt with a high-powered semiautomatic assault rifle with high-capacity clips. Real sportsmen get one, maybe two shots on the target. They don't have to mow down the entire forest to take down a deer."

He stared at me, as if deciding how serious an argument he wanted. "I like you, city boy," he said with a western movie drawl. "I can see I'm just going to have to take those smartass comments outta your hide. Maybe outta your ass right proper." He waggled his eyebrows, and it was clear where he wanted that to go. He'd laid the accent on thick, and it was perfectly believable. He should have been wearing his sheriff's badge and dusty cowboy boots with spurs.

"I'm assuming your folks are gone," I said, changing the topic. "Do you have any other family?"

He nodded. "I have a younger sister. She's a big ol' lesbian living the life in San Jose. She's some IT honcho with a salary to match. Funny, isn't it, how we both came out queer? We're good friends, though we don't see much of each other. Neither of us have partners."

He took a sip of his drink, making the ice cubes chime. "It's funny how different we are, though," he said softly. "She couldn't wait to get out of here, and the minute she could, she was gone. First to Salt Lake City, then on to San Francisco. On the other hand, I've tried to leave two or three times, but I just can't do it. I got reeled back to this house, this land, as sure as a trout that's swallowed a hook. This damn red dirt runs in my veins, I guess. Whatever the reason, I can't live without it." He looked at me sideways. "I go away sometimes, on vacation or on business, and I get restless after a few days. I don't find peace until I'm sitting here on my front porch again."

I thought about that for a moment. He'd told me something important about himself, and I honored it with silence. Nearby an owl hooted.

"You hear that?" he asked.

"What, the owl?"

"Yeah. And the silence after. I love that silence right after. It's so...real." He shifted in his chair, and the creak punctuated the silence. "You don't get owls in your yard in Denver, do you, Russ? Or that kind of electric silence after, when every small mammal freezes for a heartbeat at the sound. You don't get that in the city. This place is full of those sounds every night, and those silences, too. I need that. I'm surprised we haven't heard the coyotes yet."

"What about companionship? Evan thinks he can play your gay card to his advantage."

"That asshole. He used to blackmail me with it, you know? Whenever he was horny and stranded out here away from his precious city boys, he'd come after me. I fucked him more often than I wanted to, that's for sure."

He obviously wasn't ashamed or in the closet. That was interesting. I could tell he wasn't done with his story, so I waited for him.

"But after I had a few years on the force and made Complex Crimes, I told my sergeant I was gay. It helped that I was a local boy, part of that rural life interconnectedness we talked about earlier. We just agreed we wouldn't make much of it and I would be discreet, so it's been an open secret ever since."

He took a sip of his drink. "Anyway, Evan made a serious mistake shortly after that. He came to me looking for fun, thinking I was still in the closet, that being exposed would hurt my career." Heath chuckled into his glass as he pulled an ice cube into his mouth and crunched it into pieces. "Well, he found out different."

"He still thinks in terms of coercion, I'm afraid."

"That so?" He scratched his flat belly through the sweatshirt. "He still baits me with it, like he did the other day. He's never understood living a private life is not the same as being in the closet." He gazed out across the valley lit now only by the moon. "I don't know how having a partner would go over in our community, and I've never met anyone that I really wanted to risk everything for." He eyed me with an appraising grin. "Maybe when I meet the right guy."

"He'll consider himself very lucky, I have no doubt."

"What about you? Have you met the right guy?"

"I had a right guy, years ago. In spite of his warnings that he'd leave if I didn't quit drinking, I kept pounding it down. And sure enough, he left." I shivered at the memory as I always did. Did I believe in more than one right guy? It was a mild surprise to realize that yes, I did. "I may have found another right guy, but it's still a little too early to tell."

Heath got up from his chair with a mischievous grin. "Let's go inside. I'll fix you another of those waters, make it a triple, maybe soften you up some."

He motioned me to an easy chair and went to tinker in the kitchen. When he was done, he handed me my glass and sprawled on the couch across from me, rangy legs wide apart. It was an unmistakable invitation.

"Well, Russ," he said, running a hand down his hard chest and belly. That hand made all kinds of promises as it descended. His thumb came to rest hooked on the waistband of his jeans, with fingers ready to unbuckle his belt. "Would you like to audition for the role of my right guy?"

I smiled and shook my head, hoping I wasn't offending him. "You're a good-looking guy, Heath," I said, "and a decent one, too, I have no doubt. But I think that would be a serious mistake for both of us. I don't think there's any way you and I could end up being the right guy for each other."

I lifted my hands in a gesture of helplessness. "You said you could never leave this land, and I'd never fit in here. If the Landrys are still considered outsiders after a quarter of a century, what chance would I have when I arrived at your door with my suitcases? I don't want to spend the rest of my life as even more of an outsider than I already am."

Heath shrugged lazily. "I expect you're right," he said with a shrug. "What about Mr. Right Now then, instead of Mr. Right?"

"I still think it would be a bad idea. And I think you know that better than I do. I'm a person of interest in your investigation, after all. Thanks just the same, though."

"Well, you can't blame a guy for trying. It's pretty slim pickings out here." He sighed heavily. "There's always Denver or LA when I get an itch I can't scratch at home."

I felt the sharp bite of his ache at being alone, without a flicker of hope in his aura. I shared his sadness for a moment. I'd carried my own loneliness for a long time, too. "You said you would let me know what was in the coroner's report?"

Heath was silent for a moment, maybe taking time to give up. "Yeah. The bullet was from his own rifle. Very close range. It probably discharged during a struggle because the bullet shattered his jaw, fragmented on impact. A piece of it entered the skull through the soft tissues, not through the skull itself. Ellis probably maintained consciousness after the shot, although he would have been paralyzed or at least incapacitated. The bullet didn't kill him, though. He died of asphyxiation while he lay there helpless. It was the mud in his mouth and throat that killed him, packed in far enough to block the nasal passages, too. He couldn't close his jaw because it wasn't functional. He would have swallowed and coughed against the mud, but not for long. Whoever killed him pressed their hand over his mouth so he couldn't get rid of it— there were little scratches all around the mouth caused by grit pushed hard against the skin."

"So Ellis and his killer met outside the barn," I said. "Stanford's hands would have been occupied with the rifle and the rabbit. There was a scuffle and the rifle went off, some of the bullet lodging in Ellis's brain. He fell, and his killer then ran over to the bucket under the barn spigot, scooped up some nearby mud and packed his mouth with it, holding his hand over Ellis's mouth until he suffocated."

Heath's jaw twitched. "Or her hand. That's how I put it together, too."

"That makes it murder, doesn't it? More deliberate?"

"Not necessarily. The DA is treating it as a heat-of-passion crime, so that's usually a class 3 felony. And the burden of proof is different. Doesn't look premeditated, that's for sure." Heath grimaced. "Helluva way to die, no matter how you look at it."

"You've got to know those papers from Ellis's office had to be planted in Sarah's barn," I said. "You would've found them the first time you went through the barn."

"Yes, I would have. Or maybe they weren't planted. Maybe she left them there by mistake, thinking we wouldn't search again." He stared at me defiantly. "Criminals do some amazingly stupid things. But I guess you know that already, being a private investigator."

I was about to push back on Sarah's innocence, but Heath's cell phone rang. He must've recognized the strident ring tone, because he grabbed it immediately, all casual energy evaporated. He looked at me as he talked. I watched his aura go dark. He hung up.

"Well, it looks like you were right to expect more trouble," he said, standing up. "Evan Landry is dead."

"I wish I'd been wrong, dammit."

"I'll have my lights and siren on, so you follow me close. He pulled off the sweatshirt and shrugged into an official one hanging by the door. He pulled on socks and boots and grabbed his hat and gun belt from a peg by the door. "Let's go."

Another department car was already there when we arrived, and a deputy was hooking the lights up to the generator again, this time on the far side of the shop, away from the house. As the generators sputtered to life, the lights went on, illuminating the body of Evan Landry lying face down on the path. It looked like he'd been shot in the back of the head. I didn't see any sign of the weapon.

"Well," I grumbled to Heath. "At least now you know Sarah didn't do it. Because she's still stuck in your jail."

Heath quirked his eye at me. "Feeling pretty good about that, are you? Doesn't have to be the same one did them both, you know."

I shook my head. "The odds are way too long for it to be two different people. At least that's how I read it. As crazy as the family is, it's too small to have two killers in it."

"Well, read it however you want. I'm going to take these statements on my own tonight. Until we establish time of death that shows he died after dinner and after you left for my place, you could have done it."

I laughed. "In private practice, killing one's client is not generally considered a sound strategy for getting paid, but you're right. Do you really think I might have eaten dinner with everyone, killed Landry, and then driven to your place to talk about finding the right guy?"

Heath shook his head. "No, but it doesn't matter what I think. I've got to collect statements and evidence, let them tell me what to think."

"Evan Landry was very much alive at dinner, which is when I last saw him. He had just engaged me to clear Sarah of suspicion. I ate, left for your place immediately after getting up from the table. He'll have that food in his stomach."

"Even so."

"Okay, then." He was being stubborn, and I told myself I didn't care. "Just let me know when it's my turn."

*

As I was walking toward the house, my phone rang. To my disappointment, it wasn't Colin. It was the Mesa County Jail.

"Russ Morgan."

"Russ? It's Sarah," said the scratchy voice. I figured it was a pay phone. "Evan was supposed to pick me up here at the jail an hour ago. Do you know where he is?"

"Sarah," I said, reaching through the phone to hug her. "Evan's dead. They just found his body a little while ago."

I felt her heavy silence on the phone. "Oh, dear god."

"Look, I'll get permission from Heath to come down and get you. I'm so sorry you had to find out this way. And I'm sorry for your loss." That last sounded incongruous, but it was true. "Hang in there, will you?"

"Sure," she said. I could tell she was crying. "I don't really have any choice."

I headed back out to Heath. He glowered at me when I interrupted his interview with Marianne. "Sorry, but I just got a call from Sarah, who expected Evan to meet her at the jail an hour ago. Is it all right if I go pick her up?"

Even in the fierce glare of the klieg lights, I could see Heath's face soften. "Sure. Come straight back. I'll want to talk to her about that timing."

He turned his attention back to Marianne, and I headed for my car.

*

When I pulled into the parking lot on Rice Street, it was almost ten o'clock. Too late to call Colin and explain why he hadn't heard from me. Sarah was perched on a bench in the foyer, her eyes red from crying, looking exhausted and friendless.

She rose slowly, as if it took all her effort to get up. I hurried over and wrapped her in a hug.

"Jesus, Russ," she sobbed against my chest. "I don't even know what to say except I never expected another murder. I'm trapped in a nightmare."

"I know. We'll get it straightened out. I promise." I gave her a squeeze. "Now, let's get you out of here." I kept my arm around her all the way to the car and eased her into the passenger seat.

I got in and strapped up. Sarah tilted her seat back and stared out the window.

"Have you ever been in jail, Russ?"

"Four days of a six-day sentence for drunk driving, long ago. It's an ordeal, isn't it?"

"I don't think I've ever felt so humiliated and unwanted by the community I thought I belonged to than I have in the last forty-eight hours. And now I've lost Evan on top of that." Her voice was tired and detached, as if she were looking at everything from a great, safe distance. She pointed to her foot. "For added shame, they put a tracking device on my ankle," she said. "Arvind said it was the only way the DA would agree to bail." She lifted her foot. "Feels so weird."

"Arvind?"

"Arvind Fletcher. Evan's lawyer. Now mine, I guess."

"I thought I'd heard the name before. Look, you don't have to hold up your end of a sparkling conversation. Just relax, you don't have to say a thing."

"Thanks," she murmured, closing her eyes. By the time we were out of Grand Junction heading south, she'd opened them again, staring out the window into the darkness.

"Thank you for working with Evan," she said. "He wasn't the easiest person to be around, but he worked hard for the things he believed in. I suppose that's something, anyway."

She turned to face me as we pulled onto the ranch road. "Let's not get out of the car right away," she said. "I want to talk, and this is probably the safest place to do it."

"Then let's not even go up to the ranch house. We can stop right here," I said. I pulled over to the side of the road and shut off the engine.

"The morning of the day I was arrested, Evan came to me in the barn where I was cutting grow blocks for the new crop. He said he had a feeling someone might try to kill him. He didn't say who, but it had to be either Marianne or Stan. He wanted me to know I was his sole beneficiary. He'd already updated his will to include his voting share of the ranch. Apparently the two restaurants with his investment portfolio come to about two million."

"Wow."

"Evan told me yesterday that Stan trashed my barn, and that he'd kept you on to clear me of suspicion. I'd love it if you stayed to do that. To find Stanford's killer. And Evan's, too, I'm guessing."

"You want me to work for you, then?"

"Yes."

"Fine with me." I hesitated. I didn't want to pile on more drama on top of everything else. "Were you aware that Evan had applied for a retail license to grow, that he and Stan had a plan to compete directly with you?"

She gave a tiny shrug. "Not for certain, but I suspected something like that. Evan was way too interested in the details of production management to not be interested in the business itself. I'm not surprised. I am surprised that he was in cahoots with Stan, but I figure that's because he wanted access to ranch land. That's the only reason he would have done business with Stan."

"You don't mind?"

She looked at me thoughtfully. "No, I wouldn't have minded. Even if he had told me up front about it. He had his own way of doing business, and it's not mine. I would've been content to simply build on the operation I already had. I was making a ton of money, far more than I had imagined when I started out."

"I can see how your business styles wouldn't mix."

"He wouldn't have wanted to branch out like I do. I still see maybe setting up and running a really good farmers co-op. You know—feed, farm supplies, and groceries, or maybe a craft shop for local artists. Something to help restore soul to this community."

I chuckled. "I guess I was more outraged at his secret plans of competition than you would have been. My hat's off to you. If I wore a hat, that is."

She smiled, looking exhausted, sad, and self-reliant. "I guess we should get home. I feel like I haven't slept for days. I want to take a good shower and go straight to bed."

I turned the key and we headed up the hill. "Unfortunately, before you can do that, Heath is going to ask you some questions about when you expected Evan to show up."

"What a surprise," she groaned. "After that, then. Soon as possible."

"I can make a sandwich for you, if you like, to take up to your room when he's done." I parked the car, watched her slow determination as she climbed out.

"That sounds divine. As you can imagine, the food in the Mesa County Jail is less than wonderful." She leaned against the car and pulled in a lungful of soft night air. "Free air smells good," she said as she looked around. "Sometimes I don't know whether to love or hate this place." She stood quietly, sadness making her face heavy, empty. "Right now, I'm not feeling the love. Maybe I'm just too tired." She trudged toward the lights and the noise of the generator, and I headed inside to see what kind of sandwich I could fix her.

*

Eventually, I got Sarah settled with some food if she still wanted it, but the forensic work dragged on into the night. I finally excused myself and went to bed. I texted Colin saying good morning, that I'd explain why I hadn't called him. In a tiny flash of social media pride, I sent him a "<3" heart, which I'd learned from him.

I woke up a little after two o'clock. The lights were still on, their generator still running. I thought of Heath out there somewhere, meticulously doing what he had to do. I felt sorry for him. Sorry that he wouldn't get much sleep tonight, and sorry that he didn't have anyone to come home to when he finally made it to bed.

Chapter Fourteen

Saturday

In the morning, I went out with Billy again to feed the horses. At very least, it was therapeutic. Actually, I was surprised at how much I enjoyed it. I'd always thought I hated farm life, but breaking up bales in the horse pasture with Billy made me understand that really, I'd just hated my father and his joyless relationship with the land.

In the second pasture, Billy stopped at the back of the truck and looked around, as if he was seeing things for the first time. He took in a deep breath through his nose and blew it out his mouth. A wide, satisfied grin spread across his face.

"Can you tell me what good clean air smells like, Russ? Betcha can't. I sure can't. It just smells real and healthy. Wide open. It smells so damn good."

Billy was not joyless. Every time I was with him, he seemed to get caught up in some small moment of his work that made him smile. Today, it was fresh air. His joy was contagious, and I caught it.

I pulled a bag of feed off the truck bed with a laugh. "You keep smiling that wide, and you'll end up with dust all over your teeth before lunch."

"Wouldn't be the first time, that's certain. This dust on my teeth feels good." He stopped, suddenly serious. "Pa died with this dirt filling his mouth. Not counting the murder part, that's a pretty decent way to go, don't you think? Ironic, but still decent."

I hadn't expected him to use that term. I could feel my neck heat up at the realization I'd bought into the family myth that he wasn't very smart.

Billy must have seen my surprise, because he laughed and punched me lightly on the shoulder. "You didn't think I was smart enough to know about irony, did you, Russ? C'mon, tell me the truth now."

I looked down, embarrassed. "More like I forgot you were smarter than you let on. I'm sorry."

"Don't be. Happens all the time. But I'll tell you something true. Whether he knows the word or not, there ain't a rancher alive that don't understand irony better'n most folks. Goes with the job."

After that, we made small talk now and then, but I chewed on Billy's profound insight all the way back to the barn.

*

I had an hour or so before lunch, so I went up to my room and texted Colin to say good morning again. No answer, so I assumed he was pulling an extra shift at work. If so, he'd reply on a break. Just thinking of him made me feel lighter, stronger. More ready to dig deeper into two murders. I decided I ought to clean my gun. It had been months since I had.

I pulled a T-shirt from my duffel and spread it on the bed, broke down the gun and arranged the parts on the shirt. As I reached for the cleaning kit, I felt someone watching me. I looked up and saw Sarah, arms folded across her stomach in a self-hug.

"Hi. How are you feeling this morning?"

"Numb. Lost. I did sleep, though. That's something."

"Then I'm glad you wandered by." I pointed to the chair at the small desk next to the door. "Have a seat, if you like."

She sat down gingerly, staring at the metal pieces lying on the T-shirt. "Those things are so ugly. So carefully designed for violence."

"It's true," I said, drawing a swab through the barrel. "That's what they're for. I'm not an enthusiastic fan of them. In fact, I've never carried one on an assignment before this." I stopped putting the thing back together and looked at her. "It felt like the right thing to do this time."

"I guess sometimes it is," she said. "I hate that I'll probably have to get one, too, considering everything that's happened." She half-rose from the chair. "Can I touch it?"

I set the reassembled piece back on the bed. "Sure. Safety's on and chamber's clear."

She pointed to the hole in base of the grip. "Is that where the bullets go?"

"Yup." I held up the magazine. "This is the clip. It slides in. I'm not going to do that right now, though."

She trailed a slow finger along the barrel and down the grip. "Deadly."

"No doubt about it."

"Does Heath know you have it?"

"Yes. But I'd prefer you didn't mention it to anyone else. I should have closed my door before I started."

"They don't know?"

I put the gun back in its box, put the box in my backpack. "No reason for them to, really."

"I suppose you're right," she said, turning toward the door. "Thanks."

She stopped at the door.

"I hope to god you don't need to use it."

I smiled at her, feeling sad. "Me, too."

*

I was poking around in the fridge to see what I could fix for lunch when Billy stomped into the kitchen, looking angrier than I had ever seen him.

"I'm glad I tracked you down," he fumed. "Marianne's gone and made a news piece about the evils of weed cultivation and Sarah's arrest for Dad's death. It's a fuckin' hit piece. I've already complained to the station. It was on the noon news hour. I just watched it on the station's website."

"How did you find out about it?"

"A neighbor called. His wife always watches the noon news. What a fuckin' mess. I told the station they'd be hearing from Sarah's attorney. They gave me that bullshit line about opinions expressed in the editorials not being the opinions of the station. I told 'em I didn't care. You better look at it before they take it down. I need to go tell Sarah."

I reached over to my backpack and fired up my computer. I was sitting at the kitchen table, nearly through Marianne's editorial when Billy came back into the kitchen. "This really is a hit piece," I said.

"Sarah's already talked to Fletcher. She's also got a number of friends who will speak up for her, and she's calling them right now. She's more friends with the farming community around here than my brother or sister."

We watched the remainder of Marianne's tearful exposé of how growing marijuana had brought nothing but tragedy to her family and how the lure of easy money had pitted loving family members against each other in violence.

"I think she'll be lucky to climb out of this one without a lawsuit," I said. "Did you know that Evan and your brother were planning on going into the grow business for themselves? And that it was your brother who trashed Sarah's business because he thought she was getting too far ahead of them?"

Billy sat bolt upright and slammed the table with his fist. "That stupid jerk. No, I didn't know, and I'm glad I do. Do you think he killed Evan? I know they had a big fight the day before Evan was shot. Maybe it was because of Stan breaking up Sarah's operation. I'll bet Evan didn't know about him doing that."

"No, he didn't know until I told him Thursday, as soon as I found out. I should have told you sooner, but I assumed word got around. As it does in this family."

Billy stood up and stretched slowly, as if all his problems were far away. "Well, all this nonsense makes it a lot easier to put my personal plan into motion," he said with a glint in his eye.

His aura didn't show violence, but whatever he was thinking about was big. Broad, vigorous currents curled out from him in warm yellows. "What do you mean?"

He winked at me. "You'll hear soon enough, Russ. There are a couple of things I've gotta settle first, but it won't be long if things go well." He looked at me with an odd smile playing across his face. "Now they're not bad plans, don't you worry none. They're happy plans."

And with that cryptic statement, Billy sauntered out of the kitchen, whistling a cheerful little tune.

*

After lunch, I went outside to call Heath. He'd already heard about Marianne's ill-advised editorial and had suggested to the station they take it down, since it posed a problem for finding a solid jury.

"This mess just keeps getting bigger," he grumbled.

I looked around to make sure no one was nearby. "I still think Stan is our killer," I said quietly.

"You've shared your opinion on that before," he said. I could hear the irritation in his voice. "Even if you're right, I need evidence. We haven't found the gun used to kill Landry."

"You know that Evan and Stan were going into business together with their own marijuana operation, without benefit of a promised land subdivision. That's evidence."

The silence on the other end of the phone carried a flash of anger. "I know that."

"Well, there's more to it. Stan's black eye? Evan gave him that. They had a fight after Evan learned Stan had vandalized Sarah's grow."

"How do you know this?"

"At lunch yesterday, Stan told me Evan had given it to him. A disagreement about implementing their business plan, he'd called it. And Billy just told me he'd heard them fighting sometime Thursday afternoon. Stan was sporting it at dinner Thursday."

"Finally," Heath said. "All I need is one decent piece of evidence, but I can't do a thing until I get that. Stan lied to me about his eye, so I can go after him with that."

"You're coming out again today?"

"No, probably tomorrow morning. I'm still trying to organize some volunteers to do another sweep of the property. Somewhere there's a gun tucked away, the one that was used to kill Landry. We're not talking about a twenty-two-caliber rabbit rifle this time. This was bigger. We don't know exactly how big, but I expect it's at least a thirty caliber with ammunition that could bring down a deer. It blew out the front of Landry's head, but we found the bullet last night. I took it over to ballistics today."

Heath's voice said he was running on fumes. "I'll be glad when this is all over, Russ." After a beat of silence, "I wouldn't mind more chances to work on you to say yes to a roll in the hay, but apart from that, I'll be very glad to see the backside of this case." He laughed. "Guess I'd like to see your backside, too."

We both laughed. He hung up.

I checked my phone for a message from Colin, but nothing. As I put the phone back in my pocket, I realized I was tired, too, in need of some downtime. I went upstairs to get my backpack, filled my water bottle, and headed out behind the barns and up the hill. I passed the place where we'd spread the ashes yesterday—you could barely tell— and hiked up a little farther into the forest.

I found a quiet spot with shade and sat. The gentle quiet, the sweet absence of human turmoil, settled on my shoulders and slowed me down. The hush of air in the trees and the warm rock at my back told me I should rest. I rearranged myself and closed my eyes.

I woke with the sun shining directly into my eyes, telling me I'd dozed long enough to lose my shade completely. I checked my phone. Almost two hours had slipped by. I was a little stiff from sleeping on the ground, but I felt fully recharged. It was great.

And even better, I had a message from Colin.

Crazy here, working all weekend. We should be done with document analysis and keyword indexing tomorrow, and I'll get my life back. Missing you seriously. R U any closer to coming back?

To my surprise, I had a better signal here on the hill than I did down at the ranch house. I shifted to get the sun out of my eyes and pecked out my reply.

Am running out of ideas on this case. Haven't been able to persuade sheriff to look hard at who I suspect. May come back to town for a couple of days next week anyway. Miss you too. Looking forward to another day off we can share.

Oh. About Evan and Stan's application. Would it still go forward? I dug Rick Saxon's card out of my wallet and sent him a message.

Confirmed Evan Landry had application for a grow license, but he was killed last night. Sarah not a suspect, fortunately. Does his application continue to be processed, or is it dropped? I'm thinking he was one of two names on the application.

It was no more than ten minutes before Saxon's reply clinked through.

Only one name on an app. His is abandoned. Whoever else was involved will have to start fresh. Glad/sad for Sarah. Tragic.

I sent back my thanks and put my phone away. Yes, *tragic* was exactly the right word for this mess. But I wondered if Stan knew that if he killed Evan, he also killed his license application. Did that mean there were two killers? I was still certain Stan had killed his father, but what about Evan? That wasn't a heat of the moment crime, it seemed to me. It would have been stupid for Stan to scuttle his own business opportunity unless he had a reason more compelling than a black eye.

But as Heath had said, sometimes criminals do really stupid things. All Stan's siblings had said he was a vicious drunk. Maybe that was enough. But maybe it wasn't. I wished I knew which it was.

I gathered up my stuff and started down the hill.

Chapter Fifteen

Saturday Evening

It was comforting to hear César rattling around in the kitchen preparing dinner. I dashed upstairs to clean up. By the time I got to the dining room, everyone else who was still alive was already there, and the atmosphere was nasty. I looked at the auras, and the real heat seemed to be between Sarah and Marianne. No surprise there. I guessed they'd been arguing about the documentary.

Actually, I was surprised to see Marianne had shown up at all. From what I'd seen and heard, all three siblings had blasted her for her maudlin and deliberately misleading exposé, but she leaned against the sidebar sipping her drink as if it were just another day in paradise. And maybe for her it was, even though her aura twisted like a rattlesnake pierced by a pitchfork.

César wheeled in the trolley, and everyone sat down.

As the dishes went around the table, Marianne finally broke the angry silence. "You've caused me some real trouble at work, you know, Sarah. That's a favor I'm looking forward to returning. Tenfold. Of course, it doesn't really matter much, because you're going to go to jail for killing my father. Still, that would be even sweeter if I could cause you the same trouble on your way to jail as you caused me at the station."

I almost choked on my water.

"Marianne, I think you might be gettin' a little ahead of yourself on Sarah's bein' guilty," Billy said. "That was the problem with your mean editorial at the station, too."

The silence in the room became hard and sharp as knives.

"You made your own trouble," Sarah added calmly. She stared at Marianne, unafraid. "That was a hatchet piece, not journalism. You stretched the truth, you misrepresented facts, and carefully avoided others. Fox News would have loved it. Except that you violated your employer's policy about opinion pieces on open investigations."

She reached for a dish. "I did none of that. You didn't need my help in making your life miserable. You've done a great job of it all on your own."

And on it went. But something else was in the air tonight. I thought I saw Billy wink at Sarah at one point, but I couldn't be sure. As César was loading the dishes back on to the trolley, Marianne dabbed at her lips with her napkin. Her aura looked like a serpent ready to strike.

"I spoke to Heath Baker this afternoon," she announced like a princess sitting on her throne. "It seems as though he's no longer only focused on you as a suspect for Daddy's murder. He wouldn't say why, but I've been thinking about that." She smiled, venomous and sweet. "In the event that he can't close the deal on you, I'm going to make sure that you never reopen for business on this ranch again."

"I have a lease that will stand up in court," Sarah said, shaking her head in exasperation. "You just don't get that, do you?"

"Oh, I get it all right," Marianne snapped back. "And I've looked at your precious lease. You have no access.

There is no easement for you from the county road to the barn. Without permission from the Ellis family, that is."

Her reptilian smile got wider. She giggled. I thought it might be a simper at first, but no, she'd actually giggled at the prospect. She seemed euphoric at her cleverness.

"And I," she said, almost crowing, "am going to see that such permission is never granted to you. Among the three of us Ellises, we have the controlling votes for the ranch. I intend to see that while you may legally be allowed to live here, you will never do business here again."

Billy pushed back his chair so he could face her directly, and the loud scrape got her attention. "Well, that ain't exactly right, Marianne," he said as if discussing the number of hay bales he was going to need over the winter. "I've got seven of those votes, and you don't control me."

He stood, cleared his throat, and grinned at Sarah. "I hadn't figured to make my announcement this way, but I guess now is as good a time as any. Earlier today I proposed to Sarah, and she said yes."

All the oxygen left the room, leaving paralyzed silence in its wake.

I fought down my laughter. No one could have foreseen this development, even in their wildest machinations. And, I realized, that was why Billy had snuck away from the barn the morning Stanford had been killed. He and Sarah had been together in the barn, doing what lovers do. I shook my head. Love was always the wild card in human affairs. It would always trump the best-laid plans. And that night it had changed everything in an instant.

"You *what*?" Stan exploded. He stood, leaning on the table to keep himself steady and glowered down the table at his younger brother. Marianne still couldn't close her mouth. She just sat there staring. Betrayal was the feeling that sprang to mind when I looked at her aura, but I really didn't want to see too closely. As auras go, at that moment, hers was about the ugliest I'd seen in a long time.

"Sarah and I've been dating for months," Billy continued good-naturedly. "If either of you had paid the slightest attention to me, you would've seen. Maybe you didn't even think your dumb-ass brother was interested in dating. But whatever you might think, Sarah and I are going to be married as soon as we can work out the details. I don't suppose I need to remind you that with her four shares, counting the one she's inheriting from Evan, she and I have eleven of twenty-one shares between us. That's a majority regardless of how you two vote. And I'm telling you, she will get access to her barn whenever she damn well wants."

"How could you... You stupid little..." Apparently Stan was incapable of finishing that sentence for the moment. I knew that wouldn't last.

"You miserable little...you've just gone and fucked up everything. I—oh, fuck it. You wouldn't understand even if I explained it to you in kindergarten terms." Stan's aura boiled up in shades of rage I'd never seen before, couldn't have even imagined. He downed the last of his drink and stomped out of the room, taking his raging aura with him. It was a relief to see him go, but I had a horrible feeling about where he was headed. I stood up. I needed to be ready.

Billy and Sarah looked across the table at each other, happy relief blossoming in their auras, entwining in the space between them. Sharing a knowing grin, Billy walked around to Sarah, who stood waiting for him. They strolled out hand in hand. Marianne sat alone at the table as if welded to her chair, her eyes wide and unfocused. I decided to leave her to her rumination, or damage assessment, whatever she had going on inside her head. I really didn't want to know what it was.

I went upstairs to my room and called Heath. I told him what had happened, and that we needed him here as soon as he could possibly make it. I was certain Stan was about to do something rash.

When I'd hung up, I sat down on my bed and reluctantly pulled out the heavy black plastic case that held my gun and the smaller one that held two loaded clips. Something told me I'd be needing it tonight. I carefully slid the safety on, shoved in a clip, and loaded the chamber. I hated the way it fit so well in my hand. It felt worse in my jacket pocket, heavy and cold as a sleeping viper.

I went downstairs and out the back door, standing in the moonlight for a few minutes to get used to the darkness. I saw a light on in Sarah's barn, and the door was open. I headed toward it.

*

I entered as quietly as I could, weapon drawn. I'd hesitated before removing the safety, but with it on, all I had was an expensive and misshapen rock to throw at someone. Stan stood propped against a workbench, rifle trained on something. When I got farther into the room, I saw it was Sarah and Billy, sitting side by side on a crate.

"Just put the gun down, Stan," I said in my calmest voice. "It's over. Heath Baker's already on his way. I called him when I went up to get my gun." I moved it to make sure he saw it. "This one."

He looked at me, puzzled, and somehow offended that it pointed at him. To my surprise, he kept his rifle on Billy and Sarah.

"Just put the rifle down," I said firmly.

He didn't budge. "Oh, no. I'm gonna make sure they never get to enjoy this place, trying to turn it into their little weed-growing love nest." He sneered. "Can you believe it? Daddy wouldn't subdivide the ranch for me, but then told me he was going to cut a piece out for her!" He waved toward Sarah with the rifle barrel. Sarah and Billy both flinched, and my stomach rolled over.

"That's what he told you the day you fought, isn't it?" Stan swung his rifle barrel away from Sarah as I got his attention. "He told you he was going to deed a piece of the ranch to Sarah in his will. For her business. You fought. The rifle went off. And then you packed some of his precious ranch dirt into his mouth, didn't you?"

He laughed, careless, eyes wild. "If he was going to give her some of the ranch land, I figured it was only proper to give some of it back to him that way. Stupid, stupid old man. I could've made him rich. I could've made us all rich, but he wouldn't listen."

I took a deep breath, willing Stan to come back to earth. "There's no point in killing anyone else. Why don't you just put down the gun? Two people are dead. Isn't that more than enough?"

Stan belched. "They say death comes in threes, old fella. Do you want to be number three?"

"No, I don't." I decided I wouldn't remind him that I had my gun trained on him, too. "You don't gain anything by killing me. You don't gain anything by killing Billy or Sarah, either. You'd have to kill all three of us. Think about that. It would leave only you and Marianne as suspects. Do you think Heath Baker won't figure that out?"

"He's nothing but a faggot country hick in a uniform. He couldn't figure nothing out."

I didn't know how Stan might take disagreement, but I had to push back a little on that. "He's a whole lot smarter than you think, Stan. Is that the same rifle you used to kill Landry? Even if you kill all three of us, Baker would connect the dots faster than you can say life in prison."

Stan's eyes lost focus, and he gazed up at the barn ceiling. He wiped his nose on the back of his trigger hand, making the rifle barrel swerve all over. Not good.

"He was so angry when he found out I'd busted up her barn."

It took me a second to realize he was talking about Evan.

"I tried to explain that I'd done us a favor, but he wouldn't listen. He hit me." He looked right at me, eyes blazing. "He *hit* me!" The pained incredulity in his voice was embarrassing. "He said we weren't in business together anymore, that he was going to go partners with Sarah and make me sorry. He laughed at me and walked away. Just like that. He's laughed at me all my life." Stan hiccupped. "Well, he ain't laughing now."

I wondered how soon Heath would get here. I had to keep Stan talking.

"You do know that when you killed Evan, you also killed your grow license application, don't you? That's unfortunate."

"No way. I'm on all the papers, too."

"Sorry, but I checked with an industry guru. On the death of any named applicant, the application is thrown out. You're going to have to start all over, find someone else with money and connections."

"Fuck." He scowled at the floor for a moment, swaying slightly. The rifle bobbed and swung, as if he was using it as a balance pole. "I'll figure out something. I always do."

"But you've got serious problems this time, maybe painted yourself into a corner. You've killed two family members, and you have two more in your sights. You're quickly running out of family to kill." I saw that register. "Think about that," I said gently as I could. "Plus, you'd have to start looking over your shoulder at Marianne, because she'd know you did it. You'd be the only two left. She could turn on you in a heartbeat, and she'd have the whole ranch to herself. I suppose you'd eventually have to kill her, too." I let that sink in.

"Are you really ready to do that?" I asked. "I'll bet you aren't."

He steadied himself against the workbench again. Stan's aura, muddy as it was, showed a little grief.

"I'll bet you're really tired of all the killing. Why don't you just put the gun down?"

"Aww, fuck." Stan's shoulders sagged, and he gazed up at the barn ceiling again, anguish and desperation sparking and spiking out of his aura. He slowly brought the muzzle to rest against the inside of his jaw, never taking his eye off whatever he saw up in the rafters. I began to lower my weapon. But he wheeled, aimed the rifle at me and fired. Fortunately, he staggered at his own sudden movement and missed.

For the first time in my life, I fired at a human being. I missed. I fired again and didn't miss. Stan's eyes opened wide in surprise as a hole appeared in his chest.

"God dammit," he said softly, putting his hand up to the spurting red that came out of his chest. It gushed between his fingers.

He looked at Billy and Sarah, as if he were going to ask them for something, some kind of help or forgiveness or understanding, and fell sideways onto the floor with a groan. Transfixed, the three of us watched him die, as if we didn't know what else to do. I guess we didn't. We wouldn't have had time to do anything useful anyway. In less than a minute, his aura melted into nothing. Billy and Sarah wrapped each other in a hug. Sarah began to cry.

In the dim light of the barn, I looked down at the gun in my hand. I hefted it, wanting to examine it closer in some way I didn't understand. It still fit my hand perfectly, so alien. I'd killed a man. I couldn't feel my fingers. The numbness spread out across my body until it hit my stomach, which rebelled. Before I could lean over properly, I sagged to my knees and threw up on myself and the gun.

I was still retching when a siren sounded in the distance. Good. Heath would take over, I thought. Restore order, keep the peace. That's what good policemen did.

Chapter Sixteen

Sunday

I didn't sleep much that night. The knowledge of what I'd done kept prodding me awake. Killing someone, even for the most justifiable reasons, would be a part of me for the rest of my life. I watched the sunrise with the same heavy feeling I'd gone to bed with. I didn't want this event to change me, and I was afraid it had. Permanently. The irony was that just days earlier, Colin had told me that I was one of the kindest men he knew. I hoped he would still feel the same way when he learned what I'd done.

And maybe I hadn't killed just one. Had my pressure on Stan, goading him about the Furies and how Evan would throw him under the bus, pushed Stan to kill Evan? I'd never know, but I'd been careless in trying to accomplish a particular goal. I'd never know.

The night before, Heath had taken our statements and my gun. I couldn't remember much of our exchange except that I felt horribly ashamed, handing it to him with vomit all over it. I apologized to him for the mess it was in, but he just laughed and told me not to be embarrassed. It wasn't the first time. He'd collected other pieces of evidence, too. Stan's rifle, of course, to be shipped off for a ballistics test along with mine.

Eventually, I got up and took a long shower. So much fallout.

While my assignment was now complete, I still needed to touch base with Sarah. To my surprise, I also wanted to say goodbye to Heath. I'd been in no shape to do that properly the previous night. Even so, I wasn't too eager to see anybody right away.

Fortunately, by the time I got down to the kitchen, it was empty and there were three sets of dishes in the sink. Coffee was still in the pot, so I poured myself a cup. I made myself eggs and toast, tidied up slowly, and headed for the barn to see if I could find Sarah.

Just as I was approaching, the door flew open and Marianne burst out, tears sparkling on her face, her aura closed down in grief and shame. She was so distraught, she didn't even bother saying something nasty to me. She hadn't wept like that the night before standing in the barn gazing down at her older brother's body, so I couldn't imagine what had happened to put her in such a state.

I knocked at the open door, and Sarah called to me to come in. She and Billy were sitting on a bench under the window, holding hands, looking puzzled. No, astonished.

"What happened to Marianne?" I asked.

Billy shook his head. "You probably won't believe it," he said, "but she had the nerve to come in here to let us know she'd reconsidered. Marijuana cultivation wasn't really that bad after all, and because what was left of our family really ought to heal old wounds and stick together, she'd like to be part of the business. She had some money, she said, that she'd like to invest in a share of ownership." He ran his free hand through his hair. "Can you believe that? Sometimes humans can be dumber than farm animals."

"I have to confess," Sarah joined in, "I wasn't all that polite in telling her there was no way on earth I was going to have her as a business partner. The lease is still in place, and she'll enjoy some of the benefits of the ranch's income from it, but my business partner and I," she said, looking at Billy happily, "are going to run this as we've been planning for months."

I had to admit, I hurt a bit for Billy's sister. She'd bet on a string of slow horses, and she had less than nothing to show for it. It didn't feel right to simply dismiss her angst by saying she'd made her own trouble. That was true enough, and everyone has to accept the consequences of their actions. I still felt sorry for her.

"It's been a tough time for Marianne, hasn't it?" I said. "Do you think she'll hang on to her job at the station?"

Billy shook his head. "My guess is they won't fire her. Instead they'll give her a few months to find a new position somewhere else so she can slip away without a fracas. She'd never make it in Denver, but some of the smaller stations in the region might take her. She surely has shot herself in the foot, though. I have to say I do feel a little sorry for her, but that mess is of her own making."

"Well," I said, "I dropped by to just close my assignment with you, Sarah. I'll draw up a report and an invoice for you when I get back to Denver." I looked at the two of them sitting on that bench, so happy together. "I really hope things work out well for you. You've both been through far more than you deserved."

Sarah smiled, and I realized it was the first time I'd seen her happy smile. It made her beautiful. "I don't know what our new normal will look like, Russ, but you're welcome to drop by anytime you're in the area."

"Thanks. You do the same when you're in Denver. Please. I really do wish you every success. By the way, I was hoping to say so long to Heath. Do you know whether he's coming out this morning, or should I drive into town?"

"He'll be here before noon. He didn't have the gizmo that would take this thing off." She lifted her ankle, where the outline of her transponder showed through heavy sock. "He had to get the DA to drop the charges before he could take it off, so that's happening probably even as we speak. Why don't you just hang around until he arrives?"

I nodded. That sounded like a great suggestion to me. "Well, I'll leave you to your reconstruction plans," I said with a wink. "I'll go pack."

About an hour later, I saw Heath's car come up the road from the highway. I waited ten minutes before going down to meet him. When I got downstairs and out the back, Sarah and Billy were standing just outside the barn door with Heath, talking amiably in the late morning sunshine. He had the transponder in his hand. We exchanged greetings as I joined them.

"Well, I'd best be going," he said, touching the brim of his hat to Sarah and Billy. "I've got a ton of paperwork to catch up on, but if anything comes up, you be sure to give me a call, okay?"

He crooked his head to me to accompany him toward the car. "A word with you, Mr. Morgan. Please."

We walked in silence until we got to his car.

"Guess you're heading out today, right?"

"Yep. Time for me to stop creating paperwork for you," I said, trying to crack a joke.

"It's pointless," he said glumly. "There's always paperwork even if it's just two ranchers arguing about a dead cow. Death, taxes, and paperwork. They should add that to the list. Hell, death, and taxes have their own sets of paperwork. Maybe paperwork should come first. First and last."

I laughed and stuck out my hand. "I'm glad to have met you, Heath. I wish you well, living here on the land you can't leave. You're lucky. Most men go through their whole lives without knowing where they belong."

"I hadn't thought about it that way, but I guess you're right. It is what it is, anyway. Nothing I can do about it." He hung on to my hand for a moment longer. "You know," he said, "I get down to Denver now and again. I'd like it if we could get together when I do. I like you."

"I'd be glad to get together for coffee," I said. "I don't think we should plan on anything more than that. I'm hoping things will work out for me and my new right guy."

"Understood, loud and clear." He shrugged. "I think we could've had some good fun, though. Still, I think you're right." He let go of my hand. "All the best, Russ. I mean that. You let me know if your right guy doesn't work out, hear?"

I smiled, wincing at the burn of his loneliness. "I promise."

He climbed into his car, and I stepped back. He started the engine, backed down the drive until he could turn around, and drove off without looking back.

*

To say that I drove back to Denver in a reflective mood would be an understatement.

For the first time, at least that I knew of, someone had intended to kill me. It could have happened as easily as it didn't. Stan had got the first shot off, he'd just missed. I'd been handed my life back with a memo about my mortality, and that made a compelling reason to stop being so cautious about the future. Cautious about love, really. Life was fleeting, regardless of age.

Eventually, my thoughts returned to the case. Lives changed by lives cut short, not by age but by murder. As I pondered the distinct lack of guarantees about anyone living a long, predictable life, I realized I'd always assumed something so heinous as murder would show up in a person's aura as some kind of distinct manifestation.

I'd seen nothing like that in Stan's aura after he killed his father. Maybe that was because of the fog of alcohol, but that was only a guess. I had to admit I didn't know how to look for it, had never needed to. Or maybe I wasn't gifted enough to see it. Then again, maybe we were all blind to murder. The mark of Cain stained us all, according to my father's angry Old Testament view of the world.

After all, I'd just killed somebody, too. Would that show up in my aura as some kind of stain? Maybe murder was just part of the lens we used as we looked around at the world.

Still, conscience had to count for something—an essential part of a moral life. Maybe Stan really hadn't thought he'd done anything wrong. That was a frightening thought. Justifiable homicide, just like mine. I didn't like thinking Stan and I might be the same, yet in more ways than was comfortable to acknowledge, we were.

He'd still been drinking when he died, and I knew firsthand how a cloud of alcohol could make a man believe crazy things. I wondered how long it had been before he died that Stan had been capable of sober thought. I knew with terrible certainty that dying while lost in that delusional fog was something I did not want.

As for the other moral issues, I didn't feel qualified to resolve them. Maybe that was the problem. Maybe morality and the law were a close enough match that one could be substituted for the other, therefore leaving the judgment of moral issues to the enforcers of the law.

No, that wasn't good enough, not really. Not for the marginalized, the racially profiled. Not long ago, interracial marriages were illegal and considered immoral, yet surely love between two people of different races was never immoral.

No, the gap between morality and the law was significant, even if we presumed the law to be fundamentally good, and regardless of what some people did in its name. Same was true of love.

I watched the road unwind and stretch open in front of me. Speaking of love, it was time I gave love a chance, risks notwithstanding. Colin wanted a real relationship. I would do my damnedest to be real with him.

I stopped for gas and coffee and called Colin to let him know I'd be home in a couple of hours and would like to make him dinner. He sounded eager to get together. It made me eager, too, and I got back on the road in a hurry.

*

On the way home, I stopped at a hardware store. It seemed a strange place to prepare for a frightening threshold-crossing ceremony, but it also felt right. After, I walked out into the late afternoon heat, feeling nervous excitement I hadn't experienced for a long time. I stopped to get some food for dinner, too. That wasn't anywhere near as exciting as the hardware store.

When Colin showed up at my door promptly at six, I hauled him into a hug and kissed him, simply grateful that

I could. I was a little surprised at myself for being so unrestrained. It felt so good.

"Wow, what happened up there?" Colin asked. I guessed I'd surprised him, too. "No, don't tell me yet," he laughed. "Let me enjoy this." He closed in for another kiss.

We laughed and joked as we cooked burgers on the gas grill outside my back door and brought them inside to adorn with the usuals. The mood became more somber when I filled him in on the murders, but even then, Colin listened with a tenderness and understanding that made me hopeful. And finally, I came to the question I had to ask.

"Now that you know I've killed a man, does that change anything between us?" I watched him carefully without opening to see his aura. Somehow, I felt that would be trespassing where I had no right. "You said just a few days ago you thought I was kind. I've also committed homicide."

He reached across the table and took both my hands in his. "Russ, listen to me. Kind is what you are. Killing a man is what you did because you had to." He paused for a moment, waiting for me to meet his gaze. "I'm glad you pulled the trigger. We might not be here talking if you hadn't."

I nodded, grateful for his absolution. "Thank you." I took a deep breath and plunged forward. "Then I have a proposal for you." I saw him get ready to make a joke, but I kept going. "I feel something for you that I haven't felt for anyone in a long time. I want to give our relationship a serious chance, because I'm very serious about you."

The words tumbled out, artless and naked. I didn't care about their clumsiness. "I want us to commit to a year's exploration together. Or at least agree to a year's exploration together. Either one of us can end it before, of course, but I want to know I've got a year to clear away the underbrush that's grown up around my heart and relearn how to be with someone deeply."

I gazed at him, his eyes wide, his face and lips open. "I want to be with you. Deeply. But I think we should have a kind of trial period, where we can just explore, free of long-term obligations. To see if there's more for us when we get to that point."

Without letting go of my hands, Colin rose from his chair, leaned across the table, and kissed me on the lips sweetly, tenderly. He pulled away slowly. "I think that's a great plan," he said, kissing me again. "Let's go upstairs and celebrate."

"Not quite yet. Please." My heart thrashed out a frantic rhythm in my chest.

Colin sat again, cautious, patient. Golden, so strong, so beautiful.

I pulled my hands back with a squeeze. I took a deep breath and reached into my pocket, pulling out a set of keys, pushing them forward on the table between us. "These are for you, then. I had them made this afternoon, when I knew you should have them if you wanted. Keys for here. This one is the front door; this is the back. The alarm code is 5346, and if the security company calls, the all-clear password is 'shibboleth.' Their number is by the fridge. I'll write all that down for you. You can come any time, don't wait for an invitation." I was babbling now, but I didn't care. Some huge urgency had overtaken me, as if I had to tell him everything right away or our chance at love would fall apart, never to be reclaimed. I opened my mouth to say more, but Colin cut me off.

"Russ. Whoa." He grinned, stroked my fingers as he took the keys. "Slow down. Thank you. That's more than I'd hoped for." He laughed. "This is amazing. You're pretty amazing, too."

He looked around the kitchen. "We've got too much stuff to leave out for long. Let's clean up and then go upstairs." He grinned at me, happiness sparking off him. "Now I want to celebrate more than ever. We have more to celebrate."

So, we cleaned up the kitchen, laughing, brushing against each other, kissing, making the chore the first phase of our foreplay. Somehow going upstairs together meant more, now that we'd begun our year. That year stretched out into the misty unknown, but at that exact moment, I didn't care where it would end.

*

Colin's head lay heavy against my chest. "Now don't panic," he said, "but I want you to meet my friends soon. You've given me keys to your place, and they need to meet you."

I laughed. "I'm thinking I'll manage." I made slow designs on the side of his head with my fingers, cherishing his relaxed comfort. "And your parents?"

He snuggled in closer, draped a thigh over my hips. "In time, not right now. We don't have to do everything at once."

He propped himself up on one elbow and looked down at me. "I really like your idea of giving us a year. It was a surprise, but a nice one. It's not an impossible length of time, and at the end of the year, we can decide what's next for both of us. But I was feeling like you needed some definition of what to commit to. So we can see where we go. I'm in."

"Part of me still wishes you didn't sound so reasonable," I said. "I feel a little guilty asking for a trial period."

"Don't listen to that part. There's no rule saying we have to decide everything right now. That's the cool thing about partnership, you don't have to be the only source of answers." He poked me in the side, exactly where he'd already learned I was ticklish. "I'll hold your hand," he said with his wicked grin. "Or maybe I'll hold something else and squeeze just a little when you get spooked."

I looked up at him, seeing the affection in his eyes, seeing his love of adventure, his confidence radiating from him. His whole life stretched out in front of him like an open road. So many possible destinations. But I knew now, or rather felt in my gut, he would choose what he thought he wanted and go from there. We would share our journey for as long as it suited us. How long that shared journey might be was not up for speculation at the moment.

I raised my head and kissed him. "How did you get to be so wise?"

"I told you already. I'm an old soul, or at least that's what I was told. Maybe I am. I bet you are, too."

"I think," I said running my fingers along his cheek, "when it comes to wisdom, you must be much older than me." Once again, a wave of apology rose up through me, but it no longer had the power it had on our hike up on the Flatirons. "I think it's very brave of you to risk a year of your life with me."

His eyes took on a harder light. I could see it glinting even in the dim room. "Everything's a risk, Russ. This is what I want."

"Well, do you want to risk a camping trip to Red Feather Lakes when we can arrange it? You can show me your favorite areas."

The hardness in his face vanished, replaced by Christmas morning excitement. "Heck, yeah! That would be amazing, to go there with you. As soon as we can, right? I'll ask tomorrow. I'm owed the time off, that's for sure."

He nuzzled my neck, and I wondered if he noticed its loosening skin as he burrowed. "And now I've got you for a whole year. Mwahahahaaa."

I laughed, caressing the smooth, perfect skin of his back. "I can tell already it's going to be a challenging year. I'd better rest up." I reached to turn off the light.

"Not just yet." Colin's voice was playful, aroused again. He turned the light back on low. "You can rest later."

Acknowledgements

My thanks to the Marijuana Enforcement Division for the State of Colorado, the Mesa County Sheriff's Office, and everyone else who so generously supported my research.

Heartfelt thanks to the folks at NineStar Press who believed Russ Morgan's stories had more mileage in them. I hope to send you more.

And finally, as always, my deep gratitude to my husband Bob, my fox. Sharing life's adventures with you is the best.

About the Author

Born on a farm in the Colorado foothills and having led what can only be described as a checkered life, Lloyd Meeker can honestly say he's grateful for all of it. He's been a minister, an office worker, a janitor, a drinker, and a software developer on his way to finishing his first novel in 2004. He is a three-time cancer survivor.

Meeker and his husband have been together since 2002. Between them they have four children and five grandchildren. They live in south Florida and work hard to keep up with the astonishing life they've created.

Email: lam@lloydmeeker.com

Facebook: www.facebook.com/lloyd.a.meeker

Twitter: @LloydAMeeker

Website: www.lloydmeeker.com

Other NineStar books by this author

Stone and Shell

www.ingramcontent.com/pod-product-compliance
Lightning Source LLC
Chambersburg PA
CBHW032120180726
48284CB00002B/639